THE LAST WIFE

J. A. BAKER

Boldwood

First published in Great Britain in 2023 by Boldwood Books Ltd.

Copyright © J. A. Baker, 2023

Cover Design by Head Design

Cover Photography: Shutterstock

A CIP catalogue record for this book is available from the British Library.

Paperback ISBN 978-1-80415-377-2

Large Print ISBN 978-1-80415-378-9

Hardback ISBN 978-1-80415-376-5

Ebook ISBN 978-1-80415-379-6

Kindle ISBN 978-1-80415-380-2

Audio CD ISBN 978-1-80415-371-0

MP3 CD ISBN 978-1-80415-372-7

Digital audio download ISBN 978-1-80415-374-1

Boldwood Books Ltd
23 Bowerdean Street
London SW6 3TN
www.boldwoodbooks.com

Faith is the bird that feels the light when the dawn is still dark.

— RABINDRANATH TAGORE

To Anita and Valerie. Here's to the future, ladies. Onwards and upwards.

PROLOGUE

With hindsight, I should have gone with that inescapable gut instinct that gnawed at me on the journey there, the one that I duly ignored, pushing it away every time it reared its head. I should have persuaded Neil we had made a grave error of judgement and persuaded him to stay on the ferry for the return journey back home. So many things we should have done but didn't. So many things I shouldn't have done but did. There were too many words unsaid between us, too few conversations. And definitely too many ill-thought-out actions. We should have turned around and gone back home, that was the thing. Not that we had a home to go back to, having sold it, our possessions shipped out four weeks prior after being put into storage for a month. But we didn't turn around because I didn't say or do anything.

Instead, I just stood there, mute, fingers clasped around the metal railings, hands numb from the cold, and ignored that small, still voice in my head, the one that continually told me something was amiss with this whole venture, that something was about to go horribly wrong. Sometimes it's easier, isn't it? To ignore the subtle signs, to quell those nuanced voices inside your head and be carried along with the original planned agenda. Having to endure the upheaval of suddenly refusing to align to a prearranged schedule takes courage. Nobody likes upsetting the apple cart, least of all me. I was also feeling weak, shattered actually. I didn't have it in me to tell Neil that I'd changed my mind, that we were making a big mistake. I had no reasons to give, no tangible evidence to present to him. Just that low rumbling of discontent that swirled about in my gut making me feel queasy and out of kilter.

And yet, despite my misgivings, despite the turmoil that whirled in my head, I had to admit that it looked so beautiful that night as we sailed towards our new home: the dark water, the rugged coastline, the neat rows of rooftops in the distance, the twinkling line of street lights that flanked the roadside next to the ferry point. They were mesmerising. How intriguing it all was. How magical and exciting. How utterly terrifying and frighteningly deceptive.

Would we have stayed had we known what lay ahead? Probably not. Our first reaction would have been to turn around and head back to the place we knew so well, back to the town where we both grew up. The same place where we made our terrible mistake. Do we regret making the decision to sell our lovely home and move to a remote island off the north-east coast of England? Strangely enough, no. Why? Because we survived what took place on Winters End island and we both lived to tell the tale. We're still here, living and breathing. What doesn't kill us makes us stronger; isn't that how the old adage goes?

Living on Winters End changed us. Whether that's for the better or not, I guess only time will tell...

PART I

PART I

1

'Christ, it's so cold here. What happened to the summer?' Neil stared up at the sky, shoulders hunched, eyes narrowed against the strong north-easterly breeze that lapped around our faces. It was freezing; there was no denying it. I wondered if Neil was also having second thoughts, voicing his innermost doubts to me, skirting as we always did around the edges of the problem without saying what we actually meant. Perhaps I should have taken more notice, seized the opportunity to tell him how I was feeling, reassured him that to be reticent and frightened was okay, that it wasn't a sign of weakness and that I was feeling it too.

'It's not so bad,' I replied, trying to mask my own

fears and angst, thinking that living on an island out in the middle of the North Sea was probably going to test the pair of us both physically and mentally. I knew then that speaking openly about what was burrowing deep within my brain wouldn't work at that point. It had been my idea, moving here. I had seen the cottage for sale online and was immediately attracted to it, the longing to escape from events of late pushing me on, giving me the impetus to run away from everything I knew and loved. I wanted to draw a line under it all, start afresh. I wasn't running away. I was simply starting again. That's what I told myself. Everyone deserves a second chance, don't they? Even me. Especially me.

And yet as we stood there discussing the weather, wondering where the late-summer heat had gone to, something in the pit of my stomach continued to flap about whenever I thought about what we were doing. What we were about to take on. I squashed down those feelings, told myself that everything was too far down the line to make any major changes. I needed this new venture, was unable to go back to my old life, to face my family and friends after what I had done. Putting some distance between us was important to me if only to save face and help keep my dignity intact. Their memories of me might fade. What I did would always be there, a stark reminder of how a few minutes of stupidity and being driven by fear and desperation could alter the trajectory of our entire lives.

I slipped my hand into Neil's, his fingers dry and cold against mine. 'Come on,' I said, trying to inject some levity into my tone, 'let's get back inside, get a coffee. If we're lucky they might even have some cake on offer.' I sounded positive. I didn't feel it but, then again, lying had become my default mode. I was practically an expert.

We walked back inside the ferry through the automatic doors, away from the rough, dark water outside, away from the biting cold that stung at our exposed hands and faces, and back into the relative warmth of the old vessel that would transport us to our new lives.

We sat at a table that had seen better days. Brown tea ring stains littered its surface, the corners of the laminate top curled up at the edges, but it didn't matter. Nothing mattered at that point except arriving. We were almost there, almost at Winters End where everything would be better. Brighter. It had to be. It certainly couldn't be any worse than the life we had left behind. The life that I had ruined.

'I'll get them,' Neil said as he stood up and walked towards the small serving area where a young lad stood staring out into the vast blackness outside, boredom oozing from him in bucketloads. He had probably done this trip a hundred times before and was counting down the hours and minutes until he was on dry land again, home safe and sound and away from the whirring of the engine. Away from the bland, needy faces of demanding customers and the inescapable, lingering smell of stale food.

Neil returned minutes later carrying two large cups of coffee, tendrils of steam misting his face as he walked towards me. I thought about how patient he had been throughout all of this, adapting without question, sticking by me. Forgiving me. Just as I had forgiven him. We were made for one another, the two of us locked together in our vast pit of transgressions.

'A flat white for you and a cappuccino for me.'

We both managed a small laugh. Before us sat two large mugs of pale brown liquid that could barely pass as coffee at all. A gathering of creamy foam clung to the sides of my cup. My stomach roiled as a large wave caught us unawares, sending my drink sliding away from us. I grabbed at it and watched as brown splashes of liquid spread across the table. Neil pulled a tissue out of his pocket and mopped up the spots of coffee. Always helpful, always uncomplaining. But then, what I had done wasn't completely down to me. He played his part as well. We were in this thing together. For better for worse. For richer, for poorer. I sighed. The irony of those words wasn't lost on me.

'Everything okay?' He caught my eye, gave me a sly wink, his smile slightly lopsided.

Even after everything we'd been through, all the trauma we had endured, an event that would have pushed many couples apart, he still had the ability to stop me in my tracks, make my heart flutter ever so slightly, his turquoise eyes, his clear chestnut-brown complexion erasing my worries. Until I looked away, stared out at the never-ending expanse of sea, that is, and then they returned: the tumult of emotions that ballooned in my head day after day, week after week. I was feeling fragile and needed him by my side to steady me, to remind me to get up every day and put one foot in front of another. To just keep going, to keep on keeping on.

I closed my eyes for a second, told myself to stop it, that I should embrace this moment, remember it as a turning point, the catalyst that would help repair our broken lives. It was a positive, constructive thing we were doing, moving to the island. It had to be. All other avenues were closed off to us, our options severely limited. If we didn't make a go of this then we would be right back where we started – with nothing, all eyes feasting on the wreckage of our lives like vultures picking over a carcass. And I refused to let that happen, to be the talk of the area, shuffling around the place, wearing our misfortune like some sort of leper's bell. My dignity was important to me. To lose face would mean losing everything.

'Look,' Neil said softly, his finger pointing beyond my shoulder. 'The lights are getting closer. We're almost there.'

I spun around, my heart beginning to speed up, and stared out at the sprinkling of neon lights amidst the surrounding black water and starless dark sky. I needed this new beginning. It held such promise for me. For us. And yet, my gut was continually telling me that something wasn't quite right. Maybe it was the sense of isolation that was getting to me, trying to tear me down, my brain refusing to let me feel anything other than fear and trepidation. They had become an intrinsic part of me and I struggled to shake them off. Winters End was a small island in the middle of the North Sea. It was different to anywhere I had ever lived before, different even to the coastline on the north-east, to the town I had loved so well. The town we were now leaving behind. Deep down, I knew that it wasn't the idea of being on an island in the middle of the sea that was getting to me. I had no idea what it was that was making me feel unsettled, but I did know that I had to suppress those fears and try to forge a new life for ourselves, make new friends. Be a part of the community. Be a happy couple once again.

The judgemental faces of my family and friends sprang into my mind, the stricken expression of my parents as I explained to them what had happened. What I had done. How, with their help, I could escape without getting a criminal record. Moving to Winters End was our chance to put all that behind us, all those dark memories. A chance for Neil and me to reinvent ourselves, be the best that we could be. Not the miserable, despondent couple that we had inadvertently morphed into.

'Let's head down to the car, shall we? Don't want to hold anybody up behind us, make ourselves the most unpopular people on the island before we've even begun, eh?' His eyes sparkled and I knew he was trying to settle my doubts and reservations with his effervescent wit and charm. It wasn't working. Besides, the ferry was almost empty, just a handful of people who looked tired and weary. Hardly a throng of locals. And anyway, most of them looked like holidaymakers with their backpacks, off to spend the weekend in a remote cottage somewhere on the island. Off to lose their problems and leave the rest of the world behind them, if only for a couple of days. It didn't work like that.

Problems rarely, if ever, disappear. They mount up, increasing a hundredfold until they're tackled head-on. I should know.

I took a final sip of my coffee and nodded. We stood up and headed out of the canteen area towards the stairs, my stomach doing somersaults as we descended into the bowels of the ferry where our car sat, its bright red paintwork a refreshing sight amidst the gloom and darkness. The place stank of exhaust fumes, poisonous gases trapped within the confines of the lower deck. A tension of opposites tugged at me – I couldn't wait to disembark and yet something within me screamed to stay put.

A handful of people began to filter towards their vehicles, everyone looking tired and mildly nauseated as the sea continued to buffet us about. This was the tail end of summer on Winters End, the vestiges of the warmest and kindest season of the year still hanging around and yet the weather appeared to be doing its damnedest to punish us. I didn't want to think about how gruelling the winters would be on this small island, focusing instead on what lay ahead, convincing myself of how exciting it could all be, how beautiful our little cottage would be once we settled in there, how making new friends would be such a challenging yet exhilarating experience.

New start, new life.

That was my mantra, the thing I would use to help me though this major upheaval. I mean, how many people had suffered greater changes than this in their lives and survived? We would do the same. I thought about my great-grandmother who had lived through two world wars, my grandparents and parents who had all grown up in abject poverty, living hand to mouth for most of their childhoods. I had been lucky. No wars, enough to eat, loved always. I had had a blessed existence thus far.

But you ruined it, didn't you?

I swallowed and turned to smile at Neil. He pointed the key fob towards our car and pressed it, our vehicle responding, its elongated beep echoing around us with an eerie howl.

'We're lucky in so many ways, Fiona,' he said huskily as we clambered into our seats, me shivering against the cold of the leather upholstery, my breath misting in front of me. 'We've got a nice warm, dry house waiting for us, a car to drive us there and enough money to be able to eat. We'll be just fine.'

Even though his saccharine-sweet attitude often irritated me, I hoped he was right. We didn't ever speak openly about the huge risks we had taken to get to this point, the friends we had lost. The family who had ostracised us. So many sacrifices. So many mistakes. All we had was each other. We had to make it work.

His flesh felt warm against mine when I reached over and placed my fingers over his hand, the solidity of it a reassuring presence. I needed it, that sense of comfort, and because I needed to convince myself that everything would be fine, I believed him, fervently hoping that things would turn out for the best. My self-esteem was flagging, trailing down in the dirt, events of late continually reminding me of what a bad wife I was. A bad sister and daughter. A terrible employee. The worst.

'Come on, let's get that heater whacked up. This place is bloody Baltic. God knows what life is going to be like here in winter.' He finished his sentence with a smile, making sure I noticed it, saw that he was being sardonic and humorous. I'd forgotten what it felt like: the sensation of spontaneous laughter as it emerged unbidden; that spark of unprompted happiness exploding into the world around me. Maybe we would reach that point again, maybe we would relax and find our feet and just be ourselves, our behaviour reflexive and effortless, not the contrived and strained actions of a couple who had dodged a bullet. We could once again become the couple that we once were: trouble-free, untethered, and soft in the middle. Some might even say naïve. Regardless, I wanted to be that person again, to act without having to think it through beforehand, my motions unrehearsed and natural.

The flow of traffic off the ferry was smooth and unchallenging and we were on the road within five minutes of docking up, the tiny lanes of Winters End a far cry from what we were used to. We weren't big city slickers – far from it – but this tiny island was different to anything we had ever encountered before, everything smaller and less frenetic. A sleepy outlier, that's what it was. Separate from the rest of the country. Exactly how I wanted to be.

'The satnav says we're only six minutes away,' I said, thinking how unfamiliar it all looked in the darkness, the towering hedgerows like eerie spectres, hemming us in on all sides.

'I think I know the route there actually,' Neil said, his driving steady and effortless as we manoeuvred our way through the snaking lanes and onto a wider road that, although bigger, was still very narrow and shrouded in darkness. 'I studied it on Google Maps and anyway, it's not as if this place is big enough to get lost on, is it?'

He was right. At only six miles long and four miles wide, whichever route we took, it would always lead us back to the sea. I stared out of the window and shivered. It was impossible to separate the land from the sky, the horizon a thick blanket of darkness that stretched as far as the eye could see. Clouds hid the stars and only a tiny sliver of a watery moon was visible above us, a hazy grey crescent hanging languorously in a swathe of black.

'I hope the estate agent left the heating on.' I had emailed him before we left, explaining that we wouldn't get here until after dusk. I prayed he had read it. The thought of stepping into an ice-cold cottage that would take hours to heat filled me with gloom. Already, I was feeling tired, and that was before we had unpacked our cases and found the bed sheets and quilts. 'So much to do,' I murmured, the words escaping before I could stop them. 'It feels never-ending.'

'We'll manage.' Neil glanced at me briefly, his expression unreadable, before turning his attention back to the road ahead, his gaze fixed on the vast swathe of blackness that scared me so much. 'He said he was leaving a welcome basket so we should at least have something decent to eat.' His fingers tapped at the steering wheel, a dull rhythmic sound filling the space around us. 'Once you get some food inside you and we get that fire going, things will seem a lot easier, you'll see. Don't get overwrought. We don't want—'

He stopped mid-sentence, his words trailing off. We both knew what he was going to say: *We don't want you making yourself ill again, do we?* He was right. I was looking for problems that weren't there. Pre-empting situations. Making things worse. It had been a long day and I was tired after packing up the rest of our belongings, saying goodbye to friends and the remaining family members who were still talking to us and getting to the ferry point – small things that took on gargantuan proportions in my head. Small things that would leave a lasting impression on us. Or on me, that is. Neil seemed to be on an even keel, letting it all happen around him, remining calm and unruffled while I felt afraid and rudderless with no real place to call home.

'The Wi-Fi will be a day or two to set up but at least we've got electricity and once that roaring fire gets going, it'll be just like home.'

'That's because it *is* home, Neil. This is our life now, where we live and work and socialise. Winters End is our life now. No changing our minds or going back. This is it.' I tried to keep the sense of dread that I felt out of my voice but it managed to find a way in, muscling its way past the small bursts of excitement that kept bubbling up inside me. They were bullies, the dark emotions that festered in my gut, elbowing any happiness and optimism out of the way. Maybe I deserved to feel unhappy. Maybe moving to Winters End was my penance for what I had done.

Maybe, I thought as we turned a sharp corner into the lane that led to our small cottage, I should cheer up and stop seeing this move as a bad thing. I was miserable and anxious, I knew that. Problem was, I didn't know how to snap out of it. Neil was a patient man but he had his breaking point and me being permanently morose could be the straw that would break this particular camel's back. I needed him. He needed me.

I leaned forwards, ran my fingers through his hair, and planted a soft, dry kiss on his stubbly cheek. 'A good night's sleep is what I need. Everything will feel much brighter in the morning.'

2

I was right, I thought contentedly as I stretched my limbs and yawned, unfurling myself like an animal coming back to life after a long hibernation. My back ached when I turned over to see Neil lying staring at me, a suggestive twinkle in his eye. A new day had dawned and things did seem brighter. I sighed, laughed a little and moved his hand away from my thigh, my libido a waning thing that reared its head rarely since *that time*. He groaned and rolled onto his back.

'I'll end up a frustrated old man, you know.'

I shot him a look that said, *don't even go there*. It was something we never talked about: our almost non-existent sex life. He winked at me and leaned up on his elbows, his skin the colour of honey in the dim early-morning light.

'I'll make us some breakfast. Will scrambled eggs do you?' My voice sounded disembodied. It echoed in my head, a reminder that I was keen to get away. Keen to avoid a conversation about sex, or the lack of it. I wasn't ready. Not yet. Having sex meant relaxing and enjoying myself. I couldn't recall the last time I'd felt relaxed, both mind and body supple and yielding.

He nodded and slumped back down onto the pillow while I pulled on my dressing gown, wrapping it tightly around my body against the chill of the room and tying it in the middle.

It had taken all night for the cottage to heat up. As predicted, the estate agent had indeed left us a package of food but neglected to turn up the thermostat, resulting in us being greeted with a blast of cold air when we unlocked the old wooden front door and stepped inside.

'It needs a name.' Neil sat up in bed and looked around at the sloping ceiling and ancient oak beams. 'Something romantic and evocative to honour its past.'

'The cottage?' I frowned. We had enough to keep us busy without adding to the ever-growing list of jobs that demanded our attention. Naming this place was low on my list of priorities.

'It used to be a forge apparently, many moons ago.'

'Well, there you have it,' I said, making my way out of the room, my stomach calling to me that it needed filling. 'The Forge. Nice and easy. All sorted.'

'Too easy,' Neil shouted as I made my way down the narrow, winding stairs and into the kitchen. 'We need something more original than that. I'll put some thought into it.'

I set about making us both some breakfast, leaving him to mull over fitting names for our new abode. I slotted bread into the toaster and whisked eggs, adding a dash of pepper before pouring them into the old skillet that I found at the back of one of the cupboards. I placed it on the hob with a clank, the sheer weight of it causing my hands to shake when it landed on the gas ring. Soft morning sunshine filtered through the kitchen window, wrapping its comforting arms around me while I stood next to the cooker and stirred the eggs. My mind wandered, my eyes drawn to the garden. It wasn't so much of a garden as a large patch of scrubby wasteland that hadn't been cleared for God knows how many years. It was big, however. Workable and full of potential. Bigger than the garden we had left behind in our old house at Saltburn. That had been pretty enough but had no room for expansion, just a small, neat square of green with potted plants lining the perimeter. Maybe that was something we could consider in the future: adding an extension to the cottage, pushing out the walls a little, having extra bedrooms, maybe even a bigger, modern kitchen. I stopped, bit at my lip. Too early. Too soon. I was thinking like Neil. Still, I knew that land was cheaper here, so it was a possibility for the future. But not yet. One step at a time.

I tried to focus on the positives and what we had now, not what we could acquire in the future. Not many people would be willing to up sticks and move somewhere this remote. But we had done it. I suppose that was something we should be proud of. Neither of us were big risk-takers, me especially, so I guessed I should have been feeling gratified at the change in our lifestyle. We had done it. We were here.

Not big risk-takers.

Apart, that is, from those times when I had overstepped the mark, taking great strides towards possible oblivion.

The eggs began to sizzle. I gripped the wooden spoon tightly and stirred them, then buttered the toast, secretly enjoying the process of making our first meal in our new house. Above me, I heard

Neil's footsteps as he wandered about the bedroom, getting showered and dressed, the thud of his movements a reassuring presence. I hoped he could locate something to wear. With most of our possessions still boxed and packed up, we would have to make do with the clothes we travelled in. Today I planned on unpacking, cleaning up, and getting as much of our items in place as I could. Making this place feel like home. I knew it would take me a long time to come round to the idea of living here but I had to try. Seeing our own things dotted about, the familiarity of having them around, would help.

I spent the next five minutes or so getting used to the new kitchen, trying to familiarise myself to its shape and size, and searching for utensils left by the previous owners.

'Smells divine. I'm starving.' Neil's voice echoed behind me. A pain took hold in my belly, hunger gripping me. Last night's food package was welcome but sparse. It hadn't constituted what could be classed as a proper meal. Two bags of crisps, two apples, half a baguette each and a small slab of butter apiece. We had eaten ravenously but awoke with empty bellies.

He pulled out a chair and flopped into it like a man fatigued by life, then stood up again. 'I'll make the coffee. I need it to wake me up. Still feel a bit out of sorts, if I'm being honest.'

I knew what he meant. The sheer physicality and anxiety of the move had felt exhausting. I had to be honest and say that it was the anxiety that took it out of me, leaving me feeling washed out. I served up our food and watched as Neil poured the coffee from an old coffee pot we found last night, the dark liquid and swirl of the steam a bewitching sight.

A pocket of calm surrounded us while we ate, the hiss of the boiler in the corner of the room drowning out the sound of cutlery scraping against crockery. There was no need to say anything, no pressure to initiate a forced conversation. The food helped, the tangle in my mind loosening with every forkful. A stark contrast to my mood last night when the world felt like a darker, more hostile place.

We finished our breakfast and I stood up, crockery balanced in my grip as I walked to the sink and dropped them in. I had just turned on the taps when I heard it, the sound sending a ripple of apprehension over my skin. It was unexpected. We didn't know anybody on the island, and nobody knew us. Except they probably did. It's a small place. Tongues wag. I felt sure plenty of people knew we were moving in. According to Mike, the only estate agent on the whole of

Winters End, it had been years since anybody new had come to live on the island and I was almost certain he had informed locals about our imminent move here. The cottage had been empty for a couple of years so I was willing to guess that us buying it would have been a major source of gossip in every shop and pub for miles around.

Still, it didn't explain why somebody was knocking on our door at eight thirty on a Sunday morning. Whoever it was, I wished they would leave. I wasn't ready for visitors. It was early. I was still tired. No, not tired. Weary. That's what I was – wearied by the move, the stress of it all. Wearied by my dreadful, calamitous mistake. I wore it like a second skin, my permanent fatigue. A person browbeaten by their own heinous crime. I wasn't ready for visitors. I wasn't yet ready to turn on charm I didn't have in order to greet people I didn't know.

Before I could say or do anything, Neil was up on his feet, searching for the key that we had discarded late last night after locking up. I watched him sweep his hand across a shelf in the dining room and locate it, his fingers clutched around its small rectangular base.

'Coming,' he shouted, frantically fiddling with the lock. He flung open the door and peered outside, his head moving from side to side as he searched for our mysterious caller.

I waited, my chest tight, my breathing laboured, and watched as he stepped back inside, his face crumpled with confusion. 'I definitely heard somebody. You heard them as well, didn't you, Fi?'

A small gavel tapped at my temple, a pain shot up through my skull and lodged behind my eye, needle-like in its severity. I pushed Neil aside and stuck my head out. Nobody there. Something didn't feel right. I wasn't a fan of surprises, especially ones that disturbed me early on a Sunday morning.

'They can't get far, can they? We're only one of three houses in the lane.' My voice rose an octave. I tried to hide it, the visceral tugging sensation that was swirling deep in my abdomen, the one that told me to beware, but it was difficult to shake, that over-whelming feeling that people were always going to think the worst of me. That they were going to do something terrible to make me pay for what I had done. Even with this amount of distance between me and my old life, that unshakeable sense of dread trailed around after me, a deadweight that refused to shift. I was tired of it, living my life on the cusp of near terror at being found out, having fingers pointed at me, eyes narrowed in disapproval.

Neil smiled and shrugged his shoulders. 'Never mind. It was probably kids messing about or somebody who realised they'd got the wrong house.'

Sometimes, the way Neil dismissed things and explained them away as something they were clearly not, irritated me beyond reason. I spun around and glared at him, fury mounting in me, anger piled upon anger until it toppled like a Jenga stack.

'The wrong house? Neil, the entire island is populated by less than a hundred people! It's early on a Sunday morning. Everyone's in bed and if they're not, then maybe they should be, not snooping around here spying on us.'

If my outburst shocked him, he hid it well, his face impassive, his movements fluid and measured. He stepped to one side and made to close the door. But then, a sudden change in his demeanour, his expression altering. A lightness in his step. Twinkling eyes, his mouth twitching in amusement. Something was coming then. I saw it, felt it in my gut and prepared myself.

'Ah, that explains it,' he said softly, squatting on his haunches, his hand sweeping down onto the concrete step and lifting something with one deft movement.

I didn't ask what it was, was unable to. My heart

was still thrashing around my chest, pulsating against my ribs, leaving me breathless and slightly dizzy. Instead, I waited until he stepped back inside, a small basket tucked under his arm. He kicked the door closed and turned to face me, his smile a sly, lopsided grin, his eyes glistening triumphantly.

'Looks like we've got ourselves another little welcome package. Damn those neighbours being so cold and unfriendly towards us, eh? Makes me glad they decided to not have a lie-in.'

I ignored his sarcastic smile and underlying tone of self-satisfaction and peered over his shoulder, watching as he placed the small packet on the table and began unwrapping it, his fingers working at the cellophane packaging, casting it aside before lifting the basket to reveal the contents.

Two apples and a handful of grapes sat atop a mound of cream tissue paper surrounded by a scattering of herbal teabags, two fruit scones, a miniature pot of jam and an envelope. Curiosity piqued, I reached over and grabbed it, aware that Neil was smirking at my sudden turnabout in mood. I pulled out the slip of paper from inside and opened it, holding it up to the light to get a better view of the tiny, impeccably neat handwriting. Calligraphy in miniature.

Welcome to Winters End, where summers are brief and friendships are lasting.

Neil was grinning. I didn't have to turn to see him; I could sense it, was able to feel the heat from his body and the weight of his small victory pressing down on me. He glanced at the message, eyes narrowed, before moving away to put the items into a cupboard. He at least had the decency to say nothing, to not dent my confidence even further by highlighting my impulsive behaviour and the maddening habit I have of jumping to the wrong conclusion and always assuming the worst.

Expect the worst then everything else is a bonus.

Those words spiked me, a childhood memory of my dad and the swift but incisive ways he had of giving me perspective on life when I was a younger woman and bemoaning the lack of opportunities that came my way.

Problem was, the worst *had* happened to us. I was still waiting for the bonus to show its face, to appear in a welcome flurry and elevate my circumstances and mood. Perhaps Winters End was the bonus and I needed to start accentuating the positives.

'Maybe once we've unpacked some more of our things, we can go for a walk around the village? Find out where everything is, show our faces and say a few hellos, eh?'

I nodded and gave Neil a tight smile. My face felt stretched, like a too-tight blouse that was bursting at the seams. The unexpected knock on the door had shoved me off-kilter. The rested sensation after a long and much-needed night's sleep had already dissipated. I was back to being jumpy, my body always on the cusp of being in a state of panic. A walk, though, sounded just right. The notion of wandering around the place anonymously gave me a warm glow. No sharp words, no pursed mouths. No sets of eyes boring their way into my soul. Neil told me I had imagined it all, that nobody knew about what had happened, but I didn't believe him. People gossip. It's a natural thing to do: to take a sharp interest in other people's misfortunes, to revel in the sins of others while thanking God their own lives are running smoothly. No bumps in the road. No unexpected deviations or reroutes. I probably would have done the same. I'm not in denial about what I did. It's there every morning when I wake and it's the last thing I see each night before I close my eyes. My misdeeds have irrevocably shaped and changed my life. Our lives. Me and Neil locked together in a lifetime of humiliation and contrition.

'I'll go and tidy up a bit then we can get ready to go?' A frisson of excitement bolted through me at the thought of it, being able to be somebody new, somebody different. Somebody who wasn't the old me. A reinvention of the old Fiona: the dirty, tawdry one. The criminal. I could be a newer, fresher version, cleansed of my sins.

I ambled through the cottage, the place we now called home – a two-hundred-year-old blacksmith's forge that was so very different from our four-bedroomed, detached house in Saltburn with its top-of-the-range fixtures and fittings. An abundance of things that we hadn't really needed.

The original wooden flooring was warm beneath my feet. I padded from room to room, scanning the newness and unfamiliarity of each wall, each doorway, each window and shadowy corner. The place was surprisingly clean with some rooms recently redecorated in pastel shades. It was an optical illusion, rooms seeming brighter and bigger than they actually were. With only two bedrooms, a living room, a small study and a decent sized kitchen/diner, the cottage was a fraction of the size of our other property, but at least we could say it was all ours. No more huge debts hanging over our heads, no more sleepless nights wondering how we were ever going to pay for it all.

'Prosperity Cottage!' Neil shouted through to me, his voice a buoyant sound amidst the silence of our tiny new home.

I stopped walking, the fact he was able to read my mind a chilling thought. Maybe he too was plagued by the dark thoughts that taunted me, both of our minds full of shadows of the past. A past we could have avoided but didn't. We chose our path in life and this move here was the net result of those choices. Time to forget, to move on.

I said nothing but nodded. Maybe the name Prosperity Cottage would suit our new lifestyle. A healthy bank balance didn't always denote how rich people were. There were many different strands to happiness and a comfortable life that didn't revolve around money and possessions. We could be happy and content with less.

Later, I would ruminate over those words, those thoughts. When our lives took a catastrophic turn, I would remember to never think that the worst was ever over. Because it wasn't true. The bad things were still waiting for us. Little did we know that an even darker period of our lives was waiting in the wings, about to make a grand appearance.

3

'Oh, you'll not find many of those around here, pet.' The man behind the counter shook his head, cast his eyes downwards. He reminded me of a small, frightened animal caught in a snare. His small hands rummaged in the carrier bag, rearranging tins of beans and loaves of bread. 'You'll have to wait for the deliveries to come in from the mainland. I can put an order in for you, if yer like?'

'No, honestly, it's fine.' I stifled a sigh, wondering why something as innocuous as a packet of Bourbon biscuits would warrant a special request.

'We tend to order what we know our customers like. Saves on wastage, you know?' he murmured, clearly able to read my thoughts.

I held my card to the screen and listened to it beep. Relief bloomed in my chest. At least they had the facility for contactless payments. Our new home wasn't so far behind the rest of the world after all. Isolated geographically but able at least to keep pace with technology.

'Aye, we've managed to keep up with the latest gadgets here on Winters End. We might be small but we've got Wi-Fi and cable TV. Not so remote after all, eh?'

I shivered and hunched my shoulders at this man's ability to read my mind, pre-empting my thoughts and questions with frightening accuracy.

'So, you here on holiday then, or...?'

I shook my head. I was sure he already knew the answer, was just being delicate and well mannered, going through the motions of polite conversation. 'We've just moved here from the mainland.' I was tempted to add, *but I guess you already know that*. I remained silent, waited for him to continue.

'Ah, you'll be the couple that Mike's been talking about. Bought the old forge up on Harbour Lane?'

I nodded, wondering how much he and the other locals knew about us, how much of our lives Mike had revealed to them. Not that we had told him anything, only that we were looking for a change, were after a smaller house and after seeing the cottage for sale on-line, decided to take a chance. Some of it was true. All of it actually. Sometimes it's what people don't say that exposes who they really are. Silent souls are sinister. They make people dig deeper, look for the unknown. The unspoken.

A Google search revealed little of our lives, our digital footprint minimal. I knew that because I had tried it. On several occasions. After it all happened, I became neurotic, convinced everybody outside our social circle knew what had taken place. I would sit hour after hour, frantically typing in various permutations connected to our names and address and was always relieved to find nothing of any substance. We immediately closed our social media accounts after the event and lived a low-key life, desperate to remain anonymous and unseen. The invisible people – that's what we became. Invisible, faceless individuals who hid behind a veil of shame. Moving here felt like the only way out of that life. A way of moving forward instead of living our lives in the abyss of a black hole that sucked us in and held us hostage with no visible means of escape. We were stuck in a groove. Every day, I felt as if all eyes were upon us, judging me. Judging us. No leniency or compassion. Just puckered mouths and tight, unforgiving glances when they scurried past us, frightened of being tainted by association. I guess we didn't deserve any compassion. I was the face of our misdeeds, Neil's part in it concealed to many. Perhaps most of it was in my imagination. That's what I told myself every time I became weepy and weighed down with it all, convinced neighbours and locals could see inside my head to our misery and problems.

Nobody knows about it, Fi. They can't possibly know, can they?

Neil would say this to me time and time again but it didn't alleviate any of my worries, so convinced was I of the transparency of my thoughts and expressions, my wrongdoings discernible to all.

When I saw the cottage for sale online, it drew me in. It was a means of escape from the problems and anxieties that were running loose in my head, stampeding over rational thoughts, obliterating all reason.

'Hope you settle in okay. Winters End is a small place. Can get pretty lonely up there on Harbour Lane. Where you both from originally? You sound northern. Got the slight twang to your accent. Nowt quite like a northern dialect, is there?'

My insides shrivelled, knotting and squirming. Disguising our accents would have been impossible and draining. An intolerable burden to bear.

'We're from the north-east. That obvious, eh?' I laughed, tried to shrug off the mantle of worry that perched on my shoulder. The north-east covers an area of just under 9,000 km² with a population of over two and a half million. Why would this man know us? He couldn't see inside my head. He couldn't see my past. What I had done. My thieving, conniving ways.

I picked up my bag of groceries and shuffled away from the counter, a sudden need to leave the shop pushing me on. I was wrong about getting out and exploring. I had misjudged it. I wasn't ready to mingle with the locals just yet. My nerves were still frazzled, always anticipating an accusatory remark or comment that I could feel slighted about. I was made of fresh air; one sharp breeze, one cutting remark and I would be lifted off my feet and blown away, a stray leaf in the wind.

Neil was waiting outside, squatting on his haunches, petting a dog that was tied up to the railings.

'Ready?' I said, eager to be back indoors. I had changed my mind. Exploring the island could wait until I was feeling less jumpy, more confident of myself. The past was a heavy cloak to wear, constantly pushing me deep into the ground, driving me so low there were days when I felt as if I was being buried alive, the heavy wet loam sticking in my throat and choking me.

'This is Max,' Neil said. He stroked the small spaniel, running his hand through its thick, straggly fur. The dog swivelled over onto its back and kicked its legs in the air. 'Isn't he a cutie? We should get one. This is the perfect territory for dog walking, for getting out and about and roaming around the place with a little canine friend by our sides.'

I ignored his remark and began walking away, the carrier bag clutched tightly between my fingers. I could barely manage myself and my own needs, never mind taking on a dog that would need walking and feeding three times a day. Most days, putting one foot in front of another was an ordeal.

'Just moved in, have yer?'

I jumped at the sound behind me and spun around to see Neil standing up, his hand outstretched to the tall man standing next to him. Annoyance prickled my scalp. I had no idea why such an innocent, harmless action irritated me as much as it did. Perhaps it was because he was trying too hard, straining every sinew to make a good impression with our new neighbours. He was making us conspicuous when all I wanted at that point was to be invisible.

'That's right,' he answered, his voice cutting

through the quiet morning air. 'I'm Neil and this is my wife, Fiona.'

Like the dutiful woman and wife that I was, I walked back, decency forcing me to make my introductions to this perfect stranger who was now busy untying his dog from the wrought-iron railing that flanked the narrow road.

Rather than shake my hand, the craggy-faced stranger eyed me cautiously, eventually cracking a smile that revealed a row of yellowed, uneven teeth that looked as if they hadn't seen a toothbrush or dentist's visit since cutting through his gums decades before. He was in his mid-forties but had the hardened, weather-beaten features of somebody much older, his leathery skin crinkled and creased, a crepe-paper complexion.

'Pleased to meet you,' I whispered. My eyes were drawn to his pockmarked face and watchful expression. A stone rolled about in the pit of my stomach, ice stabbing my flesh when his gaze travelled down to my chest, lingering there for a few seconds before moving back up to my face.

'Yeah,' he replied quietly. 'You too. I'm Sam. Live back there by the patch of grass over yonder.'

He pointed to a squalid, sad-looking house nearby. It was clearly a prefab property and reminded me of a scout hut; a flimsy shed that could blow over in a strong breeze. Yellowed net curtains hung at the windows and a faded bottle-green door that looked as old and neglected as he did was half-open, fingers of darkness from within creeping out into the street. Even looking at it for more than a few seconds made my toes curl. I wanted to turn and run, to get as far away from him as possible, but instead I stood there, making small talk, listening to Neil chat about our move here, our old house in Saltburn, how we were both self-employed so looking for work on such a small island wouldn't be an issue for us.

'Good job 'cos there ain't nowt here for ya. Unless you wanna work in the shop or head out on a small boat trawling for fish.'

I cringed as Neil assured him that we were completely self-sufficient.

Why not just show him our bank details, driving licences and passports, Neil, and be done with it?

The words stayed in my head, unspoken, static fizzing and popping. Loud and unstoppable, trapped within the confines of my brain. Typical Neil: so open and friendly and approachable. And typical Fiona: a closed book riddled with negative thoughts and malice.

'You'll be used to the sea breeze and the dangers of the tide then, if you lived on the coast?'

Neil nodded sagely, a self-satisfied smile on his face. My fingers itched to wipe it clean off. Why was he doing this? He knew how much I craved anonymity. Needed it. That was why we had moved here – to escape everything, spend time forgiving one another and healing, not expose our sordid past to the first people we become acquainted with. This man was a stranger and I would rather he stayed that way. For now. I wasn't so stupid as to think we could live on such a tiny island and remain alone and unknown, but for the first few weeks I wanted some time to adjust, to get to know myself properly, the new me that I'd become, before I introduced her to anybody else.

'Yes, the North Sea is a force to be reckoned with, isn't she? No half-measures where her temperament is concerned.' Both men laughed as if they were old friends from way back.

I wanted to throw up at the sound of Neil's vomit-inducing idle chatter, his persuasive talk that would make anybody believe he was well acquainted with the ebb and flow of an entire body of water. We had a house in a coastal town. We were hardly hardy sea folk who eked out a living from it, singing sea shanties

while we emptied lobster pots and gutted fish from
barrels.

'I'm in The Bucket most nights,' Sam said, his
voice a low, husky growl. 'I can be found huddled over
me pint in the corner if ever yer fancy joining me?'

'The Bucket?' The question was out of my mouth
before I could stop it.

'Bucket of Blood,' Sam replied, his lip curled at my
interjection. 'The local pub. Good craic if you're
passing that way. When I say a pub, it's more like stepping into someone's living room, if y'know what I
mean? Right small space it is, but good atmosphere all
the same. Had some good laughs in there over the
years, we 'ave.'

I lowered my gaze. I didn't want his invitation and
hoped that Neil wouldn't accept it either, that he
would have the good sense to step away and give us
both time to settle here before he ventured out and
made new friends. We needed to talk, to ensure we
both told the same story, that nothing of our previous
life slipped out after one pint too many. Chatting to
people on a walk around the island was different to
suddenly becoming drinking buddies with them.

'That sounds great,' Neil exclaimed, my blood siz-
zling and bubbling as I listened to the undisguised excitement and childlike fervour in his tone. I knew this

would happen. He was like an overfull bottle of champagne, fizzing around, desperate to be out and about. I wanted to turn and run, to throw the bag of groceries to the floor and disappear. But I didn't. Once more I stood, meekly and submissively, too frightened to make a show of myself by protesting. I visualised Neil sitting in a crammed bar, his mouth running loose after four pints, telling everyone within earshot about our private business, him thinking these people were our friends when they were no more than strangers. 'How about it, Fi? A couple of drinks in our new local. Sounds about perfect, doesn't it?'

It didn't sound 'about perfect'. It sounded like hell. I wanted to reply that sitting plucking out my eyelashes with blunt tweezers held more appeal for me but found myself nodding in agreement, my expression set in a tight grimace, my eyes narrowed in suspicion at this Sam person who once again was mentally undressing me, his eyes roving over my breasts and down to my abdomen. I tightened my jaw and swallowed, then turned away and stared off into the clouded sky, trying to erase from my mind the look that was in his eye whenever he stared at me.

Neil's voice faded into the distance, everything becoming a blur as I struggled to contain my anger. Fingers clutched around the handle of the carrier bag, I began to walk away, no longer caring whether Neil was following me, no longer caring what sort of impression I was making by distancing myself in the middle of a conversation. I just wanted to get back to our cottage, our tiny old-fashioned prison where I could hide away from the rest of the world, skulking behind its thick ancient walls like the sorry cheap thief that I was.

I could hear Neil's voice behind me, his dull, muffled cries when I picked up my pace and he tried to catch up with me. I listened to him bid his goodbyes to his newly made friend and heard the echo of his footsteps pounding on the pavement but I didn't care and made no attempts to slow down. I was too angry, too lost in the murk of my emotions to respond to his pleas for me to wait. It was all I could to not turn round and scream at him to just fucking well stop being so nice to people when he was married to a woman who'd robbed a family of their life savings so she could bail out her husband and his astronomic credit card bills; a woman who stole from her employer so she could stop the bailiffs from kicking down their door and repossessing almost everything they owned. But no, he always felt the need to talk to anyone and everyone, pretending as if nothing had happened when, in reality, everything had happened.

Our lives had been turned upside down and none of it appeared to bother him. He continued to act as if everything was as it had been in our other life when it wasn't. Our lives were now an ill-fitting jigsaw, parts of it forced into position so we could carry on like normal people, trying to present a pretty picture to the outside world. We weren't a pretty picture. We were a disaster, a family of thieves. Criminals who had run away from their other life and were now living in relative obscurity trying to pretend that none of it had taken place. Trying to pretend that it meant nothing when in fact it meant everything.

I took a long breath and slowed down when Sam was out of earshot then turned to Neil, tears already spilling out, and hissed at him. 'Why, Neil? We agreed to lay low for a while, give ourselves time to adjust, but no! You couldn't contain yourself, could you? At the first whiff of a beer, you're there, like a fucking puppy, all doe-eyed and excited, bouncing around like a fucking idiot.'

He stopped walking, shock and hurt etched into his expression. I had overreacted, I knew that. I wasn't stupid. I wasn't so out of touch with Neil and his emotions that I didn't know when to stop, didn't see those invisible barriers that denoted his dented ego and damaged feelings, but no matter how hard I tried, I couldn't shake off my own misgivings; the dirt still clinging to me, every penny and pound I stole immediately apparent to everyone I met. The word *thief* was stamped all over my face, chiselled deep into my bones.

Like the ever-forgiving person he was, Neil wrapped his arms around me and I fell into his chest, my sobs muted by the fabric of his jacket. It was time I left it all behind me, I knew that, but it felt so damn hard, the heft of my misdeeds constantly bearing down on me. I wanted to turn back time, undo the damage I had caused, but I couldn't. What was done was done and couldn't be undone.

'Let's go home,' Neil said. His palm rested on the back of my head, light as air, his fingers stroking and separating the long strands of my knotted hair. 'Let's go home and talk. It's long overdue.'

Our fingers interlocked. We walked back over the small hillock towards Harbour Lane, to the recently and ironically named Prosperity Cottage.

4

If there is one thing I have learnt from life, it is this: aside from sudden death and major illnesses, difficulties and trauma rarely happen in one fell swoop; they gain momentum gradually, starting off as a few minor issues that snowball and increase in speed, mounting up until they're unmanageable, forcing the bearer of the problems to do terrible, tragic things in an attempt to salvage what is left of their lives. It's like a vicious circle that is too tight to break. Until it does. And when that happens, the repercussions and ripples have a lasting effect on those within the circle. And often on those standing on the outside, watching it all take place. Innocent bystanders who get injured by the shrapnel.

I think of my parents, their crumpled features as Neil and I tried to explain what had happened. What I did. Why we needed to borrow over £35,000 to stop me being arrested and appearing in court. Then Neil's sister, Kate and her partner, Chrissie: their crestfallen expressions and looks of horror when we sat them down and asked if they had £25,000 we could borrow until we sold our house, at which point we would pay them back. Remortgaging our property to raise the much-needed cash would have been impossible since I had already lost my job, having been told by my employer that I had a month to find the money and pay back what I had stolen or I would be charged. I was lucky. They had allowed me some time. Lucky that they hadn't gone straight to the police and had my name splashed all over the local newspapers, my misdeeds pronounced in bold, glaring headlines for everyone to see. Court appearances. A prison sentence. Bankruptcy. They were all possible scenarios.

But none of this happened overnight. I didn't wake up one morning and decide to steal £60,000 from my erstwhile employer. It was an act borne out of desperation. Desperation due to mounting debts that Neil and I simply couldn't find the money to pay. When I say Neil and I, what I really mean is me. I was the one who managed our finances. I was the one who realised we were living beyond our means. And I was the one who said nothing, remaining silent, allowing my husband to spend more and more money on a house that didn't need it. Lavish fixtures and fittings, expansive, opulently decorated rooms, we had them all. We had everything and yet, in the end, we had nothing.

You can never overspend on a property, was his favourite phrase, truly believing that any cash ploughed into the house would make us wealthier, believing that it was an investment. Our retirement plan. Our only pension pot. And now, all gone.

After selling our house, we had enough to pay back Kate and Chrissie and my parents, and just enough to buy our new cottage outright. Many would be forgiven for thinking that we got off lightly. I could have ended up being prosecuted but was lucky enough to work for a family firm who didn't want the humiliation or hassle of taking me to court. We could have ended up penniless, having to scrape up enough money every month to pay rent on a measly little flat somewhere that had peeling wallpaper and rising damp. We didn't. And yet, I didn't feel lucky or blessed. I felt dirty and ashamed.

It started off with me taking care of the accounts at work and having access to the company bank account.

It all seemed so innocent, so easy. I was going to pay it back. That's what I told myself every time I did it. Just £100 to see us through until payday. Then another £200 to pay off the minimum charges on one of our credit cards. On and on it went, week after week, month after month, guilt and dread biting at me whenever I transferred money over, knowing that one day it would all come back and explode in my face. Which, of course, it did. A detonation of earth-shattering proportions that blew apart our safe little lives beyond recognition.

Rick and Jerry, the company owners who spent most of their days out seeing customers, were contacted by the accountants, querying the transfers I had made. It had been going on for over two years before they made the grim discovery. Two years of anxiety and reckless spending. It was a relief, in the end, to be found out. I was glad it all came out in the open. I now faced the long haul of recovery, an endless road that would lead us back to normality with so many twists and turns it felt never-ending.

At the time it was traumatic. I had to own up to my crime and I also had to face Neil and tell him that it was all over, that our finances were built on foundations of sand, that the money we had spent on the house amounted to nothing because we had overstretched ourselves on a massive scale and, as a result, our lives were in free fall.

Now, looking back, our life in Saltburn feels like a lifetime ago. I deserve to live here in this squalid little cottage. I did this to us. It's my penance for being a thief, for almost bankrupting a decent, ethically run, small firm. Rick and Jerry worked hard to keep the company afloat, believing their profit margins weren't working when in actual fact it was me stealing from them that resulted in their bank account looking perpetually empty. They spent many sleepless nights trying to keep that company going. I didn't want to think about the damage it had done to their mental health and the unity of their families.

I was lucky that we had spotted this place on Winters End, lucky that we had been able to up sticks and leave it all behind us, all that trouble and heartache. Lucky that certain family members had been able to loan us the money and keep the wolves away from the door. So why did I feel like the most blighted person on earth?

My stomach was in knots. Neil sat opposite me on the sofa, a serious expression on his face. We had poured all our energies into surviving after that event. There had been little time for soul-bearing and long, deep, meaningful conversations. We had both known that this would test us, and there were days when I had felt utterly washed out – I still did – but the strength of our relationship was never in doubt. Regardless of what we had or hadn't both done, separation was never going to be on the cards. And yet a barrier still sat between us, an invisible but tangible wall that had stopped us from moving on from the past. Stopped me. To all intents and purposes, Neil appeared to be the same jovial old soul he had always been, whereas me – I was a changed character. Sullen, withdrawn, miserable. Family members believed that I was the sole perpetrator, the petty thief. The criminal. They knew what I had done but still didn't know anything of Neil's spending habits, his lackadaisical attitude to money. It was all my doing. All my fault. I bore the brunt of their anger and abhorrence.

'We have to put it behind us, Fi. What's done is done,' he said, his eyes full of warmth, full of love and forgiveness.

I swallowed and clutched at my knees, my fingers digging into the flesh beneath my clothes. 'I never wanted to say this.' I stopped and clenched my teeth together, swallowed hard, hoping what I was about to say next didn't set us apart, lengthening and widening that invisible wall between us, stretching it out until it was completely unsurmountable, too high to ever be scaled. 'But can you promise me we will never again get into that level of debt? That your need to have the biggest and the best of everything is behind us?' I dipped my head and glanced away. 'Behind you?'

His reply took only a couple of seconds. It felt interminably long. Neil wasn't given to temper tantrums but I knew my words had an accusatory ring to them. I was no longer prepared to carry this burden alone, was heartily sick of it in truth. Whenever I'd tried to talk to him about his spending habits in the past, he used to shrug and tell me that the money always seemed to be there so what was the problem? Except it had only been there because I was continually transferring somebody else's hard-earned cash to our account to stop us going into the red. I had given him a false sense of well-being. I was his enabler. Which one of us was the guiltiest? Me for stealing or Neil for not enquiring or caring to notice? He saw the credit card bills, knew that we didn't have the means to pay them off. Not once did he ask where the money was coming from. Not once did he stop to think of the enormous pressure his spending was putting on us. I swallowed, pushed a strand of hair out of my eyes. On me. The pressure was all on me.

He leaned over and clasped his hand around mine, lowering his head to make eye contact. 'I promise. Honestly, this is our life now and I love it. We're going to make new friends here, have a different way of living. I know you want to hide away, frightened everyone knows about us, but they don't. How can they possibly know?' He was right, I was aware of that, and I did feel buoyed up by his words. It was just a matter of taking time to heal, that's all it was. This wasn't permanent, the way I viewed life. It was just a passing phase. 'This time next year, you'll wonder why you worried. And yes, I know I was stupid and careless and got carried away by the lavish lifestyle we had, but that's the old me. The old Neil. The new Neil is a cautious character. Never again do I want us to go through anything as traumatic as that.'

The lump in my throat was a large rock, jagged and angular. My eyes burned as I fought back more tears. He hadn't done this thing alone. I was just as responsible and yet not once had he ever blamed me or turned against me. Unlike me. I'd blamed Neil plenty in my head, wanted to kick and punch him, shake him till his eyes bulged and his nose bled.

I stood up, brushed myself down, and blinked back the tears, sniffing noisily. 'You're right. Time to move on. But slowly, yes? No diving into new friendships or opening up to people about our problems? Don't let your mouth sound off after a few beers.'

Neil laughed. I laughed. Not loud, acerbic, gut-shaking hysteria but a small recognition of my words, that our secret should remain just that. No opening up to people, no hints in conversation. No mention of the real reason why we had come here.

'Scout's honour.' He lifted his fingers up to his shoulder, tapped his collarbone, and smiled.

I only hoped that he really did mean it and it wasn't simply a stream of empty words, that this conversation would balloon in his mind and ring in his ears should he ever feel the need to say anything to anybody here on Winters End. I had to trust him, but with the lapse of time, friendships would grow, metal clasps that held secrets in place would slacken, and tongues would become loose. There were some things, however, that should never be spoken of and my crime was one of them.

'Tea?' I asked, my voice light and airy. Deceptive. I said it because I couldn't think of anything else to say so we could move on from the moment. Even marriages as strong and solid as ours had awkward moments where conversation was stilted.

We sat and sipped from mismatching mugs, my thoughts beginning to free themselves from the tangle of anxiety that for so long now had wrapped itself around my brain: yards of barbed wire encasing my emotions, refusing to free me. Maybe now was the time to break out of my self-made prison, to step away from the carnage and destruction and live a little.

I wish I'd held that moment, kept the beauty of it in my head, treasured it a little more because when everything started to fall apart, I dreamed I could have turned back the clock to that time. A time when I actually believed that things could go our way, that we could clamber out of the big black hole we had dug for ourselves. Not that the troubles that came our way on Winters End were any of our doing. Far from it. It all came looking for us. And on such a small island, we found ourselves backed into a corner with nowhere to hide. We were surrounded, an army of suspicious wrongdoers determined to drive us out of our new home. Or rather, *me*. Because it was, after all, me they were after. I just didn't know why. And when I finally discovered the reason, it was too late to do anything about it.

5

We didn't venture out again until the following day. Neil managed to resist temptation and didn't join Sam in The Bucket of Blood.

Jesus. That name. The very idea of sitting in such a darkly named place filled me with gloom. I had always thought that pubs were meant to be convivial places, full of cheer and warmth. The Bucket of Blood conjured up images of misery and desolation; an unfriendly bar packed with suspicious locals, intent on harming any outsiders who dared to enter. Like something out of a low-budget horror movie.

'A walk around the place properly this time,' Neil said, a little too cheerily. 'That's what we need. To just stop and breathe in the clean air, take in the views. Good for the soul.'

He was trying too hard. I didn't want forced warmth and happiness; I wanted normality. Familiarity and routine, something to anchor us to the island, to make me feel balanced again.

Outside, the sky was an ominous shade of grey, a stretch of gunmetal, the clouds primed for rain. Soon winter would arrive, the ground turning hard as iron, the north-east wind biting at our faces. It didn't bother me, the thought of living here through the darkest months of the year. We could lock ourselves away, ignore the outside world. Watch the waves crash against the shore with shocking ferocity. It would give my broken mind time to repair itself. Or so I thought.

I slipped my feet into my old ankle boots, the feel of them a comforting thing. Something from my past. We had discarded many of our belongings before moving here, the cottage too small to house everything we owned. I trailed my hand over the worn leather, the feeling beneath my fingertips sparking memories of times spent walking on the moors, backpacks strapped on, hip flasks at the ready. Good times, untainted and free of shadows. A time before money, or rather the lack of it, filled my every waking moment, worries about how I would manage it all pushing me towards a breakdown.

'Ready?' Neil was standing next to me, holding my jacket.

I pushed my arms in and wrapped a scarf around my neck, the wool tickling the soft skin of my throat. A brisk walk was definitely needed. It would wake me up, force me into the day. This could become our new routine: starting each morning with a stroll around our village, maybe even trekking over to the other side of the island. The possibilities were endless.

A breath caught in my chest as I realised that I was experiencing true feelings of glee and positivity, senses that had been dulled in me for months and months.

'Come on,' Neil said, a twinkle taking hold in his eye. 'Race you to that post on top of the hill.'

He pushed open the front door. I walked outside and the stench immediately hit my nostrils, my feet out of sync with my senses as I stepped into something wet and slippery.

'Jesus, what is that smell?' Neil's voice filled the air.

I looked down at the smear of brown beneath my feet, a retch building in my gullet. A small note was propped up on the step behind the broken plastic milk crate gifted to us by the previous owners, an item we planned on throwing away once we had sorted out the inside of the cottage. That was the problem with leaving in a hurry: we were unprepared, everything still in disarray.

I bent down to pick up the piece of paper, curiosity winning over my need to retch at the almighty stink that was all-pervading. I opened the note and read it, the odour of the dog dirt stuck to the soles of my boots catching at the back of my throat, making me gag.

Leave this place. Better that way. You shouldn't be here.

A thudding in my head. A large boulder rolling around; acid swirling and burning in my gut.

'What is it?' Neil said resignedly. 'Another welcome note? Told you the locals were friendly.'

'Far from it.' I held out my hand, the paper flapping in the breeze, my skin flashing hot and cold. 'Whoever wrote this also dumped a pile of dog shit on our doorstep for us to step into. Not the sort of welcome I'd hoped for.'

He was quiet, his eyes glued to the paper. I knew what he was doing, what was going on in his head. He was trying to find a way of making a joke of this. This awful, sickening scenario. He would try to put some sort of stupid, insulting positive spin on it so I didn't feel unnerved. He'd have to try really hard with this one. Dog shit and threatening notes didn't sit well with me. This was something nasty, something even Neil couldn't explain away with a flap of his hand and a winning smile.

I said nothing, waiting instead for his words of wisdom, something that could possibly make all this seem better, easier to bear, even though I knew nothing would.

He sighed, sucked at his teeth. 'Look. People will probably have a strange sense of humour on an island this small. We might see this as a warped act but I don't know, maybe this is fun to some of the weirder folk around here.'

He was clutching at straws. I knew it, Neil knew it. Nothing he could say would make me think of this as funny or quirky. It was quite clearly a threat.

'Yesterday, somebody left us a welcome note and some food. Let's look at the positives here. There's bound to be a sprinkling of idiots around. Every village has them. We just got an introduction to them earlier than most.' He put his arm around me and pulled me into his chest. 'Come on, Fi. Let's not get dragged down by the small stuff, eh? We've weathered worse than this. It's just some pathetic nobody who probably lives in his mum's spare room at the ripe old age of forty and gets his kicks out of scaring the neighbours. Don't let him ruin our day.'

'He could be out there now, watching us. If it is a he. It could be a she. We don't know for sure, do we?' I took a deep breath, anxiety gathering in me like a swirling eddy, ready to suck me under. 'We don't know anything about this island or these people. We know nothing. Nothing at all.' Heat gathered around my hairline, prickled under my arms. I stared down at my boots, my sense of smell still not inured to the stench of the dog shit that was caked into my soles. I wrinkled my nose and swallowed down the vomit that threatened to rise. 'I need to take these off and hose them down.'

'I'll do it. Here,' Neil said, his voice showing his weariness, 'let me undo your laces. Step out of the boots and go back inside. I'll take them round the back and fix the hose to the outside tap while you get another pair.'

'Another pair?' I frowned, caught his eye and shook my head. 'Neil, I'm not going out now. What if this person is out there, waiting to do something horrible to us? Something unspeakable?'

There was a moment's silence, a couple of seconds

of nothingness as he watched me, his eyes narrowed in puzzlement. Then he laughed. A loud, throaty chuckle that sent shock waves over my flesh. I hated him for his flippancy and glib attitude.

'You think this is funny? You think I'm overreacting to a threatening letter and a fucking huge pile of dog shit left on our doorstep? What the fuck is wrong with you?' I didn't intend to shock him into silence, but it worked.

I waited, my breathing hot and dry. I gasped in uneven chunks of air, almost choking on them.

'Okay,' he said finally, his laughter absent, replaced instead by a furrowed brow and a thick, gravelly voice. 'Whatever. You go back inside. I'll sort all this out.'

The slamming of the door when I went back into the cottage echoed through the place and was probably heard at the end of Harbour Lane and back again. I didn't care. And yet I felt churlish for taking umbrage, for slinking back inside, my reaction childlike. Isn't that what they wanted, this individual who took time out of their day to scoop up dog shit and dump it on our step? If I acted like a fugitive in my own home then they would have won. I found another pair of walking boots and slipped them on.

'I thought you wanted to stay in the cottage?' Neil

was bending down, scrubbing at the step with a wire brush when I opened the door and leaned outside, a backpack strapped over my shoulders.

'I changed my mind.' I skirted around him and sucked in a lungful of fresh air, the stench of shit almost gone, only the faintest whiff still hanging around.

He didn't respond, smiling at me instead as he rinsed away the last greasy smears. 'I could maybe do with a coffee before we set off then. Hard work this being a scrubber business.'

He winked at me and my chest tightened. I was irritated by the fact he still had the power to do that to me but as long as we had that connection, nothing could ever come between us, could it?

'Coming up,' I said breezily. 'I'll make us a pot of strong caffeinated in preparation for a brisk walk, shall I?'

Neil nodded and turned back to finish cleaning up. It was an awful task, yet he did it without complaint. Something else that rankled me.

Less than five minutes later, we were sitting side by side on the old rickety bench beneath the bay window, steaming mugs of coffee in hand.

'You have to admit, that's some view, isn't it?'

I nodded. He was right about that. Seemed that Neil was right about a lot of things lately.

Ahead of us stretched a field and beyond that was the sea. A reflection of the sky, it was a dull grey but captivating all the same. Our view of the coastline in our old home had been limited, blocked by houses and rooftops, lines of ridge tiles obscuring what should have been a pleasant sight. The view that we now had was uninterrupted, the sort of vista many would pay to have. And here I was, bemoaning my lot in life. I was luckier than many. I had more than I deserved considering our circumstances. Considering my crime.

'Come on,' Neil said, placing his empty mug down at his feet, 'race you to that tree stump over there.'

Before I could swallow the dregs, he was up, pelting out of the garden and on to the field beyond, his willowy frame already a speck in the distance.

I darted out of the hanging crooked gate, feet twisting beneath me, legs burning as I tried to catch up with him. I watched him reach the rough-looking, broken stump, pockets of his misty breath circling in front of his face. And then I saw something else. Another figure approaching from behind the thick hedgerow to the left.

I stopped, breathing hard. Lungs burning. I was

unfit, horribly so. I watched, curious, as the figure moved towards Neil. My legs were lead. Blood pounded in my ears. I visualised something awful happening. A mugging perhaps. Some sort of attack.

The figure spoke. 'Now then. You the people who just moved into the old forge?' The voice was guttural, a rasp. Not welcoming. It had an accusatory ring to it. It made my knees weak with dread.

'That's right,' Neil replied, hand outstretched, a grin fixed on his face.

The stranger's fist hung limply by his side, his stature not dissimilar to the crooked, gnarled tree trunk that stood between us.

'Better watch out then. Better watch out is all I'll say.'

Neither of us said anything, shock rendering us mute as he loped away, disappearing once again into the dark thicket that ran parallel to the open field.

I tried to ignore my hammering heart, the voice in my head that was screaming at me to turn and head back to the cottage, to close the blinds and lock all the doors and windows behind me.

'Welcome to Winters End,' I muttered.

Neil's laugh was like the bark of an excited dog, his face creased with amusement. 'Well, that was different!'

I couldn't find it in me to reply, my thoughts a smorgasbord of clashing emotions, my voice momentarily absent.

'Come on, let's take a walk round this weird and wonderful little place. Lots of exploring to do.' Before I could reply or resist, Neil grabbed my hand, pulling me closer to him, his face the picture of contentment.

I walked beside him in silence, staring ahead at the magnificent view of the roaring sea. I felt in awe of its power, its undeniable strength and ferocity. Maybe I could learn a thing or two from its all-encompassing presence, be a force to be reckoned with instead of the cowering creature I had become of late.

'Right, let's do this,' I said eventually, doing my best to conquer my demons, nudging them aside as we trudged out onto the main path that led to the village and beyond.

6

'This is really weird, eerie actually.' My voice was a whisper, floating around the graveyard, reedy and toothless as it battled against the sound of the wind that whistled through the huge yew and sycamore trees, their thick, towering branches swaying and rustling above and around us.

'It's full of dead people,' Neil laughed. 'What d'you expect?'

I shook my head and tried to not glare. He was being evasive, overly chirpy and annoying, avoiding speaking about what I had noticed. 'Neil. Look at the names, at the inscriptions on the headstones. Don't you find it all a little odd?'

He leaned forward, craning his neck to read them.

'Okay, lovely prose, lots of history here. Don't quite see what you're getting at?'

I sighed and gritted my teeth. Was he being deliberately obtuse? Or was I simply seeing things that weren't there? 'The names, so many young women. All dead and many within such a short space of time. Recently too.' I walked along each row, stepping between the vases of flowers and rectangles of earth, my feet dancing around the shape of each plot. 'It's just a bit – I don't know – a bit unusual, don't you think?' It was jarring. These women were more or less the same age as me. Was that why I found it so unsettling? Or was I overreacting?

He spun around and began to walk in the opposite direction, hands tucked into his pockets, eyes carefully studying each one. I watched as he read stone after stone until at last he stopped and looked at me, smiling. 'Here we are,' he said, sweeping his hand out like he was performing some sort of gracious bow to a waiting audience. 'Arthur West. And another over at the end, Martin Waverley.'

'Two? And how many women are buried here compared to the number of men?'

'Oh God, you're not going to make me count them all, are you?' He was smiling now, laughing even; a gentle inoffensive chuckle that softened my tough veneer. 'And also, look at the dates, Fi. Some of them are from donkey's years ago. Yes, some are recent but there's nothing to connect them. What are you saying here – that none of the men on Winters End ever die?'

I curled up my fists, my nails digging into the soft skin on my palms. He was right. Once again, I was overplaying it, my hackles rising to a situation that didn't warrant any response. It wasn't as if there were even that many headstones dotted about. It was a small graveyard, tiny actually. Perhaps that's why the names jumped out at me. Or perhaps I was imagining things. My mind had numerous ways of punishing me, always managing to find new and innovative things to brood over. I was my own worst enemy.

'Tell you what,' he said, small wrinkles appearing at the corners of his eyes when he smiled, a sight that always steadied my nerves, 'why don't we go for a drink at the local pub? Maybe even get an early lunch?'

I shivered. The wind was picking up, the temperature dropping. Powerful gusts traversed the landscape, bringing with them a bitingly cold sea breeze. Sitting in the pub, even with its inappropriate and sinister name, seemed like an inviting option. My fingers were numb, my feet like ice.

'Have you got any money on you? Or your card?' I

was aware that we needed to keep a close eye on our finances, the pair of us earning less than we had in our previous jobs, but I was also cold and I was very hungry. Anywhere that wasn't the graveyard felt appealing. We had inadvertently stumbled across it, my curiosity piqued by its size and location, and now after standing here in the freezing cold, reading those inscriptions, it had lost its initial allure.

'I've got two ten-pound notes and a fiver stuffed into my pocket. You game?'

I couldn't say no. Once we got back to the cottage – I still couldn't bring myself to call it home – I would get into a routine of working. Tackling my new job as a freelance editor felt like an enormous task, but I was still looking forward to settling into it. Perhaps getting out whenever I could to meet and mingle with others would be something I would learn to do. I was used to being in a busy office. Working alone would bring its challenges, but it would also bring in much-needed income. Neil's job selling sportswear online hadn't changed, his income as variable as it had been in the past. This visit to the pub, as well as being our introduction to the island, could also be our last hurrah before we knuckled down to work in a bid to start bringing in a half-decent salary.

'I'm game,' I said, my voice sounding full of cheer,

the feel of mild happiness an alien sensation to me. For so long, I had felt only anxiety and dread and had forgotten what it was like to experience contentment. 'And I'm starving.'

'Right,' said Neil, his mood clearly lifted up by my new-found positivity, 'let's get going, shall we?'

* * *

The graveyard incident was relegated to the back of my mind by the time we reached the pub. My stomach ruled my thoughts, calling out for sustenance. After a twenty-minute walk, I was ready for a drink, ready to rest my aching feet. Heat gathered beneath my layers of clothing making me clammy and thirsty. We had tramped across field after field, even climbed over a couple of stiles before taking the cliff path, and we were windswept and hungry by the time we arrived.

Inside it was dim, the small windows casting a pall of darkness over everything. It was also extremely small, with many shaded corners and low beams, but even making allowances for that, it was obvious to me that our arrival was a shock to the locals. Our presence clearly unwanted. The conversation dipped as we entered, all eyes following our route to the bar. The Bucket of Blood was everything I had imagined it to be. Trepidation sat in the base of my belly, a small, heavy weight that pressed down on the soft flesh of my stomach.

'Shall I get us a table?' I nodded at Neil, and without waiting for him to reply, I left and made my way over to a small area beneath a particularly low beam. It looked private, intimate even. Far enough away from the sea of dark eyes that watched us, and yet at the same time, not quite far enough.

It was as I was pulling out one of the stools that I heard the voice behind me. Low. Menacing. Determined. 'It's reserved.'

I carried on regardless, resolutely ignoring it. There were no signs, nothing to indicate the table had been set aside for anybody else. I also didn't want the confrontation. I had only just begun to unwind, to regain my self-confidence. An altercation with a complete stranger would upset the delicate equilibrium in my little world, so I pretended I hadn't heard him and sat down regardless, pulling the other stool closer to where I was sitting for when Neil arrived back carrying the drinks and, hopefully, a menu.

His abrupt presence sent a ripple of disdain over my flesh. I sensed him before he stopped walking, this perfect stranger, his bulky frame casting a long shadow over where I was seated.

I looked up into the craggy face of a middle-aged man who was staring down at me, eyes like slits, a suspicious glint to them, a darkness there that made me shift and squirm. Even as a child, despite being cautious and reserved, there had always been a part of me that refused to be browbeaten by bullies. It was still there, that quality, buried somewhere deep inside me, hemmed in and squashed by recent events and the subsequent anxieties that followed them, but I felt it rise to the surface as he leaned down to me, his fat, saggy jowls wobbling with every tiny movement he made.

'No chicken but apparently the steak pie is a must.'

I jumped at the sound of Neil's voice. He was there as well, standing next to the man, his voice light and airy, a juxtaposition to the gruff words of the uninvited stranger standing at our table. Seemingly unaware of the new presence at our table, his attention focused on the large, laminated menu that was clutched between his fingers, Neil spoke softly, his tone easy. Effortless. 'I ordered you an orange juice. Figured you would say it was too early for a proper drink.' He turned, smiled at the stranger, suddenly aware of his presence, and placed the menu on the table, his hand outstretched. 'Hi, I'm Neil and this is my wife, Fiona. We've just moved here on to the island. Pleased to meet you.'

Neil, always relaxed, perpetually gracious. I envied him. I also hated him for it.

The man's face changed, his eyes creasing and lifting. His mouth cracked into a wide grin, the contrast from the scowling expression only a few seconds earlier so stark, I almost laughed out loud.

'Davey. Pleasure's all mine.' Still his jowls wobbled as he spoke, the darkness leaving his eyes when he chatted to Neil. I listened to his jovial banter, observed his affable ways. All boys together.

I glanced around the bar whilst continuing to listen to their conversation, my ears attuned to every word that came out of Neil's mouth. I was poised, my hackles rising, ready to interject should any slip-ups or inadvertent indiscretions occur. I suddenly took a huge dislike to the place. It had a brooding feel to it.

Neil wouldn't agree. He would argue it was warm and welcoming, its dark corners and low beams providing a comfortable, easy environment. But it was anything but welcoming. It was a cheerless, cold place. Hostile even.

In the corner, huddled together, was a group of casually dressed forty-something males, their worn tweed jackets and trousers giving them the appear-

ance of a gathering of poverty-stricken country gents. I
recognised Sam, the man with the dog who had been
outside the shop, straightaway, his slovenly appearance and greasy hair catching my eye.

My ears were still tuned in to the conversation between Neil and this Davey guy. So far, it was mundane
stuff: the weather and football and how the roads on
the island all led to the main village of Lawton where
there was a proper supermarket and a tiny old library.
Neil would hold on to this information, try to talk me
into visiting while we ate our lunch. I would refuse.
He would tell me, in his usual honeyed, affable way, to
loosen up. Start living. Socialising. I would silently
seethe, hating both myself and him. Mainly because
he was right and also because I was being overdra-
matic, imagining the worst scenario where we would
bump into somebody who recognised me. Somebody
who would rip open my past and declare what they
knew to everybody on the island.

I snatched up the laminated card and ran my
finger over the food listed there. It was limited: basic
and lacking in any finesse. Exactly what I expected.
Somehow the thought of eating a steak pie made my
stomach roil so I opted instead for a tuna baguette. A
growing resentment began to build in my belly as they
continued with their dreary dialogue, my presence

not acknowledged by either man. I was an outsider, a bystander on the periphery of their conversation. A female, and therefore unworthy of being involved in their talk. Was that how they treated the females on this island? As second-class citizens, undeserving of any attention and shoved in a corner and ignored? I thought of the row of recently placed gravestones and wondered who those women were. How they had died.

'I'll have the tuna baguette, please,' I said loudly. 'And a pot of tea.' All heads turned to stare at me, their pints of frothing beer poised in clenched, rough-looking fists. All men, no females to be seen any-where. I was a minority, every part of me feeling like an unwanted visitor. An intruder.

'Ah, sorry, yes of course,' Neil exclaimed, as if my being there was a surprise to him. 'I was just saying to Davey here about how nice it was to get a welcome package left on the doorstep when we arrived at the cottage.'

Images of the dog shit and note we found this morning jumped into my mind and for one awful mo-ment I thought that perhaps he was being facetious, trying to lure this stranger into a debate of some kind, then remembered the food package: the teabags and tiny pots of jam. I smiled and nodded, less than eager to get into a conversation with this person, the one who had seemed determined only minutes earlier to stop us from sitting here at all. 'Yes, it was a very kind gesture.'

'I'll let yer get on with ordering yer food, then,' Davey said, and before either of us could reply, he headed back to his seat, the wooden stool making a loud scraping sound on the flagstone floor as he pulled it out from under the table and sat back down with the other men.

'Right,' Neil murmured, his eyes trailing over the menu. 'I'll order the food, shall I?'

He wandered back to the bar. I watched his retreating figure, suddenly feeling alone and vulnerable. At the edge of my vision, I detected a movement. As unobtrusively as I could, I turned and saw the group of men nursing their pints, all eyes firmly fixed on me. I twisted my body around and met their gaze, refusing to let them bully me with their hard expressions and threatening postures. I had just as much right to be in the pub as they did.

It didn't take long for them to swing back around, their murmurs and mildly embarrassed hunched shoulders giving me a warm glow of victory. The Bucket of Blood may not have been the most salubrious of places, but it was our local. We would be visiting it occasionally. I wasn't a big drinker but it was unthinkable that a group of men had the power to force me to stay away from the place.

My fingers were splayed against the grain of the wood, palms outstretched on the table in a show of power and strength. I lifted up my hands, flexed my fists, stretched and smiled. Neil was right: nobody here knew about what I had done. This was our fresh beginning, and I could be anybody I wanted to be. Anybody at all. I could finally be the real me. The woman I used to be before the desperate thief inside of me took hold and ruined what I had worked hard to achieve.

'The food's going to be brought over once it's ready.' A glass of orange juice and small pot of tea was placed in front of me, making me realise how thirsty I actually was.

I wanted to mention the behaviour of the men to Neil but knew he would be blind to it, his blinkers and perpetual wish to live a mediatory life blocking out anything he considered untoward or undesirable. This was his life now that our money worries were behind us – warm halcyon days full of lightness and cheer even though it was freezing outside, the clouds were engorged with rain, and we were sitting in a dark shadowy pub amongst people who didn't want us here. I only hoped his new spending habits remained as rigid and unwavering as his belief in the good in people. Those men had clearly shown a level of animosity towards me, yet he simply couldn't, or wouldn't, see it, focusing only on the positive aspects of these people's characters: his conversations with them, their camaraderie and superficial bullish ways. Perhaps it was a male thing. Or perhaps I was being prickly and oversensitive. I hadn't imagined it, however, their staring eyes and frowns. I knew what I had seen.

'Drink your tea before it goes cold.' He picked up the silver teapot and poured it into the small porcelain cup before pushing it my way and smiling at me.

'Thanks. I need it after that walk here.'

I pulled at the neck of my sweater, a wave of warm air escaping as I yanked it to one side to cool down. Behind me, the murmuring grew, voices thickening in volume, a sudden crescendo reached as tempers frayed and anger spilled over. My muscles were tensed and ready when I felt a hit from behind, pain ricocheting up and down my spine. Amber liquid exploded out of the cup, spreading and pooling over the surface of the table.

Neil was up on his feet within seconds, face creased with confusion, crouching down at my side, his arms wrapped around me, pulling me to one side away from the fracas. My feet were lead, my legs liquid as I stood and allowed myself to be guided away from our table to another part of the pub. It was cramped in there with little or no space to escape the unfolding drama. I wanted to flee, to bolt for the door and to run and keep on running until my legs gave way but Neil held me in place, his arms wrapped around me in a protective embrace.

I heard it as we stood huddled in the corner, those words, cutting into me, frosting my skin, chilling my blood.

'I don't care what you say, she shouldn't bloody well be here! We all know it.'

Syllables echoing in my brain, pounding against my skull. It was about me. The fight that was taking place in the pub was all about me.

I broke free from Neil's vice-like hug and spun around, watching the brawl: fists flying, stools being kicked, tables and cushions scattered all over the floor. Everything in disarray. I could hardly believe that it was happening – this childish display of anger. Grown men throwing punches, chucking furniture around. Acting like a clutch of spoilt, angry toddlers.

And no matter how hard I tried to convince myself otherwise, I knew deep down that it was all because of me. I rearranged the words that I had heard them say, said them over and over in my head, tried to apply them to somebody else. But I couldn't. Because they were directed at me. This huge, stomach-churning scenario that was occurring was all because I was there.

7

'You didn't hear it? Christ almighty, Neil, what are you: completely deaf or utterly oblivious to what is happening here?' Frustration at his ignorance and lack of insight to what was taking place bit at me, digging beneath my skin and tunnelling into my bones. 'When you were at the bar, that man you were chatting to just stood at my table and stared down at me. He'd already shouted across that the table was reserved. Does the whole thing not strike you as just a teensy bit strange and disturbing?'

Neil shook his head, jutting out his bottom lip in an act of perplexity exactly as I knew he would. I could have predicted his reaction: denial and a vacuous outlook on the whole thing. They were his default emotions. If he didn't see it, then it didn't happen. It explained our prior predicament, how we had got ourselves in such a mess with our finances: Neil's denial to accept that we had a problem and his lack of concern and curiosity about where the money kept coming from. It had been the perfect storm. Or imperfect, as it turned out.

'How's your back? Do you want me to give it a rub?' I felt an ache where a chair had landed, catching me just above my coccyx. He was wide-eyed, every word that came out of his mouth brimming with innocence and sincerity. Had he always been this way or had things changed between us? Perhaps it was me. Perhaps my perception of people and situations had become skewed and tainted by our experience. Blackened and charred by my crime.

'My back is just fine, Neil.' I sounded gruff and lacking in patience. That's because I was. It was exhausting trying to get him to see the obvious, to get him on my side and stop being a constant mediator and peacekeeper. To stop seeing the world through childlike eyes.

'Okay, well the landlord of the pub was deeply apologetic and I'm sure those guys will also be really sorry and feel horrified at what they've done once the air has cleared and they've all calmed down. One bevvy too many, I suspect. Daytime drinking nearly always ends up with bother.'

I wanted to scream at him to shut up, to stop being so fucking polite and tolerant. But I didn't. Once again, I held my tongue. Rather than argue, I stood, made my way into our tiny little bathroom and ran myself a hot bath making sure the door was locked behind me. I half expected him to try the handle, see if I wanted a cup of tea while I was lying there, but he didn't. At least he was able to detect some sort of negative emotion. I visualised him skulking about in his tiny makeshift study that was actually not much larger than a small cupboard under the stairs, eyes downcast, mind in overdrive as he tried to work out what he had done wrong. What he had said or not said that had exacerbated my deteriorating mood.

When I finally got out and dried myself, pulling the towel around me before heading into the bedroom to get dressed, I could hear below me that he was watching TV, the sound echoing up through the ancient floorboards. I could see his face in my mind, eyes fixed ahead, features blank and expressionless. It was abundantly clear that he had no idea what to do or say next. I could have thought, *poor Neil*, but didn't. *Poor unaware, pathetic Neil with his lack of insight and embarrassingly meagre emotional intellect.* Two days we

had been on Winters End and already we had received a threatening note, had our doorstep smeared
with dog shit, and witnessed a pub fight that I knew
for certain had started because I had entered the bar
and dared to ignore the command to not sit down at
that table. Two days.

And yet we had also received a welcome pack with
a supportive, beautifully written note attached. I bit at
a loose nail, gnawing and tugging until it came free,
leaving behind a strip of pink, stinging skin. I sat on
the edge of the bed and pressed my fingers between
my knees, pushing them together to try to deaden the
pain. Was I overreacting and pushing the panic
button here? Coming apart again, allowing paranoia
to edge its way back into my life?

I dragged out some clean clothes and got dressed
then went downstairs, my movements muffled and
soundless, keen to put some distance between me and
Neil. I needed some time to think, to be alone and
clear my head. Sitting at the small desk in Neil's study,
I opened my computer and sifted through my emails,
noticing one from Chrissie that had arrived last night.
My heart started up: a tightening in my chest. My
finger hovered over the mouse but I couldn't bring
myself to open it. She had been furious when Kate
had offered to lend us the money to pay off our debts

and even though we paid it back as soon as our house was sold, she never forgave us. Whatever was in the email could wait until I was feeling a little less fragile. A little less breakable. Chrissie was a hothead, prone to outbursts. I knew that whatever it was she had to say, it wouldn't be pleasant.

I spent the next hour catching up with work-related emails, answering queries about prices for editing manuscripts of all manner of genres and successfully secured two new customers who returned their signed contracts almost immediately. Now that my business was up and running, I would have to dedicate more time to it, sitting at my own desk in the spare bedroom and working all day as opposed to visiting the local pub that proved only a few hours ago that it did actually live up to its name. Work could be my saviour, my escape from everything. If Neil wanted to spend every day in that pub, he could go right ahead. I had better things to be getting on with.

'I've made you some lunch if you're hungry? Soup and a sandwich since we didn't get to eat earlier.'

Neil was standing in the doorway, his face clouded over, eyes darting around the room. It would take more than an offer of a paltry snack to soften and smooth out my frayed edges. Feelings of deflation and loneliness had burrowed beneath my skin, his inability to see any issues with this place driving a wedge between us. The move to Winters End was supposed to solve all of our problems, but it was currently creating more, heaping more worries on top of those we thought we had left behind. Each time I felt able to steady myself, contentment tentatively creeping its way back in, something happened that dragged me back to the beginning. Or perhaps it wasn't anything to do with the fight in the pub or being told that I was sitting at a reserved table. Perhaps my anger was misdirected and it was the way Neil viewed things, his linear way of viewing the world that was making me feel miserable. I wished I could see inside his head, stare in awe at how well presented and clear it was, unlike mine which was a constant snarl of pent-up emotions and neuroses with a sprinkling of paranoia thrown in for good measure.

'Thanks. I'll be there in a minute. Just finishing this final email and I'll be with you.' My voice was light and airy. God, I was good at concealing things. Too good.

In a rush of bravery, I clicked on Chrissie's brief missive and inhaled, my face prickling at her angrily worded message. Neil had already left the room and I was alone. I glanced around anyway, a need to reassure myself that he hadn't hung around, all doe-eyed and needy.

I swallowed and rubbed at my face, a mist of unshed tears obscuring my vision when I attempted to read it again.

Fiona,
Don't think this is over because it isn't. Your thieving ways almost wrecked my relationship with Kate. I refused to help you out but she did it anyway and now whatever trust we had is gone, our relationship hanging by a thread. If we break up it will be your fault and I will hold you responsible. I will also make you pay for it so you'd better fucking well watch out.
Chrissie

It had been sent at 11 p.m. last night. She would have had a good drink, her thoughts loosened by the alcohol. That notion did nothing to dampen my fears or anxieties. She would still have been as angry when she awoke this morning. All the wine had done was give her the courage to send this poisonous note.

Chrissie and I never did hit it off. The money was the final straw. Still, I had no idea that her hatred of me ran that deep and was shocked and upset by the wording of the message, my head now pounding after seeing the depth of her malice printed there in black and white.

Everything felt heavy: my eyelids, my limbs, my body solid as stone. I headed into the kitchen where a plate of carefully prepared food sat waiting for me. Any hunger I had felt earlier had now dissipated. Fire burned in my gut. I stared at the plate, at the bowl of soup and the sandwich that was cut into quarters, a smattering of strategically placed lettuce and cucumber scattered around the edge of the plate for artistic effect, and swallowed down a small amount of bile, knowing I would have to make an attempt at eating some of this, the snack that Neil had thoughtfully made for me.

Chrissie's words, her inescapable fury, flickered before my eyes. Telling Neil about the email wasn't an option. It would only add to the already frosty atmosphere and make me appear even more negative, somebody who was actively looking for reasons to be miserable. Maybe I was. I wished I could work my way out of it but it felt as if life was constantly putting me under pressure, testing me, seeing how far I could be pushed before I snapped. Again.

I pulled out the chair and sat at the table, doing my utmost to appear unfazed by everything, happy even, if that was at all possible. I had to try, however.

That was what I was told by my doctor: to ignore the peripheral stuff, the things I can't change. Sometimes, though, it's so damn hard.

'A hot bath and some food always help.' It was excessively jovial, his voice, the sound of it irritating me to the point of wanting to scream. I said nothing and stared down at the food.

What was the point of arguing? We were here now, stuck on this island. Stuck with each other. There was no going back, no way of having a sudden change of heart. This was our home and I had better get used to it.

* * *

The next few days passed by in an uneventful blur of unpacking, odd painting jobs and answering more work-related emails. It gave me a sense of direction, helped me feel buoyed up even, and God knows I needed that sensation. After the past few days, my mood couldn't have been any lower. I was jumping at every shadow, every whisper of wind, convinced somebody was lurking outside, waiting to harm me. Telling me to turn around and leave. Even now, in the cold light of day, I couldn't tell you if there was anybody there or if it was all in my mind. I'm hardly a reliable source when it comes to such matters. Not with my past and my fragmented thoughts.

'I'm going to go for a walk.' I shouted through to Neil who was bent over his computer, eyes glued to the screen. 'Just to clear my head and have a break from work.'

For once, I wasn't lying. My eyes were sore. I had spent too long staring at my laptop screen, but I did have another reason for venturing out. That graveyard visit had preyed on my mind and I wanted to go there again to make sure my addled brain hadn't been playing tricks on me. Was there really a disproportionate number of dead females buried in those graves or was my imagination in overdrive? It had niggled at me and today felt like the right time to check it out. I was probably wrong but there was no harm in taking a walk over there to blow off the cobwebs.

I pulled on my jacket and stepped out into the swirling fog that appeared to have completely engulfed the whole of Winters End. How had I not noticed it when I was inside? I'd been immersed in work, my thoughts elsewhere. A freezing spread of silver surrounded me, its icy fingers digging into my pores. I shivered, pulled up my collar. It was cold but bearable. I tucked my scarf tight inside my jacket, tugging at it, straightening and rearranging my layers. Getting up a good pace would help me stay warm, freshen everything, clear away the mustiness in my brain.

The fog swallowed the path, making it difficult for me to navigate my way along the route that led to the churchyard. I carried on walking regardless, determined to make the journey on my own. Being independent was important to me, especially in this new and unfamiliar environment. I needed to find my feet, be the strong person I used to be. Not the broken one I had become. It was the first step to getting back my confidence. Green shoots that could possibly sprout buds and blossom into something promising bringing a flash of colour back into my life.

It didn't dissipate as I had hoped, the blanket of fog. If anything it thickened, gathering ahead of me until it was so dense, I couldn't be sure of where I was any more. I stopped and patted my pocket, checking I had brought my phone with me, and felt a jolt, fear ripping through my veins. I had left it behind. Such a stupid thing to do. It didn't matter too much. Getting a signal on this island was hit-and-miss at the best of times. It occurred to me as I took a few tentative steps that I hadn't seen a police station or any sort of law enforcement officers since moving here. Were there any emergency services at all on this tiny slab of land? What if I tripped and fell or, worse still, stumbled over the edge of the cliff? A sickness rose in my chest, clawing its way up my abdomen and lodging in my gullet. I had to stop with these unpalatable, irrational thoughts. It was ridiculous. I was making things worse. The graveyard was a straight route. So why did I suddenly feel so nervous?

More walking, stumbling, clutching at thin air to steady myself. More thoughts about the cliff edge.

I could have turned back, gone home, but the fact I had come this far and was so close kept me going. I hoped I was close. There was no way of knowing. I'd been walking now for some time. If I was as near to the graveyard as I kept telling myself, then why wasn't I there yet? Also, if I had accidentally deviated and wasn't on the route to the graveyard, then I wouldn't know how to get back to the cottage without getting completely and utterly lost, so I carried on, still walking and stumbling, more faltering steps, convincing myself that I was doing the right thing. And then there was the cliff path to contend with; the cliff path which, as I recalled, was as narrow as a pin and on a camber that tilted down to the crashing waves below. I should have turned back.

My heart raced, thumping wildly as if trying to beat its way out of my chest. I stopped to catch my breath. This was a stupid move, coming out in the fog, thinking I could find my way to a place I'd been to only once, in a place I barely knew, near a cliff edge with the sea roaring away below me, without my phone. Stupid, stupid, stupid.

My fingers trailed out in front of me like tentacles feeling for something – anything – firm or solid that would help guide me back to the cottage or a place of safety. Anywhere would do. Anywhere that wasn't a narrow cliff path, but there was nothing, just thick pockets of icy cold mist that enveloped my hands, freezing my fingertips.

I stopped, my breathing erratic. I was letting fear rule my head. I'd come this far. I had to keep going, to push down my growing anxieties. Ignore them. I needed to remain calm, in control. No lurching fear or sudden anxieties that would cloud my judgement and have me wandering into danger.

'You'll freeze standing there like that. 'Ere, follow me and I'll get yer back on the right track.'

A sudden, desperate shriek. I didn't have time to stop it, to hold it in and mask my fears. He had appeared out of nowhere, his silhouette emerging from a thick white cloud. An approaching stranger. A possible threat. It was when I saw his face that my knees crumpled, my legs weak and wiry. It was him. The man from the pub. Davey.

'Hold on to this. Didn't mean to scare you or nowt but it's stupid being out in this. Grab the end and I'll lead yer back to the path.'

A length of rope was placed in my hand. I almost stumbled back away from him, knowing that this person was the same man who had brusquely in-formed me that our table was reserved. The same man who had tried to intimidate me by standing over me when Neil was at the bar. The same man who had been involved in a fight where chairs were thrown around and beer spilt.

'Davey,' I said, my fear leaking out, my voice a trembling whisper. I said his name again, if only to confirm that it actually was him. 'Davey?'

'Aye. We'll get you away from the cliff path. Hold tight.'

I let myself be led along, my gait rickety and un-stable as we walked across gravel and rocks that crunched beneath our feet. I began to wonder if Davey was actually helping me or if he had other more sinister plans in mind. Turning and running wasn't something I could do, not with the mist ob-scuring my vision. Not with my lack of local naviga-tional knowledge. Not with the edge of the cliff so close by. I was trapped here with him, forced into ac-cepting his help.

To my left, I could hear the sea, the sound it made as it crashed against the rocks below us, the sheer violence of it causing me to gasp. I was closer to the edge than I had realised. Too close. Despite the freezing temperature, despite my ice-cold extremities that were turning numb, perspiration gathered under my armpits, prickling my scalp and hairline. I was filled with an overwhelming desire to get back to the cottage, to throw myself into Neil's chest and feel secure and safe in the only home I now had, the place that since moving in had made me feel rudderless and uncomfortable. A stranger in a strange place. Yet now it held a sense of calm and warmth. My fortress.

'I need to go back home to the cottage,' I said, my voice barely audible above the noise of the angry sea, its fury now scaring me almost as much as Davey and the swirling, impermeable fog.

'That's where I'm tekkin yer.'

Something in his voice reassured me, made me realise he wasn't about to harm me in any way. I had to believe that. I was lost and in danger. He was the only thing stopping me from stumbling over the edge.

We stopped walking and I could just about make out Davey's features close to where I was standing, was able to see the movements of his mouth as he spoke to me. 'If you keep on going in a straight line, follow this gravel track, it'll tek yer right up to yer front door.' He began walking away, his outline slowly disappearing into the mist. Then I heard his voice, the crunch of his boots on stone, and tried to work out if he was approaching or leaving. My body was rigid as, once again, his outline appeared through the silvery murk, his features dark and sinister. 'If yer want my advice, and if I were you, I'd pack up right now, get back to the mainland. If you want to stay safe, that is, if yer want to stay alive.'

I shivered but didn't have time to reply, to ask what he meant. He was gone in a matter of seconds and I was left standing alone, feeling cold and frightened. I definitely hadn't imagined those words, what he had said. His icy, authoritative tone. Something was very wrong here. I took a deep breath and glanced around. Nobody to be seen. No noise at all aside from the rush of the sea, the ferocious sound of a wall of water hitting the rocks below. Nothing at all. I swallowed and furled my fists into tight balls. I was completely alone. It was as if he had never been there at all.

8

I was left with just two choices: bottling everything up or telling Neil and once again coming across like a neurotic, overbearing wife who was constantly looking for cracks in her sad little existence. Neither of those options appealed to me but knowing what Neil's reaction would be, I chose the former. I couldn't stomach any more of his inane platitudes or outright denials so made the choice to keep Davey's words to myself and do my own detective work to find out what he meant by them. It would deepen my worries, having to work it all out on my own, but Neil wouldn't be any help anyway. He would brush it off, shrug his shoulders and tell me I was being too negative, that Davey was probably a good guy and just trying to look out for us, that it was what he did, taking newcomers to the island under his wing.

We stayed away from the pub and spent the following few days painting walls and working at our respective businesses, my new editorial company attracting many fresh enquiries. I managed to secure two more new customers and was delighted to receive a query from a small publishing house for my services. All of these things helped to quash my fears and left me feeling more hopeful than I had been for some time. Even the thought of Chrissie's email no longer disturbed me. I didn't reply and had no reason to feel worried. She was miles away in Durham and I was here, trapped on this tiny island with what appeared to be a population of maniacs. Her words had almost been banished from my memory anyway. A small, insignificant woman. She meant nothing to me. There was no love lost between us but plenty of animosity to be found. About as much as the maniacs on Winters End. I smiled, thinking how much easier it was to laugh at the idea of them. Better than feeling constant worry and fear, although admittedly I still woke at night with those dark shadows threatening to knock me off balance. It was like walking a tightrope, making sure I kept my footing steady and didn't plummet to the ground below.

Neil also seemed to be settling into a routine of working and carrying out DIY jobs. Our bank balance was something I kept a close eye on, a small part of me still concerned that Neil's predilection for online purchases hadn't left him. So far everything was as it should be and that was something else that afforded me a modicum of comfort.

Outside, a weak, watery sun hung amidst the surrounding haze of pale blue, the fog finally having cleared after almost three days of being blanketed in a cloud of thick mist. It was perfect walking weather. My shoulders and spine were aching after sitting for so long hunched over my laptop, my eyes as dry as sand.

I didn't let Neil know of my plans. He would have wanted to come with me, his jovial, affable ways grating on me when I needed solace and silence. Living and working in the same space, we collided regularly, the cottage too small for both purposes. I pulled on my coat and pushed my feet into my walking boots, shouting through to him that I was off out for a walk, and slipped out without waiting to hear his reply.

The sky was an azure blue. Threads of cold whirled with the breeze, an absence of clouds lowering the temperature. My intention was to go back to the graveyard again to settle my mind. Maybe I hadn't looked hard enough and saw only what my ever-suspicious mind told me to see. I was feeling out of sorts at the time, fragile and off-kilter. Today I would look harder, try to find some balance, not scare myself. I had enough on my mind at the best of times, plenty of demons perched on my shoulder. I didn't need any more.

Time passed quickly as I walked, the views impressive and the weather perfect, the chill of the breeze cooling me as my body temperature rose. It didn't take long to get there. I wondered how in that mist only a few days ago, I had managed to get so horribly lost. I must have gone around in circles, blinded and disorientated by the fog. It was practically a straight route yet, somehow, I had moved away from the track and closer to the edge of the cliff.

The churchyard was deserted and silent save for the distant cawing of a crow, its sharp cry lending a certain ambience to the surroundings. With a tiny population, the graveyard was small and easy to navigate but still, an ominous, unexplainable feeling hung over me. Set up on a small hillock, the church sat in the middle, its steeple a huge dark obelisk that spiked the sky. A thick scribble of wrought iron surrounded its perimeter, ivy snaking around it in a dark green tangle. Misty orbs of breath pulsed in front of me as I headed to the far side of the church. Row upon row of headstones stood awkwardly, many looking close to collapse. I stood to one side while trying to read the inscriptions. They were weather-beaten and reading the names was difficult but not impossible. The dates were from the late 1800s. I would learn nothing from these particular graves. I kept walking, taking tiny steps, stopping when I came to a row of what appeared to be recently laid head-stones, their creamy colour and accurately etched en-gravings incongruous against the older crumbling gravestones. I scanned them, looking closely at the names – Sarah Woodward, Phillipa Dyke, Abigail Pa-terson, Peter Swann, Joy Rollings and Julia Bristow, and the dates, all of which were recent. Sarah died in 2019, Phillipa in the same year. Julia died in 2020. Abi-gail passed away in 2021 along with Joy who died only three months later. All of them under the age of forty. I thought about the recent pandemic and the possi-bility that they had succumbed to the virus. A lack of medical care on the island, poor access for emergency vehicles, the thick swirling fog that would ground air ambulances, and the rough seas that halted ferry crossings in the winter – they could all have played a part. And yet something told me not. Something else had happened here. I don't know how I knew that. I just did.

There was only one male name nestled in between the graves of the women. I continued walking and scanning them all, trying to commit to memory the ratio of women to men. By the time I had finished reading as many as I could, my head was spinning and I was no longer able to recall whether my imagination was playing tricks on me in my susceptible, weakminded state, whether there were just as many men buried in the graveyard as there were women. So few headstones and yet the place was riddled with mystery.

I did definitely see those newer headstones though. I hadn't imagined those. Some of them were only in their early thirties when they died and they were recent. I stuffed my hands into my pockets and headed back out onto the main path. Five women, all recent and all young. Five. Was that a disproportionate amount? Perhaps if they had been elderly then I would have thought not, but the fact they were all under the age of forty made me think that something had happened on this island. Or not. I was at it again, jumping to ill-informed conclusions, my brain wary and sceptical.

Enough. I had to put a stop to this.

I shivered. A chill skittered over my skin. I pulled up my collar and started to head back. And then I heard it: the unmistakable sound of the shuffling of feet behind me, the sound of heavy breathing. I froze, my scalp tingling with dread, and began walking even faster, keen to get away. Keen to get back to the cottage.

'Sorry if I scared you back there.' He seemed to spring out of nowhere. It was a habit many men on this island seemed to have, appearing around dark corners and stepping out through clouds of mist like terrible, sinister spectres.

I coughed and spoke quietly, my throat hoarse and sore, a length of barbed wire cutting into my gullet, impeding my speech. 'It's fine. I was just heading back home.'

'I'm Father Henderson. Ewan. Father sounds far too formal, don't you think? Everyone on Winters End calls me Ewan.'

I relaxed, my shoulders sagging, my tongue ungluing itself from the roof of my mouth. I wasn't being followed. He was a priest. He'd been in the church and had seen me out here. I held out my hand, his palm warm against mine as we shook.

'I'm Fiona. We've just moved—'

'Into the old forge. Yes, I know.' He smiled, tipping

his head to one side, his nut-brown eyes crinkling up at the corners as he spoke again. 'It's always a bit strange and creepy when people know of you and you don't know them, isn't it?'

'Definitely,' I replied, slowly warming to this man, this perfect stranger I knew nothing about; aside, that is, from the fact that that he was the local priest and he hadn't acted as if I was the spawn of the devil, telling me to leave the island in a frenzied outburst.

'I feel I should apologise.' I sighed and looked at a point somewhere over his shoulder, eyes narrowed against the cold wind. 'Neil and I aren't believers and we don't go to church.' I smiled and looked back into his eyes. 'There, I've said it.'

His laughter echoed between us, disappearing quickly as the wind snatched it away, carrying it over the landscape and out to sea. 'Seems you're in the right place. Most of the people on Winters End aren't believers.'

'You must have your work cut out for you, then.'

'Every Sunday, but I guess it's my job, isn't it? To try to instil a sense of confidence and belief in people when life gets rough and things seem difficult and, at times, almost impossible.' Another wide smile, real warmth and sincerity there.

'Quite.' I cleared my throat, unsure what to say

next, thinking that he must be able to see inside my head, that his words were a little too close to the truth and resonated with me in a way he would never be able to understand. 'Well,' I murmured, looking away once more, my face heating up at his unwavering gaze, 'I guess I'd best be off. Need to get back home, get some more work done.'

'You're an editor, I hear?'

A pulse kicked at my neck. I turned to face him, about to say something in return but was cut off by his words.

'Don't worry, I'm not some sort of mad stalker. Mike, the estate agent who sold you the place, is a friend of mine. He mentioned it in passing.'

I nodded and felt myself soften even though I didn't recall mentioning it to Mike. I bit at my lip. I was doing it again, suspicion and mistrust oozing out of me. What did it matter if this guy knew what I did for a living? It wasn't the end of the world, him knowing. Me being an editor was hardly a state secret. So why did it make me feel so uncomfortable and out of sorts?

His natural warmth, easy charm and effusive manner was, however, too difficult to ignore. 'Well, since we're so well acquainted, I'd like to ask you something, Ewan.'

He smiled, his slightly overlapping teeth and clean-shaven skin giving him the appearance of somebody much younger. I guessed he was in his mid-fifties but flecks of grey hair and a small pouch of sagging skin on his neck were the only signs that he was middle-aged. 'Ask away. I'm pretty good when it comes to modern history and the environment but best steer clear of pop music. My knowledge of it stopped once Duran Duran and Spandau Ballet broke up. I'm still firmly entrenched in the eighties, I'm afraid.'

I laughed. I was growing to like this man. 'The gravestones in the churchyard.' I pointed beyond the wrought-iron gate behind him. 'The newer graves. Why did so many younger women die recently?'

I couldn't swear to it, his reflexes rapid as gunfire, but I thought I saw a change in his expression: a flicker of his eyes, a slight trembling of his mouth, a tensing of his posture. Maybe it was the cold that was getting to him, causing the sudden rigidity of his spine. Or maybe it was my question, the fact that I held his gaze and refused to look away.

'I'm not sure what you mean? Is there a discrepancy in the numbers? I've never noticed.' His voice was light as air, a hint of humour to it. I was willing to bet that Father Ewan Henderson with his twinkling eyes and clear complexion was able to bat away many an unwanted question just by smiling. He was good, I would give him that, but then I guessed he was used to dealing with people and their strange, quirky ways and I felt certain that the congregation of Winters End had more than their fair share of those.

I glanced at the church then back at Ewan, letting the silence stretch out. We became locked in a battle, me remaining resolutely mute, my eyes scrutinising his every move until, eventually, I saw him look away, noted how his posture changed, how his hands were slung in his pockets, his knuckles a clear ridge of tension through the stretched fabric. I began to feel a tad sorry for him. He barely knew me and here I was, playing mind games with him. It was unfair. He was trying to make a good impression. We were getting along nicely and then I threw him a curveball.

'Anyhow,' I said quietly. 'Maybe even a non-believer like me could perhaps be persuaded to visit St Augustine's every now and again.' I almost winked to try and alleviate the awkward atmosphere I had inadvertently created but stopped myself. Too much and too soon. He was a priest. It was too flirtatious. I wasn't at a party chatting to a close friend. I had to keep a respectful distance from this man.

'You'll always be welcome.'

His voice was soft, not full of anger like those men

in the pub. He was different. Non-threatening. Gentle. Approachable.

'Anyway, I'd best be off. Those manuscripts won't edit themselves.' I smiled and we both laughed at my weak attempt at humour.

I turned and began to walk away, stopping as I heard his voice calling after me.

'If it's information you want, you'd be best talking to Honnie. She lives in Cook Cottage, the pale-blue house next to the post office in the main village of Lawton. Although village is a fairly imprecise term to say the least. More of a hamlet.'

I spun around, intrigue gripping me. 'Honnie?'

'Honora. Honnie for short. Honora Armstrong. She knows everyone on the island and, according to local gossip, knows the business of everybody who's ever lived here, so don't be surprised if she already knows everything about you and has a pot of tea on ready for your arrival.'

I was already halfway down the path, a morbid curiosity driving me on. Ewan shouted his goodbyes, coupled with a hopeful message about seeing me and Neil in church on Sunday. I gave him a wave and replied, making no hard and fast promises. I had enough to be getting on with and didn't want to commit myself to events and visits I knew I wouldn't be able to fulfil.

We had passed the post office a few days back so I was pretty sure I knew where this Honnie woman lived. I guessed it would take me twenty minutes to get there. I zipped up my jacket against the prevailing north-easterly wind and set off at a lick.

9

I noticed it while I was walking. Or at least I thought I did. It seemed like such a stupid, irrational notion that I initially dismissed it, told myself I was being ridiculous, looking for problems where there weren't any. I tried to dampen the thought, push it away but the harder I tried, the longer it lingered. Where were all the women of the island? Yet again, The Bucket of Blood had only men in as I passed, the corner shop also contained only men. Even the estate agent was a man. If there were any other women around, then where were they? There was me and, of course, Honnie. But where were the others?

My fist was raised to knock as I stood outside her house, a mid-terrace property that was indeed that palest blue colour with small Georgian windows, when the door opened and there standing before me was the woman I presumed to be Honnie Armstrong. She was, I guessed, in her mid-seventies or possibly even her eighties, dressed in a dark woollen dress with a patterned brown pinafore tied around her waist, and a sharp scowl on her face. Her hair was scraped back into a large bun and held in place by a thick white ribbon. I almost turned and fled. Almost, but didn't. I stayed, rooted to the spot. Waiting for something to happen, for one of us to break the silence. I opened my mouth but before I had a chance to introduce myself, to tell her why I was here and who sent me, she nodded and spoke, her voice low and authoritative. 'You'd best come in, then.' Her body dipped, her hand was outstretched as she stepped to one side and gestured for me to enter, her arm sweeping behind her. 'I wondered when you'd show yer face here. Kettle's on and tea's brewin'. What kept you?'

* * *

'None at all?' Honnie's hand hovered over my teacup, a triangle of pure white sugar piled high on the spoon like a tiny, crystallised mountain peak.

I shook my head and placed my hand over the rim of my cup. 'No thank you. Haven't taken sugar for over ten years now.'

She tipped the silver grains into her own tea and stirred it vigorously. A high-pitched tinkling sound as the teaspoon hit the porcelain of the cup rang around the tiny room we were sitting in. I glanced around, immediately recognising the style and era of the décor, the lace tablecloths and overstuffed chairs reminding me of my great-grandma's house in Whitby. It was a time warp, a throwback to many decades before. Another era. Another life.

'This was my mother's house before it was mine. And her mother's before her. In case you're wondering, that is.' She raised an eyebrow and took a slurp of her tea. 'Been in the family for generations. Always lived 'ere, we 'ave. Practically own the island.'

I felt a jolt of realisation as she spoke that here was an astute woman. Trying to hide anything from her would be stupid and pointless. Insulting, even. She was old, not senile. I didn't waste any time dancing around the issue, instead going right ahead and asking the questions that had been niggling at me since moving here.

'Where are all the women on the island? I was told

by a reliable source that you had all the answers and that you were a person who's in the know.'

Relief flooded through me when she smiled and gave a little laugh. 'Oh, you young ones. I love how you dispense with all the formalities and just dive right in with your probing questions.' She slapped her knee and took another swig of her tea before placing it down on the table between us with a clatter.

I waited while she poured herself another cup and took a biscuit, offering the plate to me, a slight tremble to her otherwise solid-looking hand. I shook my head, my stomach tight with anticipation. 'No, thank you. One's enough for me.'

'You're far too skinny. Need a bit of fat around your middle, you do. Something to give you a bit of energy. You'll need it for all the walks you'll be doing from that cottage of yours on Harbour Lane.' She stared at me through rheumy eyes and bit into the shortbread, crumbs spilling onto her lap like a mini snowstorm.

'So, all the women, then?' I raised my eyebrows and waited, watching as she continued to nibble at her biscuit, her small creamy-coloured teeth working at the edges of the shortbread.

She sighed, all the while formulating an answer. Honnie wasn't the only one who was good at reading people. I knew a stalling technique when I saw one. Her mouth was wet, her tongue tracing around the outer fleshiness of her lips. She shook her head and pressed her fingertip down onto the crumbs scattered around the rim of her plate. 'What makes you think we don't have any women on the island? You're here.' She sniffed loudly, rubbing her hands on her pinny. 'And so am I.'

'Oh, come on, Honnie. Don't be so coy. You know exactly what I mean.'

Her gaze locked with mine. I held it before glancing away, the pale film that covered her eyes reminding me of a dead fish, the jellylike greyness that stretched over her irises unsettling me.

'More tea?' She grabbed the pot, its spout poised over my cup.

'Thanks, but I'd best be going. Neil will be wondering where I've got to.'

I stood and picked up my jacket, pushing my arms into it, disappointment rippling through me. I should have known Honnie wouldn't be an easy nut to crack. Sharp and shrewd, she knew how to play people and how to keep them at arm's length if needed and I was definitely being kept at arm's length. Either that or she thought me half-insane with my weird questions, asking her why there were so few females around. Because it was, after all, a strange thing to ask. A small part of me worried that she now thought me foolish. I didn't want her to think of me that way. We rubbed along together. I wanted her to think of me as a reliable individual, not someone who was dancing around the edges of lunacy, unable to differentiate between reality and fantasy.

'Feel free to call back anytime. I don't go so far these days. Not if I can help it anyway, especially if the weather's bad.'

'Is the weather ever anything other than bad on Winters End?'

'Ha!' Her mouth widened, revealing a row of remarkably straight teeth. 'Just you wait until summertime when there isn't a whisper of wind and we're all gasping for breath in the heat.' She stood up and followed me to the door. 'You'll know when it's summer around these parts. When the flowers bloom along the side of Harbour Lane and up past all the roadsides, the smell taking your breath away, then you'll know spring has left and summer has arrived in all its glory. An explosion of colour, it is. Never seen anything like it.'

I desperately wanted to turn and ask her once more, every sinew straining within me, but feared losing her trust and breaking the connection we had made. I had plenty of time to call again, to soften her up and wait for this slightly austere yet remarkably robust woman to open up to me. Because she definitely knew things. The look on her face when I asked her had been undeniable. She had closed down, become defensive. More importantly, she hadn't asked why I posed such a strange question. And it was a strange one, yet there had been no raised eyebrows or pursed lips. No crinkled brow or looks of puzzlement. She knew. Honnie Armstrong definitely knew.

My fingers were clasped around the door handle when I felt it: the heat of her body moving closer to mine, the sound of her breathing; soft, rhythmic, heavy.

'Call back later in the week and we'll talk more. You might get some answers to your questions then.'

Every fibre of my being wanted to stop and beg her to tell me there and then, but I understood the boundaries, those invisible lines that shouldn't ever be crossed. I would call back in a few days, maybe even bring her some home-made cake. I had a feeling she would appreciate such a gesture. Then we would talk. I had plenty to keep me occupied in the meantime: manuscripts to edit, paint jobs that needed doing in the cottage, a garden to be cleared. A never-ending list of DIY tasks. The thought of it made me feel slightly crushed when all I wanted was to sit here in Honnie's living room, gleaning as much information out of her as I could.

'Thank you for the tea and biscuits. I'll see you soon.'

'Aye, that you will, pet. And start eating, get a bit of weight on. You're nowt but skin and bone.'

From many, such a comment could be deemed as offensive but coming from Honnie it felt like a compliment, as if she cared about my well-being. As if she really knew me and was looking out for me. She was right. I was thin. Too thin. Eating had been the last thing on my mind in the last few months. It was time to start being kind to myself, to stop punishing myself for what I had done. It was over, all in the past. Time to move on.

'I'll bake us a cake and bring it round when I next visit. Coffee and walnut or lemon drizzle. Or I could stretch to chocolate with caramel icing if you don't mind it gooey and sticky?'

'They all sound bloody marvellous to me. I'm partial to a bit of sugar in case you hadn't noticed.' We laughed and I had to stop myself from leaning forwards and embracing her. She felt like such a familiar old soul, as if we'd known one another for decades. 'Now go on, get yourself 'ome to that husband of yours. And be careful walking back. The route to your cottage is uneven and close to the cliff path. Keep your eyes peeled and your ears open.'

It was as I was heading out of the door that I thought I heard it: a distant banging sound, like the dull pounding of a drum. I stopped, narrowed my eyes to concentrate but heard nothing else.

'Problem?' Honnie's voice was metal, taking me by surprise, her mood swiftly altering from friendly to fierce. Such an unpredictable individual. A force to be reckoned with.

'I thought I heard something. A banging sound.'

'Be those bloody builders over by the quayside. Been at it all week with those pneumatic drills. Driven me mad, it has. They're a bloody nuisance. I'm about ready for my nap so they'd better knock off and have a break or they'll get it both barrels from me.'

I stepped out into the fading light outside and turned and smiled. We said our goodbyes and she disappeared back into the dimness of her hallway. 'Go on, now,' she said gruffly. 'Get yerself off home. I'm an old woman and need my afternoon sleep. You get back and have that husband of yours cook you a hot meal, get some meat on yer bones.'

And with that, she was gone. The door closed with a muffled click, leaving me feeling strangely bereft. I turned and bathed my face in the tepid warmth of the setting sun. It would be a pleasant walk back: no howling wind, no thick fog. Just me and my thoughts. Plenty to mull over after my conversation with Honnie. Lots to think about in readiness for my next visit.

Only as I passed the wall next to the quayside did it become apparent to me. It was when the drills started up again, their noise a metallic thudding sound. That was when I knew. It definitely wasn't the sound I had heard as I left Honnie's house. It was a different tone. Very different. This sound was clearer, not a dull thudding. A sharper, louder noise.

I pushed it from my mind as I left the village and took the narrow gravel path home, Ewan and Honnie in the forefront of my thoughts. Perhaps living on Winters End wouldn't be so bad after all. Perhaps Neil and I could finally move forward with our lives, maybe even thrive on this peculiar little island where nothing and nobody made any sense. Honnie had made me feel welcome with her crotchety ways and plain yet oddly pleasant manner. A far cry from the brawling men from the pub, although admittedly, Davey did come to my rescue when I was lost in the fog. And Ewan also seemed kind and fairly normal. Perhaps things here wouldn't be so bad after all.

The views on the way back were magnificent, lifting my mood, banishing the shadows that lurked

and loitered in the corners of my mind. I turned into
Harbour Lane and that's when I saw him, his figure in
the distance: Neil tearing up and down the road as if
searching for something.

He came running towards me and I knew then
that something dreadful had happened, my limbs
stringy with fear when I saw his stricken expression,
my gut tightening as I waited for him to speak.

'It's you. You're here!' His voice cut through the
still air. He was panting, eyes wide and glassy. Beads of
perspiration were peppered over his brow.

I'd taken longer than anticipated but that wasn't it.
There was something else. Something terrible. Panic
and turmoil had never been Neil's way. He was level-
headed in a crisis. Too calm and level-headed actually,
continually jovial and ebullient while our finances
turned to ash.

'Sorry. I took a walk to the churchyard and then
went to meet an old lady who lives next to the post office. I should have called you to let you know. It's—'

'It's not that. Christ, Fiona. I thought you'd fallen
over the cliff. Here,' he said pulling me towards him.
'Somebody called to hand me these – one of the guys
from the pub, I think. Or maybe not, but he knew who
you were for sure. He said that he found them over by
the old barn next to the cliff path. Why the hell didn't

you answer your phone? I ran over to where he found them and looked down and, Jesus Christ, something was going on down on the beach, something serious and I thought—'

He stopped, pushed his fist against his mouth and dipped his head. In his other hand sat my small wallet, the one I took with me wherever I went. It contained my driving licence and a couple of credit cards. He held it out on his open palm for me to take. 'I moved closer to the edge to see what was happening and thought that I saw a body sprawled out below. Jesus, Fi, it looks like somebody has fallen over the side of the cliff...'

I stepped forward and wrapped my arms around him, slipping my wallet into my back pocket. It must have fallen out when I got lost the other day and I didn't even realise. 'I'm here safe and sound and definitely not lying at the bottom of the cliffs. You won't get rid of me that easily.'

Even as I was saying it, the idea that somebody had possibly tripped on the path I was on only recently and stumbled over the edge in that thick fog gave me pause for thought. It's a long way down, the route littered with overhanging rocks and crevices. They would be dead. Nobody could survive a fall like that.

'Fi, I just wanted to say that...' Neil stopped and shook his head, the words he was about to say remaining unspoken. Swallowed back down.

I waited, feeling almost certain he was about to speak openly about my fears, but nothing came. I wanted to think that he now believed me, that he too could see that something was amiss with this place, but with Neil being the way he was, it was unlikely he would ever say such a thing. Not until the evidence was right in front of his face.

'My phone,' I said, remembering. Grabbing it out of my jacket pocket, I saw Neil's four missed calls and shook my head. 'Really sorry. I didn't think to check. I am such a bloody klutz. I had it on silent. So sorry, Neil.'

'Come on. Let's get into the warm.' He took my hand and we walked back to the cottage, the idea of getting inside and locking the door behind us more comforting and appealing than I had ever thought possible. I knew then that I could perhaps grow to love the old place, make it my home, no longer viewing it as a prison. With a possible dead body nearby, it now felt like a sanctuary, my safe place. We could hunker down and block out the rest of the world. Angry locals with their whispers and secrets could all go to hell. Just me and Neil and a roaring fire. That was enough. For now.

'Coffee? Or would you prefer something stronger?' Without waiting for an answer, I headed into the kitchen and filled two large glasses with whisky. 'For the shock,' I said as I handed it over. The thought of that body, the height they had fallen and the boulders they had undoubtably hit on the way down, weighed heavily on me. I thought about who it could be, wondering whether it was one of the locals from the pub or if they were well known in the community. I imagined it was impossible to remain a loner on an island this small. It would have an impact on everybody, the discovery of that body. Somebody somewhere close by would be grieving. The thought of it made me unutterably sad, my heart aching for them.

If only I had known what lay ahead, that mentioning the body would be the catalyst for the events that followed, setting us on a crooked dark path that would ultimately lead to disaster.

10

It was unnerving, deafening even: the silence, the peacefulness that surrounded us. The normality of it all. We had expected to see emergency services milling around, the coastguard perhaps, a smattering of onlookers, maybe even the odd TV reporter that had caught a whiff of a story and headed straight over here on the next ferry in the hope of a headline, but there was nothing. Not a damn thing. An air of ordinariness tinged with our fear was what we felt. A smattering of dread. A big gaping hole of nothingness.

Neil and I stood hand in hand, a respectful distance away from the edge. After we had finished our drink, the amber liquid fortifying us, I had insisted we take a handful of flowers that I had managed to untangle from our overgrown, neglected garden – some dahlias and chrysanthemums – and place them next to the cliff path as a small tribute. I felt compelled to do something. Sitting at home doing nothing seemed wrong somehow; callous and uncaring.

'You're sure it was here and not farther along?' I stared at Neil, knowing how insulting my question sounded. I was doubting him. He had been here and seen it, looked over to see the body splayed out below. It's not the kind of thing anybody could forget, but what if shock had jarred his thinking? It was a possibility. He had been on the edge of hysteria when I saw him, a far cry from his usual measured self.

'It was here.' He glanced at me, his eyes dark and piercing. 'This is definitely where I saw it.'

I nodded and squeezed his hand. 'Well, maybe they were just super quick at moving the body?'

'Maybe.' Even as he said it, I could hear the threads of uncertainty in his voice. The undisguisable doubt. I felt it too: that niggling suspicion that he had made a mistake.

'I guess they're used to dealing with things like this and are pretty efficient at getting everything back to normal? The cliff is really high and...' My voice tailed off. I thought about our home town on the mainland and the local suicide spot and the poor people who were so desperate that they felt there were no other avenues open to them.

'We could call somebody?' I said, unsure if there was even, indeed, anybody to call. 'We could ring 999?'

'And tell them what? That I thought I saw a body lying on the beach and now it's gone? They'd think I was mad as a box of frogs.'

He was right. Aside from going down there and combing the entire area, there was little we could do. Besides, the tide was coming in fast. By the time we took the winding route down there, we'd be waist high in water.

He shrugged and moved back, a part of him looking mildly insulted by the lack of movement from below. The lack of a body. The lack of anything at all. His back was bent, the crests of his backbone visible through his flimsy shirt. His timbre was husky and gravelly. 'Let's get back. It's getting chilly. The wind's picking up and it's nearly dark.'

The clunk of the door behind us as we stepped back into the cottage was a welcome sound; more welcome still was the metallic click of the key as Neil locked us in and put a pile of logs on the fire. At that moment in time, the outside world felt like a place I didn't want to be a part of and the thought of shutting it all out gave me a warm glow of contentment.

I sat on the sofa, feet tucked under my backside, and opened my laptop, knowing what I was planning on doing. Work could wait. There was something I wanted to look into first.

The fire crackled and spat while I browsed the internet, searching for something – anything – that would scratch the itch that had been bothering me since moving here. I realised after over half an hour of searching that there was nothing of note that had taken place on Winters End that would explain my initial fears. Fears that, now I was comfortable and settled, seemed silly and outlandish. People die all the time. Young people, old people. Children, even. At some point, we all die. There had been a pandemic. Perhaps those women were all struck down with Covid at the same time. Anything was possible. And yet, it still didn't feel right.

Neil placed a sandwich next to me and put a cup of tea on the floor at my feet. Tea: the typically British way of solving all problems. I closed my laptop, the plastic casing making a sharp snapping noise, and picked up my snack, a small part of me still certain that my fears weren't unfounded. There was something wrong with this island, these people, and outside these four walls there was a sickness that I couldn't quite comprehend. So many strange occurrences. So many unanswered questions. And yet I had no proof. I'd asked both Ewan and Honnie and had had my questions ignored or brushed aside. Maybe that's because there were no answers and maybe that was because my questions and suspicions were unfounded, born out of fear and an overactive, partly fractured mind. My head ached just thinking about it. At some point I had to stop and rest my brain.

'We never did find out who left the small welcome basket on the doorstep, did we?'

I could feel Neil's eyes boring into me as I asked the question he didn't want to answer. He was probably wondering which way this conversation was going to go. Being peaceable was his default route, his preferred way of operating. Confrontation and dissecting situations alarmed him. I was the opposite, always wanting to get to the nub of an issue. I often wondered what it was that drew us together as a couple in the first place. We're very different beasts, Neil and I. Poles apart.

'Just a friendly neighbour, I guess.'

A silence sat between us, an expanse of emptiness that felt both relaxing and awkward in equal measure as we ate without speaking, drinking our tea and staring into space.

I stood up and carried the dishes over to the sink, the thought of how I should be working looming large in my mind. I needed to refocus, to shift my mind away from a festering darkness that was slowly bleeding into my brain. We needed another source of income to supplement Neil's money and sitting at my desk and concentrating on my new business was the only way that would happen. To his credit, since moving here Neil had managed to get his head down and get some work done. I also had new contracts to fulfil, manuscripts to edit and hadn't done nearly enough work to break the back of them. Visiting graveyards and chatting to Honnie had eaten into my time, dragging me away from my desk.

I needed to catch up. Feeling resolute, my mind batting away any lingering shadows, I sat at my desk and opened up my work file, pushing away visions of dead bodies and people falling over the side of the cliff. Every time I softened to Winters End's rough edges, it jabbed at me, reminding me who was boss, that I existed here at its mercy.

Three hours later, I glanced up from my computer screen at the surrounding room, its unfamiliarity still managing to catch me unawares, forcing me to remember exactly where I was. It was dark outside, a crescent moon hanging like a tiny silver fingernail in a vast inky-black sky. A wave of dizziness held me fast. I focused on my breathing, waiting till it passed. Despite that, I felt remarkably resilient, an ambitious, iron-like determination coursing through me, the fear of being penniless and ending up back where we were before moving here enough to motivate me and keep me on track. I had managed to secure another client and the small publishing house had informed me that they would be passing more manuscripts my way within the next week. Soon I would be too busy for supposition and worries about occurrences that may or may not have taken place on Winters End. I would be busy working and there would be no time for allowing any anxieties to muscle their way into my brain. Work and my new business would become my succour, my route to a peaceable existence. I had to forget about a string of possibly premature deaths and bodies that may or may not have been sprawled on the beach just a few hundred yards from our new home.

'I know you might not fancy it after our last visit and after the carry-on from earlier with what I saw.' Neil was standing in the doorway, his face in semi-darkness. 'Or thought I saw.' His hair was a halo of light brown. It reminded me of cinder toffee, the small wisps that were standing on end, held fast by static. 'But I was wondering if you fancy some food at the pub?' He raised his hands in mock surrender, his half-smile crooked and innocuous as if displaying anything remotely resembling happiness would be disrespectful and inappropriate. The smile of the innocent. The smile of a mystified man. 'Feel free to say no. I just thought it would save us cooking, not least since we haven't bought in any food and the cupboards are practically bare.' He rotated his hands and stared at them. 'I mean, I know I'm fairly good at cooking but even these fingers would struggle to conjure up something out of nothing.'

At the mention of food, my stomach sprang to life, reminding me it hadn't had any sustenance for some time. A sandwich a few hours ago wasn't enough to keep either of us going, and Neil was right: we hadn't organised ourselves properly. There was nothing in to eat. The thought of leaving the cottage and going back to The Bucket of Blood didn't exactly fill me with a sense of glee. There was a time the prospect of going out for a meal would have lifted my spirits but I wasn't exactly enamoured with our new local and its patrons, their aggressive ways still embedded in my brain. I dreaded their unpredictable ways, their loutish mannerisms. Their unwelcoming dark stares. I also dreaded leaving the cottage, the thought of that body at the foot of the cliffs chiselled deep into my mind. If indeed there *was* a body.

Neil's face, however, was full of anticipation and it was difficult to disappoint him, especially after what he had experienced earlier in the day. At the very least, he deserved a couple of beers. And besides, the fracas from our last visit didn't weigh as heavily on his mind as it did mine, brushing it off as laddish behaviour after a bout of midday drinking. What were the chances of it happening again? As much as I would have liked to, I knew that we couldn't stay like this, holed up at home, too fearful to go out because of the actions of a few loutish old men who should know better. Too fearful to go out because somebody fell over the edge of the cliff. I shivered and shut out that thought. I wasn't about to say anything to him, but I was starting to think that Neil had perhaps made a mistake. Winters End was our new home and, whether I liked it or not, The Bucket of Blood was our new local pub.

'So, what do you say? Sit here and starve or brave the locals and the weather and get a good meal inside us?'

* * *

Heads didn't turn as we entered, people didn't stop their conversations and watch us through tapered, suspicious eyes, but once again, the atmosphere within the place was heavy and loaded with what I felt was animosity at our presence, as if we had no right to be there.

I stood at the bar, Neil beside me, having already pleaded with him on the journey there to not leave me alone. The barman passed us a menu and took our drinks order. I asked for a gin, my nerves already getting the better of me, and much to Neil's chagrin, gulped it down in one as soon as it arrived.

'Same again, please,' I said, sounding like a hardened boozer. I passed the glass back to the barman. It slid along the countertop, the damp surface and a pocket of air trapped beneath it, expediting its arrival.

I wasn't a heavy drinker. I wasn't even a regular light drinker but needed some Dutch courage. Being in the place where only a few days ago somebody had threatened me and inadvertently hit me made my skin ruck and my scalp prickle. I needed to show these people that I was stronger than they could ever imagine. Brazening it out felt like the only way to deal with all my fears and demons. It was that or disappearing altogether, an act of cowardice and defeat that punished me and Neil only and nobody else. We'd almost lost everything once. I was determined it wasn't going to happen again.

He passed me my refill and we turned and found a table in the corner next to the window.

'I'll be over to tek yer order in a minute. Just need t'go down to the cellar and change the barrels.' He was standing over us, his face expressionless. 'I'm Vince, by the way. People round 'ere just call me Vin. Owner and sole barman. Got a cook and a kitchen assistant but just me behind the bar so you'll 'ave to excuse me if it gets a bit slow around 'ere from time to time.'

Neil smiled and held out his hand. 'No problem at all. We're nothing if not patient, aren't we, Fi?'

I nodded, gave him a tight smile, reminding myself that I needed to show a positive face. Be a smiling, happy Fiona, not the Fiona from the mainland who only a few months back had been close to a breakdown. Not just close, if I was being perfectly honest. *In the midst of* would be a more fitting description. I liked to kid myself that I had skirted around the edges of it. I hadn't. I was still recovering. Running scared in case it happened again and doing my utmost to take care of myself and not have a relapse.

'Aye, well, as I say, won't be a minute. Be as quick as I can.'

The murmuring from the group of men in the other corner of the pub filtered our way, my ears attuned to the conversation. I couldn't pick up anything that made sense and wasn't even certain if it was the same group of people that had been here the last time we came. I wondered if Vince had torn a strip off them, berating a group of grown men for their boorish drunken behaviour, or if those sorts of antics were the norm in his bar and he had continued mopping up dregs and serving them more beer, their questionable conduct gliding over him like liquid mercury.

I watched Neil. He had narrowed his eyes, his gaze following the small group of males gathered together like predators. Something about his stance, the sudden rigidity of his spine, made me anxious, the flesh on my arms prickling.

'What?' I leaned into him, my voice hoarse, a weakness washing over me. I whispered into his ear, ice lining my veins. 'What is it? What's the matter?'

'Hmm? Nothing. It's nothing, honestly. Let's just relax and enjoy our meal, shall we?'

My fear and irritation levels ratcheted up a notch. After what we had been through over the past few

years, the truth being withheld from me was something I would no longer tolerate.

'There won't be a meal if you don't tell me what
the problem is. I mean it, Neil. Don't treat me like a
bloody child. I won't stand for it.'

He pursed his lips, sighed, and lowered his gaze,
leaning into me, his head close to mine, our faces almost touching. I could smell his trepidation, was able
to feel the heat of his unease. It emanated from him in
small, pulsating waves. 'It's nothing major. Just that
I'm sure that man sitting over there with the other
guys was the one who returned your wallet. In fact,
I'm certain of it. The one with the fair hair and
glasses.'

My stool scraped across the floor, drawing attention to my movements as I stood and walked towards
the guy in question. Tension sprang from the group
when I leaned down and spoke to them, my antennae
for detecting a delicately balanced mood finely tuned.

'Hi,' I said, my projected voice belying the anxiety
that punched at my throat. 'I just wanted to say thank
you for returning my wallet earlier. I really appreciate
it.'

'S'nothing,' he replied without even turning
around to look at me. 'I'd a done the same for anyone.
We're an honest bunch around 'ere.'

'I don't doubt it. Thanks again.' I began walking away and stopped. 'Really awful news about that body on the beach, isn't it? What a terrible tragedy.' I couldn't help myself. It had to be said. I had to say something.

'No body found on the beach. Don't know what yer on about.' Murmurs of agreement from everyone in the group. Nodding of heads. Eyes all lowered away from mine, sweeping and scouring the floor.

I felt a kick to my solar plexus, the force causing me to gasp. 'Sorry? Neil, my husband, said he saw it earlier. It looked as if somebody had fallen from the top of the cliff?'

Or been pushed.

I blocked out those final few words, pretended they didn't exist in my head. More murmuring. A rumble of low laughter from one of them that made my hackles rise in indignation. 'Aye, well, he must be mistaken, pet. Dougie here is a fisherman. Brought his trawl in earlier today and saw nothing and Ron lives in the old coastguard cottage at t'end of your lane and he saw nowt either. No body. Not sure what your husband thought he saw but it definitely weren't a dead body.'

A breath caught in my throat. I suppressed a coughing fit, swallowing repeatedly to stem the rush of saliva that filled my mouth. I suddenly felt weak and helpless, coupled with deep frustration that burned at my face, my skin patchy with fury. They were lying. I don't know how I knew it, but something about their body language, their inability to look me in the eye, made me think they were either patronising me, which in itself added to my growing irritation, or they were being deliberately deceitful. Why, I didn't know, but it was there, evident by their hunched backs and conspiratorial glances at one another when they thought I wasn't looking. It screamed dishonesty and a collective sense of concealment. And to think, I had begun to doubt my husband. I would sooner believe him than this lot.

I could have stayed, told them that I hadn't given any times or locations and that he had been quick to jump in to disprove my story without even checking with his pals as to whether or not they had seen anything, but didn't have the energy for it. It would have been a pointless endeavour, I could see that. His mind was made up, the rigidity of his posture telling me exactly what I needed to know: that the matter was well and truly closed.

Neil's hands were clasped around his pint when I sat back down, his knuckles white. I started to speak but he stopped me, shaking his head and briefly closing his eyes.

'I know what I saw, Fi,' he said once the conversation in the other group had risen to a volume that was loud enough to drown out our whispered words. 'Earlier, I had begun to doubt myself but I know what I saw. I just know it.'

'And I believe you. I have no idea what's going on around here but I do know that they were lying. Too quick to bat away the idea when I mentioned it.' I placed my hand over his arm and squeezed it. 'Let's order our food, eat up and get out of here, shall we, eh? Back to our little cottage with its crooked walls and open fire. We'll close the curtains and block out the rest of the world. Everything will make more sense in the morning.'

I wished I could believe my own words. There was a strange kind of comfort to be had from them but I knew even then that something big, something monumentally tragic, was going to happen. I just didn't know what it was or when it would take place. I didn't even know how I knew it; I just did. It was a fire burning in my gut. Flames that couldn't be dampened or put out. Flames that would eventually consume us.

11

If I could have stayed in our cottage for the next few days, salted myself away from the rest of the world, then I would have, but empty cupboards determined that one of us had to visit the local supermarket. Neil was busy with work and I was loath to drag him away from it, which left me to be the one to go and get our weekly grocery shopping.

The term 'supermarket' could only have been very loosely applied to the building before me as I pulled up in the car. I yanked at the handbrake and sat for a short while, thinking how dated everything looked. Dated and shabby. Large, wide cracks ran across the car park, many stretches of it unusable. Gaping holes and mounds of rubble were strewn across the concrete. It was a world away from the modern shops we were used to back on the mainland. I tried to see beyond the peeling paint, the faded signage and filthy windows. As long as they had enough essentials to see us through the rest of the week, that would be enough to satisfy me. Even before I was through the doors, I was already mentally planning monthly visits on the ferry to bulk-buy our food and toiletries. If this place was all Winters End had to offer, I needed a contingency plan.

Relief rippled through me when I stepped inside. I was faced with row upon row of well-stocked shelves. Piped music played in the background and although it was a supermarket in miniature, a glimmer of hope that we didn't live in a place that was so remote that the most essential items of food were hard to come by sparked to life in my abdomen. I was rapidly becoming grateful for the smallest of mercies.

The place was almost empty. I had the shop to myself save for an elderly man who was engrossed by the racks of beer and didn't appear to even notice me standing close by, and a young lad dressed in a pale-blue uniform of sorts who was busy stacking shelves full of fresh bread. Nobody else. No other females. I shook that thought away. No brooding today. I hadn't the stomach for it.

It took me just ten minutes to fill my trolley. For all that the shop was peaceful, I still didn't want to be there. Buying groceries had never been one of my favourite pastimes, but it was a means to an end.

The checkout operator was the same young lad who had been stocking the shelves when I arrived. He wiped his hands on his shirt and began scanning my items, his eyes clouded over as if I wasn't even there. Disinterest stemmed from him, his movements sleepy and torpid. I tried to catch his eye, thinking I should introduce myself, but stopped. Something about his body language told me he wasn't remotely interested in my presence, the sweeping gesture he made when he scanned in my items slow and sluggish as if my being there was causing him actual physical pain.

I didn't want to appear churlish or aloof so made a point of catching his eye and saying 'thank you' when I paid and snatched up my receipt. My words were met with a stony silence. It didn't bother me. He was a young lad, pimples lining his face, soft bristles pushing through his pale, baby-soft skin. So many years ahead of him. So much still to learn.

I heard it as I was walking away: a muttering, monosyllabic, low and rumbling, but it was there all the same.

'Y'must be mad comin' to live here. You should go back to where you came from.'

My footsteps faltered and for a brief period I considered retracing my steps, confronting him, asking him exactly what he meant by those words, but in the end decided to keep my dignity intact and do the right thing: I continued walking and left him behind. He was a callow, spotty youth, surly and lacking in the necessary social graces. My energies were best spent on other issues. There is a certain truism to picking one's battles carefully.

It was a challenge, pushing the trolley over the expanse of broken tarmac to my vehicle, having to manoeuvre it this way and that to avoid the potholes and large cracks. I didn't see it at first, the damage to my car. It was only as I stepped back to open the boot hatch that I spotted it. My pulse raced, my heart sank, until anger took over, that is, blocking out all logic, all sensibilities and rational thought.

Leaving the trolley, I strode back into the shop ready to have that battle that I had been so keen to avoid just a few minutes ago.

My face must have given me away, my anger evident in my features and gait, seeping out of me in visible waves. He seemed to dip in the middle when I approached, his face leached of all colour. 'Was it you?' I barked. His eyes fluttered, darting away from mine, sweeping across the dusty floor. 'Did you scratch my fucking car?' I knew it wasn't him. He had been here, hadn't left the building. It was impossible. That fact didn't matter. Fury doesn't sit alongside logic. It's a wild beast, snarling, lacking in sense and decorum.

He looked around, I guessed, for assistance. None would come. He knew it, I knew it. We were alone and I was unfurling, like magma bursting out of its chamber. If assistance had arrived, it wouldn't have held me back. Everything was too far gone. I was too far gone. Dead bodies that mysteriously disappeared, locals who made threats towards me, dog shit left on my doorstep, and now a deep scratch on my car. I could see it all in my head, every insult, every little offence mapped out, line upon line etched into my brain. I imagined a hammer smashing them all to pieces, tiny, jagged shards of my problems splintering and fragmenting, slicing at my flesh, stabbing at me and drawing blood.

'What was it you said to me as I left? You told me to leave, didn't you? You said I was mad to live here and that I should leave. Why the fuck did you say that? Why?' My voice echoed above us, reverberating around the high vaulted ceiling, bouncing off the tiled flooring and bare brick walls.

He moved away from me, falling backwards onto a pile of empty boxes that cracked and collapsed beneath his weight. Broken and empty, they toppled and rolled around the floor like large, solid tumbleweeds.

'I... I don't...' He scrambled to his feet, his face puckered with fear. A crimson web crept up his neck. 'My dad, he said...'

'What?' I edged closer, curiosity pushing me on, directing my movements. I wanted to hear his words of defence, what it was that drove him to say it. He stumbled away again, his skinny legs scurrying with spider-like movements. I took a silent breath, softening my features and body language. I needed to keep him on side. He was scared. His had let his mouth run loose and now he was frightened. 'What exactly did your dad say...' I scanned his chest and eyed his badge. '...Liam? Look, I'm sorry I shouted at you. Tell me what your dad said and I promise I'll leave you alone.'

He saw me as deranged. I sounded it, looked it. I knew I appeared unhinged with my wide eyes and clenched fists. It didn't matter. Whatever he was about to say, I needed to hear it. I would listen to every word, every syllable, and dissect it, try to work out what was going on, on this godforsaken island.

'He said that you must be mad coming here to live, that you should leave or you'll end up dead. All the women here, they nearly all end up dead.'

I was relieved to hear him say it out loud, for him to voice my suspicions about this place. I wasn't imagining it. I wasn't going insane, suffering another breakdown, my mind cracked and broken by the near collapse of our finances and my bouts of thieving. It was real. There was something dark and sinister about Winters End, an invisible enemy that lurked around corners and danced in the shadows, avoiding detection and scrutiny. They all knew. The people here knew that something was going on and in their own strange and irksome little way, had been trying to warn us.

Tears bit at the back of my eyelids, frustration and relief colliding. I smiled at young Liam, stepping away from him and his tangible terror. He didn't deserve my anger. He also didn't have to tell me, yet he had. He could have feigned ignorance, hid himself away in the warehouse at the back of the shop away from my boiling fury, but hadn't. He had stayed put, told me what I needed to hear.

'Thank you,' I managed to whisper, my voice

croaky with emotion. 'You're a brave lad owning up to that and speaking out. Thank you.'

He didn't reply, the colour slowly returning to his thin, pallid face. He stared at me with dull, frightened eyes before lowering his gaze. I didn't break contact, keeping my focus firmly fixed on him before turning around and almost leaving. Something stopped me. A low voice inside my head, willing me to say it, to ask the question.

'Who's your dad? What's his name?'

An intake of breath. Then his reply.

'Dave is his name. Everyone calls him Davey,' he said with a shrug, his eyes suddenly veiled with darkness. 'Why d'you ask?'

'Well, I think I have a right to ask the name of the man who told his son that I might end up dead if I don't leave the island, don't you? What's his surname?'

A pink web rose up his neck, settling on his cheeks. Tufts of facial hair were peppered in small patches on his face. A smattering of whiskers sat in a thin line above his top lip. He was young, afraid. Startled by my outburst. 'Fairhurst. Davey Fairhurst.' His voice was a squeak, a scratch in the surrounding emptiness.

'And what about your mother?' I couldn't help myself. I should have stopped at that point, turned and left. I didn't. My mouth was running loose. I'd over-stepped a boundary. Leaving without more answers was pointless. This was my opportunity to glean as much out of him as I could.

'My... my mother?' He was stammering now, his jaw slack, tongue lapping at his wet, fleshy lips.

'Yes, you know, the woman who gave birth to you?' My nails dug into my palms as I waited, my own jaw rigid, teeth clamped together.

Part of me thought that this poor kid didn't de-serve my wrath but then another part of me remem-bered that he'd started this whole thing with his throwaway comment.

He shrugged, placed his hands on either side of the large crate next to where he stood and began pushing it down the aisle. He was making his escape, trying to shift away from me and my endless ques-tions. My unfolding madness. 'She left years ago when I was a kid. Lives in Durham near the river.'

My temple developed its own heartbeat. My mouth was dry. I wanted to ask more, for him to tell me why she had left, but he was already putting all his weight behind pushing the half-loaded crate towards the double doors at the other end of the shop, his back turned away from me. He was desperate to es-cape my lunacy and white-hot rage.

This was my final chance to find out just one vital piece of information before he disappeared altogether, his slim body soon to be completely obscured by the large trolley as it vanished into the darkness of the warehouse. 'What's she called? Your mum?'

He stopped moving and turned, eyes narrowed, a small quizzical line appearing on his brow. 'Catherine. Why d'you want to know?'

'No reason,' I murmured, the actual reason for wanting to know boring a hole in my brain. 'I was just wondering, that's all.'

I left the supermarket before he could question me any further. I had enough to be going on with. My mind was alight with these new pieces of information. I could have stayed, pressed young Liam even further, asked why his dad had said what he said, cornered him about the reasons why his mum had left the island, but I was treading a fine line between being inquisitive and terrorising him. I could have also asked him why the women of Winters End ended up dead and what he knew about it but I'd said enough.

My trolley was where I left it. I almost laughed. At least that was one positive of living here. No thieves. Inspecting the deep scratch on the car was pointless, a waste of time and energy. It was there and there was nothing I could about it. Somebody had seen fit to drag a knife or a key across the paintwork of our vehicle for reasons known only to themselves.

I rummaged in my bag for my keys, Liam's words going round and round in my head. My initial fears about this place weren't unfounded after all. I wasn't going mad, on the cusp of a breakdown. I was right. From the beginning, the very first moment we set off on our travels to Winters End, all my doubts and anxieties and unspoken moments of dread that had sat like rocks in the base of my belly had now been proven to be real. I had worried that they knew about my wrongdoings, these people, and thought of me as untrustworthy, a criminal in their midst. But that wasn't it at all. It was something else. Something bigger and more dangerous. Something far worse than stealing money to pay off credit cards and huge debts. I just didn't know what it was but was certain that it was precarious and would have a negative impact on our lives.

I loaded the shopping bags into the car. My focus was elsewhere, his voice causing me to jump, my scalp crinkling in response to the sudden sound behind me.

'Looks like you could do with a hand. Here,' the voice said, 'let me help you.'

I spun around to see Ewan standing there, his body silhouetted against the pale sky and stretch of clouds. Before I could protest that I was managing perfectly well, my anger and sadness at my predicament making me wish I was alone, he gently nudged me to one side and placed the rest of the bags in the boot, repositioning them so they fitted in easily without squashing anything, like a huge grocery jigsaw puzzle. A stray apple fell out and rolled around the plastic surface of the boot. I snatched it up and stuffed it down the bottom of a half-empty bag, pushing it between a loaf of bread and a carton of milk.

'Thank you.' I said, staring up at him. My voice was cool and clipped. I wanted to speak calmly but it was so damn difficult, fury and frustration building in my chest, bubbling like hot oil in my throat.

He noticed my pinched expression, the darkness in my gaze. I too, saw his face, the compassion there. He made to speak but I held up my hand and closed my eyes, shaking my head for him to stop. 'Please, Ewan, don't say anything. I know that none of this is your fault, but as a religious man, you're duty bound to tell me the truth. No lies, no fobbing me off, no evading the question or smiling inanely, telling me there's nothing wrong on this island and that it's all in my mind. I need to know one thing – just one thing.' I took a shaky breath and blurted it out, my face burn-

ing. Hearing it spoken out loud gave everything that
had happened a sense of reality, turning it from something ethereal to a tangible thing. A threat. 'Why do
the residents on this island hate me so much and why
do they think I'll end up dead?'

12

'Fiona, I can see you're upset and, having heard what you've endured, I understand why you're worried and frightened, but I'm afraid I don't have the answer to your question, and I'm almost certain they don't want you to come to any harm. The people of Winters End are a strange, quirky lot, I'll give you that, but I can say with complete sureness that they don't think you're going to die.'

Was he lying, covering up for the residents of this island? It was too difficult to tell, my usually precise antennae for detecting bullshit and deceit blurred and woefully off frequency after this morning's events. I almost laughed at the way he had of saying so much without actually saying anything at all. Like a politician, his job was to placate the masses, make sure they remained calm and didn't make any rash decisions.

'How long have you been here on Winters End, Ewan?' I expected him to tell me that he'd been here for many, many years, that he knew each member of his congregation inside out and that he had never seen or heard anything untoward, that he treated each and every one of them like a close sibling and that none of them had a bad bone in their body; they were simply eccentric and misunderstood.

He didn't. Instead, he shrugged his shoulders and pursed his lips in thought as he counted off the dates in his head. 'One year and nine months.'

I watched him silently, my heart a heavy pendulum banging at my chest. I scrutinised his expression, every line on his face. I stared into his eyes, into the depth of his pinprick pupils and bronze irises, searching for cracks and lies. I stood and watched and waited. And saw nothing. I thought this man could possibly be the one person who could help me see the truth of this place. I was wrong. He didn't know anything about this island or these people and their thoughts and intentions any better than I did. With his dwindling congregation, how could he possibly know what went on in their lives, let alone their heads? He didn't know them at all.

At a loss as to what to say next, I thanked him with a vague promise that I would visit the church again sometime in the near future and made to get in the driver's seat. I felt the warmth of his hand on my shoulder; gentle yet persuasive. Firm enough to stop me in my tracks.

'There is something. It may help you with your worries but it may be nothing at all.'

I opened my mouth to say something but the weight of his touch increased, his grip tightening ever so slightly as he shook his head and smiled.

'Not here. This isn't the right place to speak of such things. If you can call around to the church tomorrow morning, we can talk then. I live in the house next to St Augustine's chapel.'

My heart continued its rhythmic thump. I was finally getting somewhere, making headway with this man who, like me, was a stranger in a strange place. Apart from the cashier in the supermarket, he was the first person on Winters End to open up to me, to speak kindly to me and actually believe my fears about what was going on, on this beautifully hideous place I now called home.

A lump rose in my throat. Maybe it was the confrontation in the supermarket or the scratch on the car or Ewan's kindness or maybe it was a combination of all three, but by the time I bid my goodbyes and began the drive home, the tears were flowing freely.

I took a longer route back, allowing for some time to pull myself together. It was also a chance to become familiar with the roads and hamlets of Winters End. Although we had been out and about since moving here, I hadn't really explored the place and decided to use the opportunity to see as much as possible. I soon wished I hadn't. Afterwards, what I saw sat in my mind like a dead weight, refusing to move, reminding me that none of my initial fears or suspicions were unfounded. I had been right all along. Something on Winters End was awry, skewed and out of kilter. I just didn't know what it was or why.

* * *

'Benches.' I stared at Ewan, closely observing his face for his reaction, for any signs that he understood what I was getting at.

His eyes fluttered slightly; he cleared his throat repeatedly as I spoke. Had I seen him do those things before or were they signs that he knew what I was implying?

'Yesterday after I left you, I went for a drive around the island. I decided to stop, get a good view of the sea. There was a long line of wooden benches on the path next to the beach. They had inscriptions on them. I stopped to read those inscriptions on the brass plaques that were on the backs of the benches and do you know what was written on them?'

He shook his head, then nodded, lowering his eyes and sighing.

'Names of the dead women who are buried in the graveyard. Tributes to them from friends and families. But I'm guessing you already knew that?'

Another nod. Another sigh. Some hand-wringing.

'Okay, maybe we need to chat. I'll make some tea first.' He headed off into the kitchen, his movements silent, ghost-like.

I didn't follow him, instead sitting rigidly, steeling myself for whatever it was he was about to tell me. With only a tiny population to begin with, I began to wonder how many of the people on Winters End were female. Perhaps we should have given the move here more thought, visited, got a feel for what it was like on this tiny, demonic slab of land. Except we hadn't. I'd seen the cottage advertised online, liked the look of the island, its remoteness appealing to my need for anonymity, and we made a snap decision. I thought I had achieved my desire to be unknown and unseen after my major indiscretion. Except that hadn't happened. Everyone here knew about our arrival. They may not have actually known us but it was clear that they didn't want us around. *Me* around. It was me. Everything, whether I wanted it to be or not, was about me and my presence here on Winters End.

He said that you must be mad coming here to live, that you should leave or you'll end up dead. All the women here, they nearly all end up dead.

'Here we are, biscuits as well for good measure. A little bit of what you fancy does you good.' Ewan placed the tray down on the table between us.

The room in which we were seated was a minimalistic throwback to the 1980s with an oak Adam-style fire surround and pale green and peach curtains, the pattern a mishmash of washed-out, smudged colours. There were no pictures or mirrors around, just a small pine bookcase and a scuffed coffee table with a couple of magazines tucked on the shelf underneath.

The house itself was an old Victorian building and seemed particularly large for just one person and, although the living room was sparse, it was in better condition than the hallway with its threadbare, dirt-brown carpet and the front garden which consisted of a tangle of weeds that stood high and proud, snagging at my trousers as I had made my way to the front door.

I guessed that housekeepers, gardeners and general maintenance people were hard to come by with such a small population, although why Ewan didn't tackle it himself was anybody's guess.

'Thank you,' I said, picking up my cup and taking a sip. I couldn't face eating anything until I'd spoken to him. I wanted solid answers, not nuanced nonsense. A hundred words with no substance to them.

My stomach was a fist of anxiety, folds of flesh tightly knotted together. I decided to come out with it, no preamble. Straight to the point. 'Before we talk about the benches, I wanted to ask you about something that I saw last night on the news.'

He raised an eyebrow and nodded, surveying me carefully with a precise, protracted gaze that had me shifting in my seat, perspiration coating my neck and back. Clearly, I wasn't the only one determined to hold my position and not be browbeaten into submission.

I looked away and spoke. 'The other day, Neil swore blind he saw a body at the foot of the cliffs but when we mentioned it in the pub, the men in there said that there definitely hadn't been a body found. And then last night, on the North East News, a woman was reported missing. Her family said her disappearance was totally out of character. They said she was an ornithologist and was thinking of getting the ferry over here. The police have said they're going to check to see if she ever made it to the island.' I stopped speaking, my heart beginning to thump now that my words were out there, being heard, my suspicions voiced out loud. All of a sudden, it was real, no longer just an idle, scary thought rattling around in my head. Heat seared over my skin. My limbs felt heavy and cumbersome. I looked back at Ewan, who was still sitting watching me, his face soft but expressionless. Why was this man so difficult to fathom?

'And as for those benches, they were all dedicated to women.' I sighed and took another sip of the tea despite the sickly sensation in my abdomen. 'But I guess you already knew that, didn't you?'

It was Ewan's turn to look uncomfortable. He cleared his throat, his expressionless mask slipping, and put down his cup. His eyes were glassy, his shoulders curved into a gentle arc.

'Fiona, I'm so sorry you're worried about this. I know that isn't going to help but I'm not sure what else to say to alleviate your concerns.'

'Try telling me exactly what you know. Try telling me the truth about this island.'

He sat back in his chair and looked up at the ceiling, fingers interlaced, knuckles chalk white, his skin taut and waxy. I waited, knowing that hurrying him would dilute the story. I needed to know this, whatever *this* was. The time he took to speak, his hooded eyes, the groove between his brows when he finally came out with it, they were the giveaways. I knew then that I needed to prepare myself, be ready to absorb every single word and analyse the information he was about to give me.

'Before I say anything, can I please ask that you don't think too badly of me for not being entirely truthful when we first met? Like you, I've not lived here that long and I've had to tread carefully around some of the locals, many of whom I've still not met. It doesn't do to upset a dwindling congregation.' Ewan stared at his hands and sighed. 'I'm a peacemaker, a religious diplomat for want for a better phrase, and I do all I can to keep people happy and calm. I didn't, and still don't, want to unearth their pasts or any secrets they may have. My job is to settle their fears, give them some spiritual guidance, a glimmer of hope in an often callous and cruel world.'

I thought of some of the islanders unburdening themselves to Ewan, trying to absolve themselves of their sins, and wondered just how much Ewan actually knew of these people's wrongdoings. More, I suspect, than he was willing to admit. More than he would ever tell me, his vow of confidentiality forcing him into an unshakeable silence.

'Okay,' I said quietly. 'I understand that and I get it, I really do, but you're the only one who's really talked to me openly since we got here. Honnie held her cards close to her chest when I visited. Whatever you say, I can promise, will stay in this room.'

I hoped I sounded sincere. I couldn't guarantee I wouldn't overreact. It depended on what it was he was about to tell me. I swallowed and waited, my hands icy cold with anticipation. How bad could it be, this piece of information he was about to reveal? Exactly how bad were things on this craggy piece of rock in the middle of the North Sea? Mildly upsetting, really awful or horribly catastrophic?

'Winters End hasn't always been kind to its female inhabitants.' He stopped, took an unsteady breath and continued. 'There have been some deaths. Some awful, tragic accidents on the island.'

'Such as?' I spoke quickly, cutting in, afraid he would omit any details. I needed to know everything. I needed to know it all no matter how dreadful or grisly.

The furrow between his eyebrows deepened. Another heavy sigh. 'Abigail Paterson fell down the stairs while her husband was away working in Newcastle.'

'The woman buried in the graveyard?' I remembered the name, saw it on a bench, the epitaph on her headstone. *Wife, sister, daughter. Dead at 29 years of age.*

Ewan nodded. 'Yes, that's right. Abigail was a lovely woman, always ready to help people. Such a terrible thing to happen. Her husband moved away afterwards. They hadn't lived here that long and he needed the support of his family back in Sunderland.'

'And?' I waited. There was more to come. I could sense it. This wasn't an isolated incident. It was there in his eyes, his inability to look at me directly. Something was amiss.

'It came just before the death of Julia Bristow. Who also fell and died.'

'Two women fell down the stairs within months of each other?'

Ewan shook his head. 'No, Julia fell down the cliff edge. She was out walking and slipped.'

'Did she slip, though?'

He didn't answer me, speaking now as if I wasn't even there. As if he was thinking out loud, trying to make sense of it all.

'And then there was Joy. Joy Rollings. She was a member of our choir.'

'Please don't tell me she also slipped over the edge of the cliff to her death or fell down the stairs at home?' I was breathless, my chest rattling and wheezing in a concertina fashion.

'No. She was at home. She had sustained a blow to the head and was found dead in her garage.'

The room began to spin around me, the wallpaper and curtains blurring as I blinked repeatedly to clear the grit that had lodged behind my eyelids, my lashes fluttering like the wings of a distressed bird.

'Nobody was ever held responsible. Police came over from Newcastle and Durham but the perpetrator was never found.'

'That was only last year though, wasn't it?' That was what had struck me about the headstones – how recently some of them had died. I thought about the pandemic, Covid-19. It did indeed look as if some mysterious plague had struck them down, wiping out those poor women one by one until hardly anybody was left. On an island this small, just a few deaths can leave a huge dent. But somehow, I had known that it wasn't that. And I was right.

Ewan nodded. 'Their enquiries are still ongoing but the last I heard, there wasn't any evidence left at the scene. They seemed to think that the perpetrator was probably a tourist who left on a boat after they murdered poor Joy.'

'And what do you think, Ewan?' I kept my voice

sharp, letting him know that I refused to be fed any lies and wouldn't be fobbed off with stories about how God takes the best and that coincidences do happen. It was bullshit and we both knew it.

'I honestly don't know. I really don't.'

'What about...' I stopped, trying to recall the names of the other women buried in the same place. They refused to come to me. I tapped my fingers against my knee, impatience ballooning in my chest.

'Sarah and Phillipa?'

'Yes!' My voice was loud, bouncing around the room.

Ewan looked as if he had aged ten years in just ten minutes, his body shrivelled, his skin suddenly turning a deathly grey colour. 'Sarah drowned. I think she died before any of the others. She was a proficient swimmer but the sea was rough that day and the coroner said it was an accident. Misadventure.'

Before he had finished speaking, I had already decided that the coroner's verdict was nonsense. All these deaths in such a short space of time. There was something else going on here.

'And Phillipa, well...' He shook his head and wrung his hands together. 'Phillipa liked to drink. Too much, as it turned out. She got in her car and it hit a tree at speed.'

My head was buzzing. Were these deaths connected? A woman who drinks and drives, that can't be
seen as suspicious, can it? But what about those other
deaths? Were they really accidents?

'And of course, there was Myra Simons.'

Ewan's voice cut through my thoughts. My skin
flashed hot at the intonation in his words.

'Myra? Who's Myra?' I thought about those other
names on the benches by the sea, tried to remember
the people who were on them.

He turned to look at me, eyes full of sorrow. 'You
won't have seen her name anywhere, I don't suppose.
As far as I'm aware, there aren't any mentions of her
on the island. All the posters enquiring after her
whereabouts have faded away, battered and shredded
by the elements.'

The buzzing in my head increased a hundredfold,
bolts of electricity surging through me. 'Posters? What
do you mean, posters?' Even as I was saying it, I already guessed what his answer was going to be. I just
knew. It was the only thing that fitted.

This time, Ewan stared at me, our gazes locking, a
look of gloom evident in his face. 'Myra went missing
over two years ago. Just disappeared. No signs of a
struggle in her house, no goodbye note. Nothing at all.
She simply vanished into thin air.'

That was when I knew that Ewan suspected, just as I did, that something dreadful had happened to that woman. I hadn't imagined it at all. It was real. Winters End, the place I now called home, was a horribly dangerous place with a dark past. And unless Neil and I decided to sell up and move away, we were stuck here with a person or peoples unknown who, it appeared, wanted me dead.

13

I decided when I arrived home that I would start driving everywhere. It felt safer, somehow. Even though I was battling an invisible enemy, being tucked inside a vehicle, albeit a damaged one, felt far more secure than travelling everywhere on foot, although after speaking to Ewan and discovering that one of the women died in a car accident, maybe I was wrong to think that the security of my car would be enough to keep me safe. I had almost run home after my meeting with him, a feeling of vulnerability pushing me on, the fear that somebody was following me, ready to harm me, giving me surges of strength I didn't know I possessed.

Neil was sitting in his study when I got back. I

could hear the tapping of his keyboard, the dull sound of it making me feel grateful to be inside our little cottage. My prison. My safe place.

'Fiona, is that you?' Even the sound of his voice was enough to make me want to weep with gratitude.

On instinct, I turned and locked the door, sliding the bolt across with a heavy, solid clunk.

'Yes, just been to see Ewan. I was thinking about joining the choir and wanted to get some details from him.' I winced at my own pathetic attempt at lying. I should have been adept at it after what I had done, yet still found being dishonest a deeply uncomfortable thing to do. I had dug into my reserves over the past year and was now empty, a husk with nothing left to offer. There was a gaping hole inside me where my decency and integrity used to be. I wasn't ready to tell him what Ewan had told me just yet. I needed more. Neil would think Ewan's words empty, the evidence flimsy. He would tell me that I was jumping to conclusions, that I was worrying over nothing. Even seeing a dead body at the foot of the cliffs and outright denial from locals wouldn't be enough to convince him. Neil dealt in cold, hard facts. He didn't hold any truck with conjecture and supposition. It had to slap him in the face to get his attention.

'I've sorted that scratch on the car. I polished it

out. You can still see it a bit if you look really closely but it's not that noticeable now.'

The floor felt unsteady beneath me. I gripped the banister for balance. Neil had insisted the scratch was just kids messing about and, as always, had fixed it without any fuss. But after seeing Ewan, I was convinced it was more than that, a sinister act carried out by one of the locals, somebody who hoped to remain anonymous. They wouldn't remain that way for long because I was going to find out who did it. I didn't care about bar brawls or people trying to stop me from entering our local pub or leaving dog shit on our doorstep; I cared about what had taken place on this island in the past few years, why young women were dying and disappearing without a trace. And I also cared about what might happen to me. I didn't want to be next. Living made me nervous but the thought of dying scared the hell out of me.

'You're back just in time. There's a pot of coffee on the stove. I thought you'd need it after the walk there and back.'

On instinct, I went through to Neil's study, placed my arms around his shoulders and rested my head on his back, my cheeks pressed into his warm flesh. He felt so steady and strong, I could have stayed there for an age. His effervescent, bubbly nature that lately had irritated me beyond words now made me feel safe and comforted. He was a robust presence in my life, exactly what I needed.

'Well, that was unexpected. I'll have to polish the car and make coffee more often if this is my reward.'

I smiled and planted a kiss on his cheek before heading into the kitchen to pour myself a coffee.

'Oh, and I also found out who the welcome basket was from.'

The coffee pot was poised in my hand, its spout hanging over the edge the mug. I visualised that note, the stench of the dog shit. I had forgotten about the basket of food. It had been nudged aside by other, less palatable events.

'And?' My own voice sounded alien: false and contrived. I wasn't that interested in the person who had sent that basket. I was more intrigued by the mystery dog-shit smearer and the car scratcher and why Davey in the pub didn't want me there.

You should leave or you'll end up dead.

'I was out walking along the cliff path again and somebody shouted over to me. Said he and his wife lived in the small bungalow at the end of the lane and asked if we got the basket of food. I didn't catch his name, just told him thanks.'

I turned and almost walked into Neil, splashes of hot coffee spurting out of the pot.

'God, sorry! I didn't know you were behind me.' I slammed the glass container down onto the kitchen counter and shrieked as it exploded, sending shards of glass and boiling liquid everywhere.

'Hey, hey! What's up? You're a nervous wreck.'

I slumped down onto one of the chairs while Neil set about wiping up the hot coffee and picking up the pieces of glass, sweeping them up with a small brush and dustpan and depositing them in the bin.

'Right,' he said, after the place had been cleared, 'what's up? You're jittery as hell. It wasn't that incident with the body on the beach, was it? Because the more I think about it, the more convinced I am that I must have made a mistake.'

I wanted to pound his chest, to tell him that he hadn't made a mistake, that somebody probably pulled that body out of view to conceal it, but I couldn't find the energy to speak. A weariness had me in its grip, some sort of lethargy after speaking with Ewan earlier. It was all I could do to not scream at him and fall to the floor in a heap.

I closed my eyes, waited until the moment had passed, then took his hand and led him into the living room where we sat next to each other on the sofa.

And that's when I told him.

* * *

'I don't know what to say, Fi.'

We sat in silence for a few seconds, both of us unable to articulate our reactions and feelings.

'Do you still think you didn't see a body down there? Or has what I've just told you made you think again?'

He ran his hands through his hair and shook his head. 'I honestly don't know. I really don't. I mean, it's not as if there's been a whole load of murders or deaths since getting here, is it? The ones you've told me about were from last year and the year before and only one of them was classed as an actual attack. The others were ruled as accidents and misadventure, weren't they?'

I spun around and faced him. 'So you believe that they were just coincidences then? Those women dying so close together is one big fucking coincidence?'

He held up his hands and stared at me with glassy eyes. 'Whoa! Hold on here. I have no idea what to think! I mean, looking at what you've told me, three of those women died accidentally, one was murdered, and one went missing. For all we know, she could have eloped or decided that Winters End wasn't the place for her. Right now, she could be living the high life in the Bahamas or she could be working somewhere – anywhere – in the UK, or the world, for that matter. We just don't know, do we? People go missing all the time. People die all the time. Honestly, Fi, we can't go around saying things, making accusations and putting two and two together and coming up with five before we've even properly settled here. We need to be careful with our words, watch what we say. Winters End is tiny. We don't want to risk upsetting people before we've even got to know them, do we?'

Something unravelled inside of me on hearing Neil's words, my previous strands of strength loosening and falling away. It took so little these days to dent my confidence, the slightest of pushes causing me to stagger and fall. Was I going mad? Imagining all of this? Listening to him say it out loud, putting a sensible perspective on it, my fears and suspicions suddenly seemed disproportionate and outlandish. I was struggling to think straight, my mind a dark mesh of tightly woven thoughts. I wanted to be wrong and maybe I was. Had the near bankruptcy and subsequent move to a completely alien place pushed my thinking into the darkest of corners again? I had thought I was on the mend but what if I was wrong, my thinking skewed by the upheaval and move here? Do people who are on the brink of a breakdown know they are at that point? I didn't think I had known last time. Maybe it was happening again. I was still able to rationalise and function on a daily basis. Perhaps that was how mental illness manifested itself, by creeping in disguised as something else, something that blind-sided us and caught us off guard. An insidious creature with sharp teeth and jagged claws.

I nibbled at my nails, something I hadn't done since I was a teenager, and stared down at my feet, feeling shamefaced and embarrassed. I thought that Neil was probably right; I had overreacted to Ewan's explanation. Tomorrow I would go and see him again, apologise for my intrusive questions and behaviour. I'd forced him into a corner, made him play my little game of thinking something was amiss with the deaths of those women. But then he had been the one who said he had something to tell me, hadn't he? I didn't set up the meeting. It was all his doing. I shut my eyes, exhaustion washing over me, and squashed that thought. I was tired of it all. Tired of looking for faults and flaws, tired of feeling paranoid, thinking people were trying to get rid of me, off the island. I was just so damn tired of everything. I wanted to curl up and sleep for an age, wake up to a brighter, better day where none of this had happened. I just wanted an easy, comfortable life. Was that such a difficult and rare thing to wish for or achieve? Others had it. Why not me?

My shoes slipped off my feet and onto the rug with a dull thud as I pushed at them with cold, desperate fingers. I tucked my legs up under a cushion and lay down, placing my head on the arm of the sofa. An overload of information had left me feeling indescribably fatigued. I felt as if I could sleep for a thousand years. How lovely would it have been, I thought as exhaustion and a blanket of nothingness enveloped me, if I woke up back in our old house in Saltburn, debt-free, crime-free and with all of our friends and family still talking to us?

I felt myself falling, going down, down, down into that safe space in my head, my body floating, all worries absent. Just dreams and a sense of weightlessness that carried me away to somewhere where nobody could harm or threaten me. When blackness finally descended, I embraced it.

* * *

I awoke with a start, my head thumping, blood pounding in my ears. My eyes were heavy, my body a dead weight, lethargy rendering me awkward and clumsy. Cushions fell and scattered across the floor as I sat up and looked around. I stared at the clock. An hour. I had slept for an hour, possibly longer. I should have felt rested, lighter. Happier. I didn't. What I felt was frightened, out of sorts, as if something untoward had taken place while I was napping.

Neil was no longer in the room and a breeze lapped around my feet. I stood up and followed the trail of cold air until I was standing in front of the door in the hallway. It was ajar – not wide open, but neither was it properly closed.

I turned and called out Neil's name, but even before I did that I knew that he wasn't in the house. Dread skittered over my skin, icy water closing around me, pushing me under, stopping me from breathing properly.

My hands trembled as I pulled on my boots and jacket and stepped outside. A sharp wind caught me unawares, forcing me to stagger backwards. I righted myself and pulled up my collar, pushing strands of loose hair back from my face. I knew it would have been pointless to call out his name; my voice would get lost in the wind, masked by the strength of the strong gusts that whipped around me, my words carried out to sea, unheard and unanswered, so I walked out onto the narrow lane instead, craning my neck around corners and over hedgerows to try and catch sight of him.

I have no idea how long I spent wandering up and down like that, fighting against the elements, but I did know that the longer it took to find him, the greater my fears were that something terrible had happened.

'You'll catch yer death out here, pet. There's a storm heading our way.'

I whirled around and was standing almost face to face with a short, elderly man, his eyes screwed up against the howling wind.

'I'm Wilf. Live in the bungalow at the of the lane with our Neave.'

'Ah,' I said, my voice a feeble protest against the rage of the wind. 'The basket of food. Thank you. That was really kind.'

'It's the least we could do. Not many of us on this little island. Got to be as friendly as we can to each other, don't we? Not as if we can go far or hide for long if there's a fall out, can we?' He chuckled softly, his face suddenly sombre. 'Anyway, get yerself inside, pet. And don't be wandering over to the cliff path. If that rain starts up, it's a treacherous route. Slippery as hell.' He held out his hand for me to shake and I couldn't help but feel warmed by the gesture. His mannerisms were a stark reminder that not all of the locals were gruff and unwelcoming. 'Neave don't get out much with her being housebound and all, but she passes on her best wishes.' And with that he was gone, a speck in the distance, the sound of his footfall on loose gravel drowned out by the roaring wind. I felt slightly bereft. He seemed kind, his voice genuine.

I had to find Neil, however, work out where he had gone. All we had was this narrow lane, an empty field. And that cliff path. The thought of heading out onto it made me feel horribly sick. Wilf was right. It was treacherous. Deadly, even.

I stared ahead but couldn't see Neil across the open field and he wasn't at the end of the lane either. So where the hell was he?

My attempts at remaining positive were just beginning to dip when I saw him – a crooked figure in the distance, body bent over as he fought his way back home against the raging elements. Fat splatters of rain began to fall, light initially but turning within a matter of seconds into a cascade of water, the sound it made as it hit the ground drowning out the deep thud of my own heartbeat that pulsed in my ears.

My legs felt disconnected from the rest of my

body. I ran towards him, arms outstretched, blinking and rubbing at my eyes, spluttering and coughing as drops hit my face and ran down my neck, blurring my vision.

'Oh my God!' The downpour, as bad as it was, wasn't so heavy that it washed away the blood that coated his face and head. Rivulets of pink bled into his shirt and jacket, small veins that spread down his torso while the rain fell around us.

I held in my shriek, my splayed fingers covering my mouth. He staggered towards me, mouth twitching, his face contorted in a battle against the howling wind.

'Jesus Christ, Neil! What the hell?'

Together we ran down the path and into the cottage. I slammed and locked the door behind us while Neil slumped down on the bottom stair, his right hand pressed firmly against the side of his head.

It was then that I let it out, the hiccupping scream accompanied by tears and hysteria that I felt welling up inside of me. I fell down next to him on the floor, knees buckling, head lowered as I cried into his bloodstained lap.

14

Neil stared at me from under his dark, wet lashes, head lowered and twisted at an angle, an ice pack held to his temple. 'The wind was getting up, I was bent over in a dark crevice underneath some overhanging rocks. I can't remember if I fell or what happened. I honestly can't say.'

'What, so you're telling me that you slipped on dry sand?'

He glowered at me, impatience and exhaustion oozing out of him. He was shivering, possibly in shock. I should have been treading carefully around him, been gentler, more understanding, but worry and the terror of almost losing him far outweighed my need to be patient and tender.

'I'm saying that I was down on the beach and I saw something, a piece of jewellery buried in the sand. Or at least I thought I did. There was something glittering and when I bent down to get it, I must have slipped.' He pressed his head back onto the cushion that was lodged behind him, a sudden weariness evident in his expression. His face was grey. Dark rings sat under his eyes.

'Here,' I murmured, doing my utmost to be kinder to him. He was injured. Cold and weary. 'Let me have another look.'

I wiped away the blood and was able to see that there was a small cut on the side of his head and one on the back of his skull behind his ear. He winced when I dabbed them with an antiseptic wipe, his body shivering.

'I'll run you a hot bath. It'll warm you up. I'll put your clothes straight into the machine, try to get those bloodstains off before they become permanent.' I stood up and started to head out of the room before stopping and turning to look at him. 'By the way, did you know you left the front door open?'

He shuffled farther down into the sofa, shut his eyes and heaved a sigh. 'Sorry. It must have blown open after I left.'

'Why did you go down there, Neil?'

He shrugged and narrowed his eyes. 'You were sleeping and I fancied a walk. I had no idea a storm was on its way. It was all blue skies when I left. Good job I came back up when I did, eh? Before it turned really nasty.'

He was lying. I knew it and he knew that I knew it. I didn't want to play this game any more.

'Where's the jewellery?' I watched his reaction. Waited patiently. He had gone down there because he was still certain he saw something last week. A body. I had been prepared to let this go, to let it all slide away – my suspicions, my fears and worries about the premature deaths of so many females on this island. I was even prepared to ignore Davey and his strange little son and their even stranger threats, putting it down to immaturity and alcohol, but now his actions had dragged me back to that dark place. The one I had tried to ignore and escape from.

'I was obviously mistaken. After I got back up, I couldn't find it. Probably just grains of sand catching the sunlight.'

I let it go. I didn't have the energy to pursue it any further. I could have stayed, argued, forced him to tell me the truth but what was the point? It wouldn't help us any. It wouldn't tell us whether Neil had actually seen a body down there. It wouldn't make me feel any happier or easier about what was going on, so rather than press him for answers, I left the room, ran him a hot bath and made some coffee, the memory of the smashed pot still a vivid imprint in my mind.

For my own sanity, I blocked out all thoughts of dead people and murder and focused on my new business. After filling the washing machine with Neil's bloodied clothes, I took my coffee, sat at my computer and worked for a couple of hours solidly until my back was locked in place, my spine rigid, a rod of iron running through it. Work was the answer to all of this. My escape. It was something I could control.

I stretched, my eyes sore and heavy. I thought about Ewan and his revelations and how I had considered going to visit him again to apologise for imposing on him. I decided against it. He was a grown-up. He could handle my anxieties. He was a priest after all, used to listening to everyone's woes and worries and being the absolver of their sins.

Neil was also at his desk when I popped my head around the corner, his eyes glued to the screen. A recent check of our bank account confirmed that we were still well in the black. No more unnecessary online purchases being made, no more horrendous bills that we couldn't possibly pay being pushed though the letter box. No visits from the bailiff. I swallowed and pushed my hair away from my eyes.

Deciding to leave him be, I went into the kitchen, opening cupboard doors, trying to work out what to cook for our evening meal. It caught my eye in the sudden gloom that descended as a large cloud moved in, obscuring the light through the window – a glint in my peripheral vision. I bent down, opened the door of the washing machine, and lifted out the silver necklace that was pressed up against the glass. A familiar arrhythmic thump started up in my chest. A tic in my jaw forced me to clamp my teeth together. I studied the silver chain, eyes screwed up to see its finer details, already knowing that it wasn't mine. It had come out of Neil's pocket. These were the clothes from the beach, his bloodied, wet clothes. The same clothes he was wearing when he told me that he was mistaken and there hadn't been any jewellery buried in the sand after all.

I had two choices – ignore it and stuff this piece back into the pocket of his shirt, or march into his study and confront him, ask him what the hell he was playing at. I opted for the latter. Despite my assurances to myself to forget about possible dead bodies and missing people, I would not go down the route of us lying to one another again.

No more secrets or deceit.

That was our new mantra, the promise we made to each other to make sure our marriage remained intact, to make sure our lives didn't break and shatter beyond repair, and I intended to keep it.

I edged around the corner of his desk and stood in front of him, the silver chain laid out on my palm. He looked up, blinked, sighed, leaned back and ran his fingers over the stubble on his chin, a flicker of recognition in his eyes at what he had done, plain for me to see.

'I thought we promised there would be no more lies?' My voice was clipped. Crystal sharp. Unforgiving.

He didn't reply. I waited. The one thing we had on this island was time and plenty of it. I was prepared to stand there all evening if needed, right through to the wee small hours. I was not going to let this one slide.

'Look, I'm sorry, okay? I knew you were really worried and I didn't want you to be. I shouldn't have lied. It was stupid and I should have thrown the bloody thing away.' He leaned forward and tried to take hold of the necklace. I shook my head and snatched it away. 'Fiona, it's probably been there for years and years. I only picked it up on instinct. I was going to dispose of it at some point anyway.'

It wasn't enough to stop my irritation from spilling out, the weak explanation that he had given. Had he not been in such a bloodied and fatigued state, he would have hidden this piece of jewellery from me. And we agreed there would be no more hiding of things. No more dishonesty.

'It belongs to her, that woman who's gone missing. That was her at the bottom of the cliff that day. I just know it.'

I watched him suppress an eye-roll and felt overwhelmed with such ferocity that I ended up backing out of the room. Unleashed anger is never a pretty thing and mine at that point was a raging furnace. I needed some space to breathe, to calm myself down, not say something I would later regret.

I was at my desk when he came to find me, his footfall quiet and muffled. Walking round the house like a monk who had taken a vow of silence wouldn't be enough to mollify me. I sensed him standing a few feet away, trying to work out how best to make his approach. My flinch was almost violent, a visceral reaction as he placed his hands on my shoulders. I pulled away and flicked his fingers off my collarbone, the sound of his low breathing evoking even more anger in me.

'It's not just the necklace, Neil. It's the lying. I can't handle it. Not again.'

'I know, and I'm sorry, I really am, but let's both start being honest here, shall we? I'm not the only one who's been telling a few white lies, am I?'

I spun around, dizziness at his words gripping me, making me queasy. 'Excuse me?'

'I called at the shop before I went down to the beach. The local priest was there. He seemed to know who I was and introduced himself. I mentioned about you joining the choir and he seemed taken aback as if he didn't know what I was talking about. Flustered, even. He wasn't sure how to reply to me because apparently there isn't a choir any more; it was disbanded earlier in the year, but of course, you already know that, don't you?'

My face flushed hot, my skin grew cold and clammy. A fib about joining the choir wasn't quite in the same league as concealing a dead woman's necklace, was it? And yet it was still an untruth. Deceit whichever way you looked at it. I had lied. There was no escaping that fact.

'I'm sorry.' I had to say it. No attempting to wriggle my way out of it. It would insult his intelligence. However, it came with a disclaimer. 'But I did also tell you about the chat I had with him about those other women. I told you initially that it was about the choir but then later, when I got upset, I told you the real reason why I went to see him.'

I stopped, looked up at him and waited. Perhaps our sins were equally matched. I didn't have the energy to be angry any more. Despite my daytime nap, I still felt completely drained.

'Look,' Neil said softly, squatting down beside me, 'I'll throw the necklace away. It was stupid of me to keep it. I don't know about you but I'm tired of treading on eggshells. What happened to the fun in our lives? Where did it go to, Fi?'

I rested my head on his shoulder and we stayed like that for the next few minutes, the sound of our breathing, the rush of the wind outside and the accompanying splatters of raindrops against the window the only things to be heard. It felt comfortable, serene and welcoming. I savoured that moment, thought of it later when things became violent. When our lives were tipped upside down and shaken about like a snow globe. I remembered those few minutes and that was what kept me going through one of the darkest periods of my life.

15

It went in the bin, that necklace. I tried to stop him throwing it away, even making an attempt to salvage it when his back was turned, but it was a messy task, the chain sliding to the bottom of the large metal container and disappearing out of sight. Retrieving it was almost impossible. It was buried somewhere amongst the many discarded eggshells and scraps of food, a mishmash of slimy, stinking rubbish swamping it, so I gave it up as a bad job.

Every few days, I checked up on the missing woman from the mainland, and also carried out some research on Myra Simons, the other lady who had disappeared, although there was, I discovered grimly, very little to go on.

The recently missing lady who was interested in ornithology was called Sian Dupre and police were saying that they were going to concentrate their efforts on searching the area close to the ferry terminal in North Shields as there were no clear sightings of her aboard the ferry. That piece of news gave me some hope that Neil had indeed been mistaken about the body on the beach, although my heart went out to her and her family. She was still missing. There were people out there praying for the safe return of their mother/daughter/sister/friend.

I decided, after reading that piece of news, to have faith in the police's theory and concentrate my efforts on reading up as much as I could about Myra Simons. Articles about her were scant, the north-east newspapers filled mainly with stories about incidents that had happened in Newcastle, Durham, Sunderland and Teesside. Winters End was small potatoes compared to those places. It was saddening to see that her disappearance warranted a tiny column in only two of the newspapers, one of them putting her vanishing down to mental health problems brought about by difficulties in her home life. That was the problem with living near a body of water – people always assumed the worst, that the missing people had taken it upon themselves to end everything in the unforgiving icy waters, but seas and rivers rarely keep the dead; they spit them out somewhere further along the coast or riverbank. And Myra had never been found. I tried to be positive, thinking that perhaps she had got the ferry over to Newcastle and was currently living in a little flat somewhere on the outskirts of the city, living hand to mouth but surviving all the same. Not dead in the water, her bones embedded in the sand at the bottom of the North Sea.

Life ticked along at a steady pace. Neil and I put full effort into our respective businesses and in our spare time we worked on the cottage, painting doors and skirting boards a brilliant shade of white to lighten up the rooms. We dug the garden, pulling out weeds despite the adverse weather conditions, and cut the lawn and pruned old rose bushes. After only a week and a half, the place had undergone a mini facelift, giving it a more homely ambience. It was finally starting to feel like we truly belonged there. Memories of our life in Saltburn dulled. Even the final few years when our lives had spun out of control, dipping lower and lower into a place filled with fear and menacing shadows, seemed far in the past. We had a roof over our heads, our bills were getting paid. We had enough money to eat. It was simple and basic, our current existence, a rudimentary way of living compared to what we used to have, but at the same time, a vast improvement on the financial worries we had left behind.

It was a calm Friday morning when I decided to go and see Honnie again. My visit was long overdue. She had been in my thoughts on and off for the past week or so, the promise of me baking a cake for her pushing me on to go back to her quaint chocolate-box house. Thursday evening, I baked a lemon drizzle cake and packed it into a tin in my backpack, deciding I would walk there again. It was clear outside, the weather calm with no fog or howling gales. I had a change of heart and refused to be browbeaten into travelling everywhere by car because of a murder from over two years ago. My mind had settled into the idea of Winters End being a relatively safe place to live. In the space of just a few weeks, I had experienced every possible emotion and, in the end, decided to settle with contentment. Not because I felt particularly content but because it was easier. Less exhausting. We had stayed away from the pub and ventured out only for groceries and petrol. It hadn't been intentional, holing ourselves away; it was simply that we became busy with our cottage and our respective jobs. We were finally settling into a routine and, as far as I could tell, that had to be a positive thing. No more idle threats from locals. No more unwelcome gifts left on our doorstep. We were coping.

Neil was deep in thought, hunched over his computer, when I left. I didn't disturb him. I checked that my phone was charged and tucked it into my pocket. With a spring in my step that I had forgotten I possessed, a simple reflex action borne out of a sense of ease and safety, I set off to Honnie's. For the first time in a long time, I felt relaxed and happy. Maybe not happy. That suggests spontaneous laughter and it had been some time since I had experienced that, but I was definitely relaxed.

The walk took just over fifteen minutes. No swirling mists. No driving wind and rain but I did have the strangest sense that I wasn't alone. At least twice I stopped and turned, staring into the distance, the feeling that somebody was somewhere behind me, lurking in the shadows, so strong that I half expected to spin around and see somebody standing right behind me. I was definitely alone. Or at least, I hoped I was. There were plenty of hiding places on the route there – large boulders and tall trees, and more than enough shrubbery to allow a stalker to crouch behind while they waited for the right moment to pounce. With the roar of the sea below me, it was almost impossible to listen out for footsteps and I had to rely on my instinct and that undefinable sense we all have that alerts us to danger. My senses told me I wasn't alone but with no sign of anybody else in the immediate vicinity, I had to ignore them and keep on walking.

In a matter of minutes, I had left the wilderness of the rugged landscape behind and was close to civilisation. That thought made me smile. Civilisation on this rugged strip of land with its unfriendly residents and disconcerting past. I'm not sure Winters End could ever have been described as civilised. It was many things – bewildering, mysterious. Occasionally terrifying. But definitely not civilised.

I had no idea whether or not Honnie would be in but felt sure that her trips outdoors were infrequent. I was willing to bet she visited the local shop just once a week, although I could see her standing on her doorstep on an almost daily basis, chatting to passers-by, arms crossed and hefted under her ample bosom while she put the world to rights. I was willing to bet that—

The collision almost sent me spiralling to the floor. I righted myself and looked up into the face of one of the men from the pub. It was him. Davey. A hundred thoughts spun and reeled around my head – was he angry about the way I had spoken to his son in

the supermarket last week? Was he full of hell because I had asked where his wife was? After finding
out about her that day at the supermarket, I went
home, tried to find out more about Catherine, see if I
could work out why she'd left and where she was now
living but found nothing. I had ideas of calling her,
asking her a stream of questions, forcing her to tell me
why she no longer lived on the island. It appeared that
there were other people out there who, like me,
simply wanted to live an anonymous existence. She
was clearly one of them, hidden and living her life
somewhere where she couldn't ever be found.

I stared at him, at his craggy features and wavy,
unkempt hair. For once, his face wasn't contorted with
fury and resentment, his mouth moulded into an aggressive pout. He didn't look as if he was ready to
throw me into the wild, foaming sea. I took a step
back, inching away from him, stepping closer to the
quayside where the roar of the crashing waves made
me shiver. I had nothing to say to this man, no words
that could convey my feelings towards him. He had
been rude before, aggressive even. I had no idea what
to expect. But then, he had also helped me when I was
lost. He wasn't all bad, was he? Unpredictable perhaps, and gruff for sure, but if he had wanted to harm
me, he had had his opportunity in the fog. But still I

didn't know how to take him, what to expect as he moved closer to me, his face impassive and un-fathomable.

'Sorry,' he said softly, catching me off guard. 'I was miles away. You okay?'

I swallowed and looked into his eyes. Who the hell was this man? This now softly-spoken individual who, shortly after we moved here, looked as if he wanted to kill me. The same man with his wildly oscillating moods who had told me to leave the island and yet, only days later, went out of his way to help me find my way home in the thick fog.

'I'm fine,' I replied, dumbfounded. 'Just a bit shaken up, I think. I was miles away too.'

I had no idea how to react. Should I strike up a conversation, get to know him a little better? Or would that be a step too far for this strange person? A step too far for me? I began to walk away and stopped as I heard his voice again, still quiet and unassuming, re-morseful even. 'I want to apologise for that carry-on in The Bucket. It was out of order. We'd all had a bit too much to drink and, well – anyway, I won't keep you. Alls I wanna say is, just take care.' His voice dropped an octave, was almost a growl even as he uttered the last few words. 'I mean, it's not as if you haven't been warned, is it?'

Seconds. That was all it took for a hundred thoughts to balloon in my brain: ways in which I could or should respond to him. I considered ignoring him, leaving his veiled threats behind, but didn't. I couldn't. Instead, I spun around, a flame igniting in my veins, taking hold and refusing to die down. I had had enough of his esoteric words and aggressive ways. Enough of him and his threats and the way I had been treated since arriving here. I had every right to be on this island. It was my home, whether I liked it or not.

'What do you mean by that? Why do I need to take care? What exactly should I be scared of?'

'Nothing. Nothing at all. It's just an expression. Ignore me.' His hands were shoved deep in his jacket pockets, his body bent like a trapped feline, cornered by a predator that was poised and ready to pounce.

'Do you know what? I've tried ignoring it since moving here – the threats, the dog shit smeared on our doorstep, the scratch on my car, the pathetic attempt to stop us going into the pub for a drink. I've tried getting on with my life but every time I do, fucking idiots like you keep reminding me that there's something wrong with this place!' My voice was raised. I didn't care who could hear me. I had some things I wanted to ask him, things that needed to be said. 'Where's your wife, Davey? Why doesn't she live on the island any longer, eh? Did all these threats drive her away too?'

I'd said too much, it was obvious by his reaction, but there was no going back. His mouth twitched. His face turned the colour of ash. His large hands were clenched into fists as he removed them from his pockets and pressed them against his thighs. I stared at him, at his long arms, his hands, imagining the power they could wield. Imagining them being driven into my face.

A moment's silence. I waited, my breathing laboured. He could easily do it – grab at me with those large hands, his filthy fingernails digging into my flesh, our faces pushed close together as he contemplated doing something terrible to me, something unthinkable. He didn't do any of those things. What he did was scowl at me, a darkness in his expression that made me fearful. Of what, I didn't quite know. Whether it was the man himself and his capabilities, or the fact I had probed into his private life, reminded him of things he would sooner forget. Regardless, I knew then that I had spoken out of turn, that my queries about his wife would remain unanswered.

Or so I thought.

He took a step closer. Then another. I flinched, quickly glancing around to see if there were any witnesses to observe what was about to take place. We were alone, the tiny quayside deserted. The drills and building work had been completed, everything cleared away. Nobody in the vicinity to stop him doing whatever he wanted. Was he the one who I felt sure had followed me on the route here? Was he walking in my shadow, darting behind tree trunks and lying low amongst the shrubbery, hoping to catch me unawares?

I noticed his fists still furled at his sides and felt my stomach somersault. He dipped his gaze away from me and when he looked up again, there was something in his expression that I couldn't pinpoint – fear, regret? Hatred perhaps? His face suddenly softened as if somebody had opened a valve somewhere in his body and let out all the air.

'She upped and left. Just me and the boy now. We're managing fine, we are. She couldn't stay here on Winters End. Wouldn't. Don't ask why, just take my advice and leave this place. Something's not right 'ere. It's bad. There's a nastiness lurking. An awful, awful nastiness. Think about what I say and get gone.'

My legs were planted wide as I responded, my head thrust forwards. His words scared me more than he did. My fear of him was dissipating but my curiosity was now fused with a simmering anger at the way I had been treated by the people of this island and it was proving to be a savage combination.

'And that body on the beach that you denied existed?' The question spilled out of me. I had to know. His words may have held me in fear but I could now see that he wasn't going to harm me. He was the one who was hurting, his voice beginning to break, his eyes heavy with misery. 'What was all that about? Who was it and where has the body gone?' There was now a pleading quality to my tone. I wanted him to break his silence, to help me work out what was going on around here. Help me feel settled, as if I truly belonged, and not spend every waking minute glancing over my shoulder, afraid somebody was about to harm me. I wanted to believe there was never a body. I wanted to believe I was safe.

He didn't reply, just shook his head and walked away, muttering under his breath, a steady stream of indistinct words that tailed off behind him.

I stood for a short while, wondering whether I should follow him, whether I should turn and head home, or whether I should carry on with my planned visit to Honnie's house. Deciding I wouldn't let that man knock me off balance, I carried on walking. I crossed the road and stood outside Cook Cottage, its pale-blue exterior having a calming effect on me. Everything would feel better, lighter and easier to bear once I was inside and sitting chatting to Honnie. I hoped that this time she would also be able to respond to my questions, be more receptive to my probing and pushing. I felt that after what I'd endured since arriving here, I at least deserved that much. I wanted some proper answers and had it in my mind that I wouldn't leave until I had them. At some point, the people of Winters End would have to speak to me, to explain their bizarre and often frightening behaviour. I was a resident of their community now. Whether they wanted me to be or not.

It took a while for her to answer. After two loud knocks, I was almost on the verge of giving up and leaving when the door was pulled open. I wasn't sure if it was because I was standing in the shadows or because I had possibly disturbed her afternoon nap, but it took a few seconds for her to recognise me and allow me inside, her features pinched and angry-looking.

'There you are. Best come in, then.' She turned and shuffled away with me following meekly behind, a chastised child, desperate for any scraps of attention she cared to throw my way.

In the living room she sprang to life, back to her

animated self, telling me how good it was to see me. 'Hope you've brought that cake you promised me.'

I reached into my backpack and pulled out the tin that contained the lemon drizzle I had baked for her last night, her face mellowing as I handed it over, her soft cheeks the colour and texture of warm putty.

'Ah, good girl. I'll go and cut us a slice and put the kettle on. You make yourself comfortable. Still as thin as a rake, I see, eh?' Her footfall was a muted thump on the ageing rugs as she carried the cake and headed into the kitchen. 'I'll cut yer an extra thick slice, see if we can put some fat on those bones of yours.'

It felt good to sit there, safe and warm in her home, surrounded by her knick-knacks, the things that defined her. Had I not been in somebody else's house, I would have been inclined to lay back my head and close my eyes, let sleep envelop me. After my encounter with Davey and now being here with Honnie, the contrast in how they treated me felt so stark, their unadorned ways and brash mannerisms evoking such a wide range of emotions in me that my eyes were leaden with fatigue. Honnie's warmth and hospitality was a feeling so powerful and all-encompassing that I had to fight to stay awake.

I stood up and looked around the room, determined to find something that would pique my interest, something that would keep my mind ticking over and force me into a state of wakefulness.

I didn't have to look too far. I picked up the photograph and felt an unwelcome tightness in my chest as I stared at the small monochrome image, wishing at that point, that I had stayed in my seat.

16

'She was beautiful. My little baby. My gorgeous girl.'

Honnie was standing in the doorway watching me, her voice catching me off guard. I twisted around and placed the photograph back on the walnut cabinet, a flush of discomfiture at being caught snooping around her living room creeping up over my neck and face. My flesh burned with shame. This was her home, her private space. I should have remained seated and didn't. I had been caught looking at her photographs – a photograph that had been deliberately half-hidden behind a stack of envelopes – and now I was going to have to cover up my humiliation by acting as if nothing had just happened.

I cleared my throat, tried to keep my voice low, to a respectful whisper, as if raising it to a normal level would shatter the moment. 'Where is she now?' I hoped the toddler in the picture was an adult and living a good life somewhere but my gut told me otherwise. Something in Honnie's face, her words, the sudden greyness of her pallor, told me that this story didn't have a good ending.

'Where is she now?' she said flatly. 'In the church-yard at St Augustine's. Been there for decades, she has.' Honnie shuffled forwards, the tea tray wobbling in her hands. 'So many years of my little girl being buried in the ground. Through every wonderful warm summer and through the deepest, darkest and coldest winters, she has been there. All on her own. Nobody to look after her. Nobody by her side.'

I took the tray from her grip and placed it down on the small coffee table. My heart was a heavy rock hammering against bone. A rhythmic *thud thud thud* that echoed in my ears. I should have remained seated, kept my hands to myself. Look what I had done. What I had started. Making her remember. Forcing her to talk about it.

'Sorry.' My voice sounded faraway, an underwater gurgling sound coming from elsewhere in the room. 'I shouldn't have been looking. Rude of me. I'm so sorry,

Honnie.' A buzzing filled my head. I sat back down, my spine ramrod straight, guilt embedded deep within me.

'I don't mind.' Her voice sounded light, unperturbed. She sat opposite and picked up her teacup, slurping and smacking her lips together as she drank. 'Does me good to talk of her now and again. We shouldn't ever forget the dead. They were once as we were: alive and breathing in the clean air around us. They don't deserve to be forgotten.'

'Indeed, they don't.'

My breathing felt noisy and onerous. I didn't ask how she had died, her little girl, trying instead to include her in the conversation, not nudge her aside as if she was a thing to be forgotten or ignored. Not focusing only on her demise. 'What is she called?'

'Theresa. Our little Terry. A blessing, she was. A joy to be around.'

Glazed eyes. A protracted stillness. I let her sit and ruminate, didn't ask anything else or try to engage her in conversation. I didn't want to pry. I let the subject be, gladdened by the silence.

'Come on, tuck into that cake, lassie,' she said after a short while. 'You've baked enough for an army and I can't eat it all by meself.'

We ate and drank our tea, chatting about the

weather and my new business, an established warmth settling between us, as if we'd known one another for years.

'So, yer'll be kept busy then?'

I nodded and smiled. 'Always. Rarely a minute to spare. Except to come and visit you, of course.' I made no mention of how my dark thoughts often intruded on my work, stopping me from focusing, dragging my mind off to places that are best left unexplored.

She grinned, a twinkle of humour and possibly even sarcasm in her eyes. 'Aye, well people always make time for us oldies. We're the ones with all the answers.' And there it was – an open invitation to ask her those questions, the ones she evaded last time I was here.

'To everything?'

She took another bite of the cake and raised her eyebrows at me. 'Maybe. Depends on what the question is, doesn't it?'

I wondered whether that was my cue to ask or whether she would take umbrage, clam up, and we would lose our connection. It was a fine balance, working her out, making sure I didn't get on the wrong side of her. Honnie was a force to be reckoned with. I tried to imagine her as a younger woman, how she had looked, acted.

A sudden gust of wind rattled the windowpanes. Behind me, a clock chimed, its sound a ghostly cry cutting into the quiet of the room. I decided to go ahead, grasp the nettle and try to find out what was going on around me, why everyone on Winters End saw me as their enemy or, if not their enemy, then at least an outsider who wasn't wanted and would never be welcome here. Apart from Ewan and Honnie, that is. She was warm, funny and generous, and the more I saw of her, the fonder I became of her quirky and straightforward ways. She was both gracious and blunt in equal measure and I respected her for it. Welcomed it, even. Honesty had been sadly lacking in my life for many years. It was good to spend time with somebody who didn't mince their words.

'Funny thing really.' I nibbled at my cake and tried to control my breathing. 'I bumped into Davey out there. Not for the first time, he more or less told me I should pack up and go, leave Winters End and head back to the mainland. Why? Why would he say such things to me?'

She waved her hand dismissively and made a harrumphing sound, tiny crumbs spewing out of her mouth and landing on her lap. 'Ach, Davey Fairhurst talks nonsense. Doesn't know his arse from his elbow once he's got a drink inside of him. Best ignored if you ask me.'

It didn't answer my question and we both knew it. I needed more from her. I wanted some background on this island and its inhabitants. 'Why did his wife leave him?'

Honnie took a quick slurp of her tea and stared out of the window, a faraway look in her eyes. 'It's obvious, isn't it? I mean what sort of a woman would stay with a man who drank away the week's wages, leaving you with next to nothing? Have you seen where he lives? In an old cottage that could have been so much more. It's a ramshackle old joint up on top of Hill Rock Point. Has the best views on the island, it does. If he'd looked after it, the place would've been right beautiful. As it is, it's a bloody wreck. The man's an idiot. So deep in the drink he barely knows what day it is. Mind you, he also lost his girl quite a few years back. Adored her, he did. Many say that's what set him on the road to binging the alcohol.'

I didn't know how to reply. Was that what had driven him and his wife apart? The tragic loss of their daughter? And how did she die? Was her grave set alongside those other women in the graveyard? Was that why he was so bitter – because his own daughter succumbed to the dark forces and sickness of Winters End? I couldn't begin to imagine the stress such an awful event would put on a marriage. Neil and I had shouldered our own fair share of problems but nothing as devastating as losing a child. Maybe Honnie was right; Davey Fairhurst did look like a man addicted to the drink but it still didn't answer my question as to why he kept giving me obscure warnings and veiled threats.

I decided to steer the conversation away from the collective loss of their children and back to the names on those benches and gravestones. 'Seems like there were a lot of accidents befell quite a few of the young women of this island in recent years.' I nibbled at my cake, trying to appear nonchalant and relaxed when in reality my heart was thrashing around my chest like a fish on dry land. 'So many deaths. It seems so heartbreaking and tragic, don't you think? So unusual.'

She clicked her tongue and turned to stare at me, disapproval etched into her features. Her pupils bore a hole into me, causing me to look away. I shivered and clenched my teeth together. 'There was a pandemic. Lots of people died around that period. All the time and all over the world. The deaths on Winters End were no different.'

I shook my head, my eyes narrowed. I would keep going with these questions; I wouldn't allow my fears and queries to be brushed aside. 'But none of their deaths were linked to the pandemic, were they? And they were all female. All young women. And all dead.'

'Not all.' Her voice was quick and sharp, cutting in before I had a chance to continue. I watched and waited; a breath suspended in my chest.

'Oh?'

'Aye. I mean just look at my boy. Taken before his time. Another tragic death. My lad, my only final living child, gone. Just like that.' She looked away and a silence hung between us.

I swallowed, too scared to speak, to breathe. I had no idea. All of Honnie's children, deceased. I didn't know what to say. I sat tight-lipped, unable to comprehend the heartache that this poor woman had endured. Life could be so unbearably tragic at times, doling out suffering in horribly unequal measures.

'What, I mean, how...?' I couldn't say anything else, the lump in my throat making it impossible for me to speak. I blinked away the film that had gathered over my eyes, fogging my vision. Nobody had spoken of this. They could have warned me. Ewan could have given me some sort of indication. I should have known, and now I had inadvertently stumbled into an awkward situation, more than awkward. It was horribly tragic. A catastrophic turn of events.

'Fishing accident a few years back. He took the boat out in clear skies and a storm came in. Happens a lot round these parts – unpredictable weather. Catches the best of them out. Even the most experienced of fishermen can struggle in rough seas.' She cleared her throat and stared at me, the look in her eyes making me shiver. 'So a few dead females isn't the only thing that's happened on this island. Men die too. All the time.'

I nodded, a vibration in my head so strong, so real, I felt certain it would knock me to the ground, pieces of me falling away and shattering into tiny fragments. I wanted to hug Honnie, to feel the heft of her warm body next to mine, let her know that I cared. To show some kinship towards this poor woman, this wise old lady whose family were all gone, leaving her alone in her twilight years. She would swat it away, my support and displays of affection, but I felt those emotions all the same, the tug of friendship drawing me closer to her, an invisible twine pulling me toward her. There may have been decades between us but a bond between two people transcended time. It was at that point that I made the firm decision to cease with my constant thoughts about the premature deaths of those women. Like Honnie said, people pass away all the time. There's no pattern to it, no set rules that death sticks to. It just takes people whenever it feels like it, striking when we least expect it. As my old grandma used to say, *man makes plans and God smiles.*

We spent the next ten minutes in easy companionship, finishing our tea and eating another slice of cake. Even my inappropriate questions that unearthed difficult memories for her didn't stop the flow of conversation or turn her against me. I was lucky in more ways than I would ever know.

'I'll leave this with you, Honnie,' I said as I stood and gathered up our cups and saucers, pointing at the remnants of the cake. 'I've got another slab of coconut cake at home. And yes,' I said, smiling and rolling my eyes, 'I'll start eating more and get a bit of weight on.'

'That's my girl,' she barked. Her voice was a clap of thunder in the small room. She pressed her hands onto her knees and hauled herself upright.

I washed the few pots we'd used, standing at the sink as if I'd lived there for decades. I stared around at the old-fashioned kitchen, at its chunky Bakelite handles and yellow tiles, marvelling at how clean and tidy something could be, how it could emanate such warmth and not reek of neglect despite its age.

'Right,' I said, brushing past her and picking up my backpack once I'd dried my hands and stacked everything in the cupboards. 'I'll be off, then. Expect to see me again soon enough.'

'Back to your editing job, eh?'

I nodded, feeling a small burst of pride and excitement at the prospect of taking on the new clients and forging ahead with my career. 'Yes, a few hours at my laptop before settling in for the night.'

'Aye. Get your fire roaring. Tonight's going to be a cold one by all accounts. Autumn's on its way.'

It felt wrong to not lean in and hug her, but I managed to restrain myself all the same and opted instead for a touch of her hand, her skin dry and cool against mine. Embracing people was something I had always done until a global pandemic made us all step back, the sense of touch suddenly a thing to fear.

We waved goodbye and I set off, the brisk breeze a welcome sensation, cooling me while I got up a steady pace and headed home.

Later, I would ruminate over my final words to Honnie about seeing her again soon enough and how I was looking forward to getting home to get some work done. They would loom large in my mind, taunting me, reminding me that something terrible was lying in wait for me.

Because after leaving Honnie's house that cold and blustery day, something happened, something dreadful. Something foul and unspeakable. I stumbled into a dark and terrifying situation and never made it home at all.

17

I didn't sense that anything was wrong as I turned right and stepped into the shadows of a dilapidated, derelict farmhouse. I'd seen it before, thought nothing of the place. It was just another ageing edifice. Crumbling walls, slanted roof, broken windows. It looked right for its setting. All tracts of isolated countryside had ramshackle old buildings dotted around. Everything felt normal, my mood light and buoyant. I was feeling upbeat about the future. Seeing Honnie had given me some perspective on my worries, and on life in general. If she had managed to get on with things after losing both of her children then I could damn well get on with mine. My trauma paled into insignificance beside hers and mine was self-made, not thrust upon me by the random hand of fate or just sheer bad luck. Even Davey's misfortune preyed on my mind. He was a damaged man and maybe he had every reason to drink as much as he did. No daughter, no wife. Just him and his son living together in an old house up on the hill. Such a lonely, insular life.

I decided at that point that every time anxiety crept its way into my head, I would banish it with thoughts of Honnie and her family and how she lost them before their time yet carried on regardless, welcoming near-strangers into her home. Always gracious and kind. Gruff and humorous, yes, but that only made her more endearing, reassuringly normal and prone to the same moods and nuanced temperaments and reactions as the rest of us.

The breeze picked up and the light began to fade, my vision dimming, everything doused with a wash of grey, a fractional edging towards dusk when the light would fade completely, plunging us into an inky blackness. A cloud appeared, momentarily obscuring the sun. Swathes of green fields rapidly lost their hue, their vibrant colours leaching, turning into something less attractive. Something menacing, sinister even.

I pulled up my collar and shivered. Fifteen minutes and I would be home. I stopped briefly and checked my phone. No calls from Neil but I did notice that the battery was running low so slipped it back into my bag and set off again, keen to conserve what little life was left in it. Thick fog and a poor sense of direction had taught me to be more cautious. It wasn't anything like the mainland around these parts. There were fewer roads and paths, plenty of potholes and a vast array of fields which after a while all looked the same. Getting lost would be easy. And then there was the cliff edge. Always the cliff edge and the sea below. The brutal, unforgiving sea.

I didn't dwell on it, how quickly a lack of light could change the landscape, altering its shape and appearance, giving it a look of somewhere fraught with tension and peril. I pushed it out of my mind, was vigilant, aware of my surroundings, less troubled than I had been just a week ago. Not frightened or fearful. I hoped that this is how it would go, my confidence slowly beginning to rebuild itself. Ideas drifted in and out of my head: things we could do to the cottage to make it feel like a proper home, ways in which I could increase my business portfolio. Somewhere in my chest, hope unfurled and began to blossom, the promise of better times ahead flowering in my veins. I was happy. It had been such a long time since I had felt that way that I didn't immediately recognise the sensation. It was alien to me, a strange and unfamiliar feeling that didn't immediately register in my brain, but I welcomed its return, felt ready to cling on to it and hold it close for safekeeping.

The sound of something behind me – the unmistakable pounding of somebody else's footsteps, the crunch of gravel and twigs being broken underfoot, they all cut into my thoughts. I wasn't alarmed. Being with Honnie had calmed me, given me enough confidence to believe that nothing bad could ever happen to me. The worst had already happened, was well behind me. If I could exude a sense of well-being and certainty, be bold and brash, then everything else would surely follow. Look at what Honnie had been through, I told myself. And she had survived. The death of one child is probably the worst thing a person would ever have to endure, let alone two, and yet she was still here, being strong and determined. Being herself. Why shouldn't I be the same way?

I stopped anyway to listen to the noises behind me but heard nothing else save for the distant twitter of birdsong and the cawing of crows in the nearby trees. Even as I set off again, I felt no fear. Perhaps that was my undoing, my usually acute sense for danger dulled and deadened by my visit, my mind filled with other things, no room left for anything else. No thoughts for my own safety and well-being.

The track that led to the small bothy I had passed on my route here was uneven, causing me to dip to one side, my gait awkward and off balance. I felt it then more than heard it: breathing coming from behind me, the heat of it filtering its way on to the side of my face.

It was at that point that fear did finally begin to rear its head, unfolding inside of me. My head thumped, a pulse tapped at my throat. I attempted to spin around, my feet twisting, ankles bending, and expected or at least hoped to see Neil behind me, concerned for my safety after being away from home for the best part of the afternoon, yet knowing deep down that it wouldn't be him but somebody who wished me harm. I even thought of Davey and our earlier encounter. Had he followed me home, intent of having it out with me? Telling me yet again how I should leave the island. I didn't get a chance to see the face of the person behind me because before I managed to turn around completely to see who it was, I felt it: a sudden pain on the back of my head. It travelled through my skull, whistling behind my eyes, a bomb detonating deep within my brain. Vomit rose. I saw stars, dizziness rendering me unable to do anything except stand there, lifeless, focusing only on the pain. A sound came from close by, a deep, guttural splutter. Then a sudden sickening realisation that it was coming from me. Another thump, an arrow splicing my head into two. An eruption of unutterable agony. I recall my legs turning to liquid, my body crashing to the floor. Then nothing.

PART II

PART II

18

BEFORE

'Stupid boy. Stupid, bastard boy. Now look what you've done.'

He stared up at her, a dead-eyed look that gave nothing away. Ever since the funeral, everything had turned to dust. Before it, actually. Long before. It was after the birth. All about the baby, that's what it became. Everything was always about that damn stupid child.

She bent down and swept up the shards of glass. He watched in silence, saw how she bustled about, cleaned it all away with such brusqueness and efficiency it took the breath right out of him, her strength on show for him to see. Like a bull she was, a big, headstrong bull that bucked and kicked at a gate when held captive. What would his punishment be this time, he wondered. A slap, a kick? Or worse. He didn't like that one, being shut away on his own. A slap or even a punch was preferable to being stuck in the darkness for days at a time, his meals slid under the door, orders barked out at him as if he were a disobedient dog.

'Was only a glass o' juice, Mam. Wasn't nowt important.'

'It was important to me!'

The silence was heavy. He didn't speak, wasn't sure what to say to make it all better. Easier to sit tight-lipped, say nothing at all rather than uttering the wrong thing and seeing her wrath multiply a hundredfold.

'Go on, now. Up to yer room. I'll be glad to see back of yer.'

He traipsed up the stairs, feet clumping on the thick carpet. He thought about his dad, wished he was around to help.

Old memories and thoughts jumped into his brain. Those awful, awful memories. The ones he had tried to forget. They wouldn't go. Every night when he shut his eyes, he saw her face, heard her crying. That's why she hated him. Because of those memories. Because of what he had done.

It was a game, that's all. She hadn't understood the rules. He hadn't wanted to play with her anyway. His mam had made him, so in a way, what followed was her fault. If he hadn't been made to look after her then she wouldn't have died and there wouldn't have been a funeral and his mam wouldn't hate him and he wouldn't have smashed that glass.

The bedroom door slammed behind him. He made sure to do it loud enough so she would hear. It would probably result in a beating later but he didn't care. He was going to get one anyway so an extra slap wouldn't make any difference. Pain was pain whichever way you looked at it.

His bed creaked when he lay down on it, like one of those boats he'd seen on television, the wooden ones from years ago when pirates ruled the seas, the sort that rocked from side to side, squeaking and groaning in the vast, open seas as they sailed to foreign lands, looking for treasure. He raised his arm, mock sword in his hand, swishing it in a circular motion, fighting off invisible enemies who had dared to try and trespass on his boat, and then sighed, resting his head back on the pillow. It was boring up here on his own. Boring boring boring. And stupid. She was stupid. Everything was idiotic, stupid, and horribly boring. Like school. That was a waste of time as well.

They couldn't teach him anything he didn't already know. And he had to get on a boat to get there. He couldn't just walk to school like kids did on the mainland; he had to get in a rotten old fishing boat and be rowed over there, and then when the weather was bad and the sea rough, he had to actually sleep at the school and wasn't allowed back home. It was all just rubbish, and he hated his school and he hated his mam and he hated everyone.

A sound outside his bedroom. Footsteps. She tried to tiptoe sometimes, thinking she was as light as a feather when she was actually a big, thumping elephant parading around on bare floorboards. That made him smile. A big, fat elephant. He rested his chin on his shoulder and swung his arm out like a trunk, swishing it up and down in front of his face. No noise, no honking trumpet sounds 'cos she would hear him, but it was fun to do it quietly, to pretend in his head, that she was a big, fat animal living in a zoo somewhere far away from here.

The door flew open mid trunk swing. A bubble of air got trapped in his throat, a big chunk of nothingness that stopped him from breathing properly. Sometimes that happened when she appeared. His eyes would mist over and his heart would gallop around his chest. He would gulp and try to get more oxygen into his lungs but nothing happened and he would just sit there staring at her, mouth agape, nothing going in, nothing coming out. Like now.

'Here,' she said, throwing a piece of material his way. 'Put this on. You've got jobs to do in the kitchen. Yer need to help me do some baking and then we'll clean up together afterwards.' A smile split her face in half. 'Hurry up, if you get a move on, I'll let yer lick the bowl out once we've finished.'

The galloping in his chest increased. The fabric slipped between his fingers like water, too soft, too delicate to hold on to. It slid onto his lap while his eyes followed her, watching as she backed out of the door and slammed it shut behind her. No key this time. No being locked in for days at a time. He didn't know which was worse – being trapped in the bedroom or being forced to take part in her awful, stomach-churning ritual. He hated it. It made him feel sick and stupid all at the same time. What if his friends came knocking and saw him? The thought of it made his skin prickle, made the ants inside his head crawl about in a mad frenzy, nipping and biting at his brain.

The heap of fabric sat beside him on the bed. He had two choices – either he put it on and then he would get to lick the baking bowl of all that lovely creamy, sugary stuff once they'd put the cake in the oven, or he refused and set himself up for a sound beating and probably no supper either. A pain in his belly accompanied by a loud gurgling sound forced him into action.

The soft, silky fabric slipped easily over his head. He unzipped his trousers and stepped out of them, noticing as he looked down how ragged and dirty his socks were. Maybe he could ask her for some new ones and she would say, 'Oh yes, of course!' And maybe the sky would turn bright green and cows would dance on the moon.

A reflection of a lumbering boy dressed in a pink satin dress caught his eye as he stood opposite the mirror. A roar formed in his gut, travelling up his throat. He pushed his fist in his mouth to stop it escaping. She wouldn't like that, if the loud noise got out and disturbed her. She would pound her way up the stairs, yelling that he was bad boy. A terrible boy. The worst. And then he wouldn't get any cake mixture. Probably no food for the rest of the day. It wasn't so bad being made to wear this stuff if he got fed, was it? Once he'd eaten, he could get changed again, curl up on his bed and go to sleep with a belly full of sugar and buttercream icing. So wearing the outfit was worth it really, feeling that sugar rush, the heady sensation of having his belly lined with gooey dollops of food. Half an hour, that was all it would be. Half an hour of pretending to be somebody else in order to pacify her and stave off his hunger. A jagged rock of resistance rose in his throat. He swallowed it down. Sometimes it was easier to obey and be the person she wanted him to be rather than put up a fight. He had done that in the past and it never worked. She always won. But one day, he would turn it all around and he would be the winner, doing exactly whatever he wanted, whenever he wanted. Nobody would ever dare to try and stop him. Nobody.

He was being punished for what he had done, he knew that. She hated him for it and he hated her right back. He couldn't even remember which came first, where it all started. It was long before the death, well before the funeral where she cried and screamed and pounded the floor and had to be helped back up by the priest and the mourners who watched her aghast, unable to say or do anything to make things better, back to how they used to be before it all went wrong. Before he made it go wrong. What the funeral did was make an indelible mark in his brain, gave him a point in time, something he could use to measure their lives and how fast things had gone downhill, like a perforated piece of paper slowly tearing and shredding, the holes in their existence too damaged to ever be repaired again. That was his doing. He'd punched the holes in their life, weakened their strength, stripping it away bit by bit. The day she died. That was the first hole. A big black gaping void. The other holes came quickly after that, appearing daily. Every time he showed his face she would find another fault, scream at him. Give him something to cry about. That was her favourite phrase. 'I'll gi' you something to cry about, lad. As if you know what real heartache is. You know nowt.'

She was wrong about that, though. He did know things. Lots of things. He knew that tomatoes were a fruit and not a vegetable and that apples floated in water even though they were really heavy. He also knew that frogs drank water through their skin and that Russia was the biggest country in the world. It's just that she never asked him if he knew any of those things.

He also knew what had happened that day – the day she died. He knew how she had tripped over in the churchyard as they wove their way through the graves, dancing and jumping over the rectangular mounds of old soil, her loud giggling filling the grave-yard as he chased her, arms outstretched, mouth set in a rictus grin.

'Ninety-eight, ninety-nine – one hundred. Coming, ready or not!'

He hadn't planned it. It just happened. Sometimes that was how things went, events taking over. Fate, it was called. He'd read about it in one of his mam's daft magazines, how fate had brought people together or how it was fate that they were meant to be apart. There were pictures of people smiling out at him, their faces all glossy and happy. And then there were other pictures of people sitting with their heads lowered, sadness in their expressions because fate had driven them apart from the people they wanted to be with. Sometimes things were just meant to be.

The crack of her head on the paving stone as she slipped was so loud it echoed around the empty churchyard. He had stood over her, watching. Waiting for her to get back up. Except she didn't. She continued lying there, all soft and floppy and stupid as if she was dead. It didn't matter if she was dead because he'd never really liked her that much anyway. He had been made to bring her here, told to play with her because there were things to be done in the house. 'Lots of jobs to be getting on with.'

And so they had headed out, him resentful, her bouncing around like an overexcited puppy on its first outing.

'Get up.' He kicked his foot at her, his toe touching the hem of her dress. 'Time to head home. I'm bored and you're being stupid.'

No response. He kicked at her again, saw her eyes flicker, shouted even louder. 'Up, up, up. Now!' He bent down, a fist of fear grasping at his throat, its cold, tight fingers furled around his windpipe, stopping enough air from getting in.

A flickering of her eyes, a cold, callous smile.

She'd been trying to trick him. He didn't like being tricked, hated it in fact. It made him feel stupid. Worthless. Like the time the boys at school had told him that Susan French wanted to be his girlfriend. He had walked over to her, tried to hold her hand and watched, his stomach knotted with humiliation and shame, as she pulled away, her palm pressing at his chest, screaming at him to get away and leave her alone, calling him a freak.

'Stupid, ugly freak. Weird, ugly freak-boy.'

He had heard the laughter, it rang in his ears, the sound of embarrassment and rejection. The sound of his credibility being slowly crushed for the amusement and titillation of others. Later that day, he waited until she was in the middle of the playground, her legs scissored in the air as she did a handstand, unaware that he was close by, and ran over, pulling down her knickers, sniggering as he listened to her screams and cries of humiliation before he headed off to hide in the bushes.

That day proved to be a turning point. He knew then that he could fight back.

'You thought I was dead, didn't you?' Her mouth twisted into a grimace just like Susan French's had that day: a wicked, contorted snarl. 'You thought I was dead! You thought I was dead!' On and on it went, her voice a sing-song shriek that bounced around his head. It woke the ants in his head. They started their journey, marching around his brain, biting and scurrying, biting and scurrying.

He knew the churchyard like the back of his hand. It was his play area, his sanctuary. She was lying right next to it, the wobbly gravestone that had never been fixed despite everyone saying how dangerous it was. All it took was one quick movement, a slight push and it gave way, falling to the ground.

The ants didn't bite at him for a while after that. They went back to their nest and stayed put.

* * *

'I'm here, Mammy.'

She spun around, her arms a powdery white

colour, her smile as wide as an ocean. 'Come here, my precious. Come to Mammy, my gorgeous little girl, and let me hold you for a while.'

The soft satin dress rode up his back as he was lifted into the air and pressed deep into the folds of her soft, ample bosom. Dressing up wasn't so bad after all, he thought as the warmth of her embrace surrounded him, her doughy limbs pressing into his flesh. He could do this. He could do it.

19

NEIL

It was getting dark out. Time had run away with him, work filling his day, keeping him busy, keeping him glued to his computer screen. By the time he realised that Fiona hadn't arrived back home, daylight was slipping away, a veil of darkness spreading across the horizon. She had mentioned previously about visiting Honnie again at some point during the day. Was that where she had gone? If so, shouldn't she be back by now?

He stood at the sink, staring out into the garden before deciding to head out and drive around the island, see if he could spot her walking back. He knew Fiona, knew what she was like. She'd have been caught up in some conversation or other with Honnie, hadn't noticed the light ebbing away. That's how she was – sometimes prone to getting wrapped up in things to the point of being slightly obsessed. It wasn't a criticism. Just an observation. They both had their foibles and quirks. She would have sat and chatted, probed Honnie about the island. Possibly even ended up leafing through old photo albums. Talking and drinking tea, oblivious to the setting sun, to the loss of light outside. The gloom that enveloped the island after sunset. Minimum light pollution. Absolute darkness. And the sea. The cliff path and the sea. And, of course, there was the Fiona of old. The agitated, nervous Fiona. The one who suffered a massive breakdown. She was so much better now but the signs were occasionally still there. He was able to spot them and had always tried to put her at ease. Sometimes it worked and sometimes it didn't. He didn't for one minute think she would do anything to herself, but it was getting late. And it was dark.

Neil sighed, his chest tight, and pulled out his phone, hoping Fiona had remembered to take hers with her. He tapped in her number. A pulse started up in his neck when it rang. She would answer soon enough, her voice a gruff shriek, cross at him for making her stop to speak when she could be making headway. He counted the rings, his heart pattering away as the answer machine cut in, Fiona's voice asking him to leave a message, telling him that she'll get back to him just as soon as she can.

His keys jangled, a jarring metallic scrape as he snatched them up and stuffed his phone into his back pocket. He would drive around the nearby lanes and if he didn't see her, he would call her once more; that is, if she didn't ring him back before then, harrumphing at him for disturbing her, telling him she was a grown woman and that she was perfectly fine and didn't need him checking up on her and that she would be home in just a few minutes. He would stand at the gate, smiling as her face appeared around the corner, her small, silhouetted figure growing closer until she was standing in front of him, wondering what all the fuss was about.

The rapid lowering of the sun, replaced by a vast swathe of darkness that covered the fields and nearby landscape, made him fearful. He shivered and pulled up his collar, thinking he should have brought a torch. It was quiet out. He would hear her before he saw her.

Gravel crunched under his feet when he walked up and down Harbour Lane, eyes narrowed, scanning for any signs of life. A quick walk about before he took the car for a wider search. There wasn't anyone around, the area deserted. He could knock on doors but knew that she wouldn't be in either of the other two properties. Besides, what would he say?

Have you seen Fiona?

Hello, my name's Neil. We've just moved in down the lane and I appear to have lost my wife.

No, it was unthinkable. There were too many other options open to him before he went down that route. It would make him look silly and small. Desperate. Which was how he was actually beginning to feel. Desperate and terribly afraid. It was one thing to go for a mid-afternoon walk but quite another to not arrive home after dark.

His skin prickled, his scalp tingled with fear. Keys clasped between his fingers so tightly until metal cut into the soft flesh on the underside of his fingers, he unlocked the car and slipped inside. Did Fiona have her keys with her? What if he missed her, took a wrong turn and she slipped past him unnoticed? What if she arrived home to a locked cottage, had to stand outside in the dark, exposed and vulnerable?

He had to stop it, get a grip on his emotions. His usually rational brain was turning to jelly.

The engine growled, a low rumble in the silence

of the night. The tyres spun on gravel, spitting stones aside when he headed on to the road, the white beam of the headlights giving everything ahead of him an unnatural ghostly glow. Grey fields, a black, starless sky. A long stretch of roughly tarmacked road. Nothing else. Not a soul to be seen. Just darkness and silence. Just him and his thoughts and fears.

In the distance, trees swayed, their gnarled, spindly branches toing and froing. It was cold out. Windy. The calm daytime weather had morphed into something menacing. The sea would be rough. A threat to all nearby.

Oh God, Fiona, where the hell are you? Use your phone! For once, pick up your phone and call me.

Neil blinked, his eyes bulging and sore as he edged his car along, scanning the roadside, the fields, the small cut that led to the cliff path. He saw nothing. That's because there wasn't anything to see. No shadows, no movement. Just a wash of grey, peppered with the occasional swaying tree and the odd dense thicket of undergrowth.

What next? Would he have to drive the entire perimeter of the island to find her? Honnie's house was next to the post office. Or opposite. He couldn't quite remember. Should have taken more notice.

Should have listened when she spoke to him about where she had been.

Shit, shit, shit!

The journey there took five minutes or so, even driving as he did at a snail's pace, frantically searching for any signs of his wife along the way, hands clutching the steering wheel, fingers curled around the leather, hooked and tight, a reptilian quality to them, like claws clinging on to its prey.

It was empty, the entire area dead. To his right was a tiny quayside, to the left a handful of houses. What was the name of the place anyway? It had a name, Honnie's house. He remembered being told that. And it was blue, that much he did recall. In the dullness of the night, they all looked the same colour, lines of slate-grey houses, the small dimly lit windows showing some signs of life inside. Should he knock? Ask if anybody had seen his wife? Christ, it occurred to him that he didn't even know what she had been wearing when she left home. Jeans? A sweater or an anorak? Did she even have a coat with her?

Once again, her tried to ring her. This time, it was turned off.

Oh God, Fiona, where the hell are you? Just answer your bloody phone!

Myriad murky thoughts crept into his head. She had been happy when she left, hadn't she? Visions of Fiona boarding the ferry and heading back to Salt-burn filled his mind. Things were getting better be-tween them. Weren't they? Had he missed some signs, a subliminal signal that things were still awry? That she was still upset, depressed even. He could be trite sometimes. He knew that. Flippant and bloody deter-mined in his refusal to see the obvious. Sometimes the obvious was just too damn difficult to tackle, that was the thing. Too big a problem to solve. Carrying on as if nothing was wrong was far easier. Not necessarily the correct way to do things but definitely easier. In the short term, that is. If anything was wrong, if his wife had suddenly taken it upon herself to leave this place and head back to the mainland, then it was all on him. This was all his fault. He would never forgive himself.

He fought back tears and killed the engine. Knocking on doors was what he would do, starting with this Honnie woman. The previous evening, Fiona had baked cakes, telling him she was going to visit her new friend. She was even excited about it. Could she still be in there? Surely not? Tentative green shoots of hope sprung up in him, rapidly with-ering and wilting as logic took hold. Of course she wouldn't still be in there. Fiona wouldn't walk back in the dark. Would she?

The clip of his heels on the pavement reverberated into the night. Even the sea was uncharacteristically quiet, as if in anticipation of something dreadful happening. The calm before the storm. And anyway, would she still be up, this elderly lady, or had she already gone to bed? He wasn't even aware of the time. Not that it mattered. It was dark. Fiona hadn't come home. She was walking, had no torch, and her phone was now switched off. That was enough to send him into a tailspin, for panic to make him dizzy and sweaty, perspiration coating his back, his armpits, trailing a wet line down the back of his neck.

Please let her still be in here. Please let her have lost track of time.

The first knock made no impact, the sound stolen away by a crashing noise as a wave suddenly hit the rocks below the quayside. Neil shivered, hoped the sudden awakening of the sea was a good omen, a premonition that everything was going to be all right after all. He tried again, bashing the knocker against the wood with as much force as he could muster. This time he heard it, a dull thump that filled his head, made him rigid with a sickening realisation that this was very real, that it was happening. That his wife was missing and he was out here, banging on the doors of perfect strangers, asking if anybody had seen her.

A shock wave cut through him at the sight before him once the door swung open. Vince the barman was standing there, his features masked by the darkness of the long, unlit hallway behind him. Neil stepped forward at the same time that Vince moved farther back into the shadows.

'I was looking for Honnie's house. I know she—'

'Two doors down.' Vince pointed with his left hand, a long, bony finger outstretched.

'Okay. Thank you. I'm Neil, not sure if you remem—'

'I remember yer. Two doors down.'

He made to close the door but Neil was too fast for him, shoving his foot inside, jamming it open. 'I'm looking for Fiona, my wife. Have you seen her at all? She was round here earlier and hasn't come home.' The pressure on his ankle grew as Vince continued tugging at the handle. 'Please? Any signs of her at all?'

Vince shook his head, lowering his eyes and glancing over his shoulder behind him into the stretch of darkness. 'Told yer. Not seen nowt. I need to get ready to go and serve them people in the pub. Now if yer don't mind?'

Neil removed his foot from the doorway, discontent and anger rippling through him. Was this the same amiable man from the pub or had he suddenly undergone a personality transplant, transforming him into this cold, calculating creature who was refusing to come to Neil's aid? Or was there something else happening here? Maybe Vince was hiding something. It would explain his abrupt manner, his reticence to get involved, to offer any help.

Visions of Fiona trapped inside the house sprang into Neil's head, saturating his brain.

Before he had a chance to voice his queries, to shout that this was a serious matter and his wife could possibly be in danger, the door was slammed shut in his face, the sound of it ringing in his ears, the image of Vince's scowling face and sharp words embedded in his mind. When this was over, when Fiona was finally found safe and sound, he wouldn't forgive or forget. He would let Vince know exactly what he thought of him.

He moved back off the step and stood in front of the house next door, looking up at the windows, surveying the tiny front garden, trying to work out what sort of person lived there. A sudden movement behind a crack in the curtains caught his eye. Was he being watched? Somebody was home. He rapped against the wooden door, this time not allowing discretion or politeness to get in the way. He needed to find Fiona; he needed help and he needed it now.

'All right, all right. Gimme a minute.' The voice on the other side of the door was faint, weak and reedy with age.

Hope unfurled in his chest, his worries slackening, falling away like confetti. This must be Honnie's house. This was it; this was where it all ended. She would know what to do, how to locate Fiona. She would tell him that his wife only set off barely more than ten minutes ago and that he must have missed her on the route here, that if he turned and drove back, Fiona would already be at the cottage, standing in the kitchen making coffee, her brow knitted with discontent, wondering what all the fuss was about.

'Where is she?' The words tumbled out of him; garbled sounds aimed at the crooked lady standing there, arms folded tightly under her bosom, a formidable stance that said, *Make this fast. I'm old and tired. I have neither the time nor the patience for this nonsense.*

The hope he felt only seconds earlier withered and died within him. Dust particles swirling in his belly as he listened to her response.

'Eh? What you on about?' Her brow was crinkled, her mouth set in a disapproving pout.

Neil swallowed, tried to still his thrashing heart. Part of him had hoped that as soon as she opened the door, she would recognise him, know why he was here and shoo him away, telling him not to be so stupid and that Fiona was already at home. Another part wanted to see his wife standing behind Honnie, eyes wide at his appearance, realisation dawning that she had lost track of time and caused him no end of problems and worry. But it was clear that Fiona wasn't there, that Honnie was alone and that she had no idea why he had knocked and disturbed her.

A sickness welled up in him as he stood there in the darkness. This lady was about to deny all knowledge of his wife's disappearance. Just like Vince, she would soon close her door and go back to her comfortable, safe little life while he would be left to roam the island alone, calling out Fiona's name, wondering what to do next, working out how to find her in the impenetrable blackness of the night.

'Fiona. My wife. She came to visit you earlier today. She hasn't come home.' He was panting now, his breath misting in front of his face as the temperature plummeted. It was starting to get cold. Freezing, actually. And Fiona was possibly out in it. Without a coat. He didn't know that for certain, but neither was he sure that she did have one with her.

'She in't 'ere. Long since left. Probably called at the shop on the way back. 'Ave you tried asking in there?'

He hadn't asked in there, hadn't even thought of it. Would it still be open at this hour? This wasn't like the mainland where supermarkets stayed open twenty-four hours a day. This was Winters End where people locked their doors at the first sign of dusk, closing their blinds to the outside world. The place where people scurried home against the brisk north-easterly wind and shops pulled down the shutters at the first sign of the dying light.

Neil shook his head, Fiona's fears about this place tumbling around in his mind. The ones he'd ignored and denied. The ones he should have listened to. Maybe she was right. Maybe there was something sinister going on around here. And maybe if he had taken notice, not dismissed her fears as nonsense and a sign she was slowly lapsing once again into the dark place she had worked hard to leave behind, then he wouldn't be here. They would both be at home, curled up on the sofa in front of the fire. He rejected those thoughts, blocked them out. Now wasn't the time. All his energies had to be poured into finding her, making sure he got her home safe and sound. God, he would tell her a thousand times over how much he loved her once she was found. He would hold her close and

apologise for his previous misdeeds until his throat
was raw, while stroking her hair and kissing away her
tears. He had been such a fool. Such an ignorant and
blind fool refusing to lift his head out of the sand and
see the obvious. His stupidity had brought them here
and now his wife was lost and he had no idea what to
do about it, how to go about finding her and bringing
her home. Was there even a policeman on this godforsaken, dark and cold island? The place that only a few
days and weeks ago held such promise. It now felt like
an unforgiving, ignorant place, the local community
turning their backs on him when he needed them
most.

'That's where she'll be, no doubt. If the doors
locked, just give 'em a knock. They can tell yer if
they've seen 'er or not.'

The door was slammed shut before he had time to
protest, to beg for assistance from a lady he barely
knew. A lady his wife had warmed to. If she wasn't
prepared to help, he felt certain that nobody would.

The wind lashed at his face. He turned and zipped
up his coat, misery and confusion gnawing at him. He
would go to the shop, ask if they had seen Fiona, and
if they hadn't, then what? He wouldn't jump ahead.
One thing at a time. Maybe they could point him in
the direction of where she had gone, tell him cheer-

fully that she had called in to buy a bottle of wine and was on her way home. Or maybe not.

The car was a welcome barrier against the sea air. He put on his belt and turned up the heater, stones and pieces of loose tarmac spitting out from under his wheels as he revved the engine and set off, his tyres screeching against the road.

20

Darkness all around me. Solid, impenetrable. I widened my eyes, still nothing. No change, no gradual adjustment. Just complete blackness and a coldness behind my eyes as I stretched them wide and waited. A freezing damp surface beneath me. Too much pain to move, to think straight. To make sense of the situation; to try to work out where I was and what had happened, why I was here in this place. Buzzing in my head, dizziness when I tried to sit up. Too painful, too much effort. I felt as if death would take me if I tried. I blinked, waited, still saw nothing so shut my eyes, tried to sink back into unconsciousness. Had I fallen? Banged my head, rolled into a ditch? A voice in my head told me not but I couldn't be certain. Everything was a blur, a jumble of snarled thoughts, tightly meshed together. And the exhaustion – it was overwhelming, my body like lead, my limbs watery and useless.

A sudden roar when I inhaled, saliva catching in my throat. I began to gag, suffocate, every movement, every breath a desperate struggle. Was I dying? Choking to death on my own blood?

Seconds passed, minutes perhaps. I could focus only on the pain, how to stem it. Nothing in reserve, nothing left to help me to think clearly, to get any sense of what was happening. Everything surreal. I tried to hone in on my breathing, *in out, in out, in out*, make sure I kept the rhythm going. Make sure I stayed alive.

I think perhaps I slept a little, dipping in and out of consciousness. A series of images filled my head: visions of dying here, dreams of speaking to Neil, begging him for help. Screaming at him down the phone.

My phone!

I tried to sit up, to grapple for my phone. Grit filled my throat, my mouth; my tongue thick and furred when I called out Neil's name. A boom in my head like a clap of thunder when I tried once more to reposition myself. Pain whistling through my skull, pin-balling up and down my spine.

I needed to find my phone, to ring Neil and tell him to come and help me, to take me home where I would be safe and warm. Where was it? Where the fuck was my phone? I wanted to move but couldn't, my body cumbersome and restricted, my legs solid, held in place, one of my arms stretched up behind my head. Had I been like this earlier? I tried to remember, my mind clouded, everything misshapen and ill-fitting.

I fought back tears, realisation dawning that something horrific had taken place, something far worse than a fall or a bump to the head. I wasn't lying in a ditch after slipping on the way home. I hadn't fallen over the cliff path. And I definitely wasn't dead. I'd been attacked. The word jolted me awake, fizzing through my brain. I remembered then, the heavy breathing behind me, the hit to the back of my head. The blinding pain as if a vice was slowly being tightened around my skull. It flashed into my mind, white sparks of recognition, the horror of it. The reality of what had taken place. Somebody had followed me. I had been calm, happy even, thought I was safe. I wasn't. I relaxed and let a bad thing take place. That was what happened when you let down your guard, became soft and unassuming. Death and terror crept close, saw your exposed underbelly and pounced. I should have run home, taken a different route, been more alert. I should have taken the car. And now I was paying the price.

Where was I? Every ragged thought that passed through my head made my brain hurt, making me dizzy and nauseous. I tried to shift about and couldn't. I was tied up, my feet tightly bound, one of my wrists shackled. My senses, however, were slowly returning, everything becoming clearer to me. I could feel the rope cutting into my skin, chafing the soft flesh of my ankles. A burning sensation ricocheted up and down my arm. A rattling sound when I tried to move away from the wall. Heat gathered around my face, everything finally coming into focus. It was no accident. I'd been right all along. Something hideous was taking place on the island. And now it was happening to me too. The thought that I might die here in the dark and the cold spurred me into action. I shuffled about blindly, trying to ignore the pain, the sickening streaks of agony that tore through me, every movement robbing me of breath. I would rail against this situation, make the person who did this to me wish they hadn't chosen me. I would—

'Don't move.' The voice was deep, throaty. Threatening.

A hand pushed me back against the wall. I could feel the squareness of their palm on my chest, the strength and solidity of it. The undeniable power behind that push. I let myself go floppy. Be pliable. Easier that way. I was exhausted, wracked with pain. But I wasn't browbeaten just yet. The old Fiona had begun to slink back before I was attacked. She was still there. I could feel her building inside of me, growing in strength. I was resilient. Determined. I wasn't going to die here. I wouldn't. Thoughts of Neil filled my mind. Had he noticed I was late home? Was he out looking for me or did he trust me to find my own way back in my own good time? I hoped it was the former. I hoped he was out there searching the island. I hoped he would mistakenly stumble upon this place and free me.

I had no idea how long I had been here. Minutes? Hours? Not days. I felt certain of that. I guessed at hours, thought about whether or not it would be dark outside by now. If it was, then alarm bells without question would be ringing with Neil. He would definitely be out there, calling my name, scouring the immediate vicinity. He would be thinking I had fallen, stumbled over the cliff. Been swallowed by the vast, icy sea.

Rapid shallow breaths as I tried to hold back the tears, attempting to quash unpalatable thoughts of what could happen next. I made a feeble attempt to control myself, to control my breathing, biting down on my bottom lip and gnawing at a loose piece of skin. Anything but tears. Crying was a sign of weakness. I couldn't be weak. I needed to save my strength. I needed to get out of here. Wherever *here* was. So no weeping, just anger and a latent source of strength I could build upon. Something I could use to my advantage.

The pain still shrieked through my head but was slowly waning to a dull ache. A physical reminder that I had been attacked and was currently slumped somewhere on the island, held here by a madman. Or a woman. The voice was low, gruff but impossible to be sure if it was male or female.

Did I know them? Possibly. Had I met them since moving here? Again, it was a possibility. The population of the island was tiny. I thought about the men from The Bucket of Blood, their anger at my presence, their furious features. Their violence.

I used the fingers of my free hand to trace a path

up to my other wrist. I could feel the cold metal that cuffed me. I winced and tentatively crept farther up to touch the metal clasps of the heavy chain that was bolted to the wall behind me. A prisoner. I was being held prisoner against my will, death perhaps just minutes away. Ice flooded my veins, that thought cutting through my steely resolve to remain calm and strong. I couldn't stop them then, the tears. They ran down my face, sobs catching in my throat, my chest compressed. Death. After all I had railed against since moving here, the arguments I had had with the locals, the conversations with Ewan and Honnie about my suspicions, it had come to this. I was probably going to die here.

Oh God.

Snot streamed, sobs welled up in my abdomen, my throat. I had to stop it. Crying solved nothing. It was futile, draining me, leaving me even weaker than I already was and yet it was so hard to stop it. I took a deep breath, retching as I inhaled. The lower half of my body ached when I tried to shuffle about, every part of me hurting, but I wasn't about to die. Not yet. I would fight off my attacker with every ounce of strength I had. I was nothing if not tenacious. Neil would say stubborn. I smiled at that notion, my body softening at the thought of him then stiffening again, preparing myself. With no idea where I was or who was watching me, anything was possible. Anything. I had to be ready. Alert, not inert.

My own breathing roared in my ears. My heart banged in my chest. I sniffed, stopped the crying, tried to be quiet, controlled. I wasn't managing to be either of those things. I was terrified. I was also furious. My brain ached. I tried to work out what to do, whether I should sit silently or thrash about, make a nuisance of myself. I had no idea who or what I was up against. I didn't doubt that I was in danger and had to be careful. I remembered the ferocity of that push, the power behind it. And yet, I couldn't just sit and do nothing, be a victim, quietly accepting my fate. I wanted to gnash my teeth, to scream to the heavens that I was being held here against my will and buck my body about to break free of the ties that were binding me.

I didn't do any of those things. Instead, I sat patiently, doing my best to stem my fear, waiting for my vision to adjust to the darkness, to allow me to see just a fraction. Anything was better than nothing and timing was everything. It was all about precision and knowledge, knowing when to move and when to stay still. When to take my chances and when to be malleable and accepting. I thought about screaming, remembering the fist that knocked me unconscious, and remained silent instead.

Seconds passed, turning into minutes. I heard nothing but the thump of my heart, the sound of my blood as it gushed through my veins. At first. But then something else. A rustle of clothing perhaps. A movement close by. I listened again, blocking out other extraneous noises, honing in on this new sound. Definitely the rustling echoes of somebody moving. And a low murmur. Another person close by. A female voice, higher than before. A frightened whimper. Almost a shriek.

My scalp prickled, the hairs on the back of my neck stood on end. I wanted to speak but didn't dare. I thought about what I would say. How I would break the silence. Was this woman my captor? Or was she, like me, bound and helpless? I guessed that she too was being held here against her will, the rapidity of her breathing, the pitch and quality of her murmurs too timid, too submissive to be my aggressor.

I needed a couple of seconds to think, to assimilate it all in my head, work out what to do next; whether to make a noise, let this person who had done this to me know that I was aware there was somebody else in this place, or to remain quiet, as silent and still as death itself. They could be unpredictable, close to breaking point. Close to doing something terrible either to me or this other person. Something final.

I damned to hell and back the impermeable darkness, the fact my vision still hadn't adjusted enough to allow me to see properly. I was incapacitated, my limbs bound, my senses dulled by pain and a lack of natural light. In my mind, I raged and railed. Physically, I was useless, my body unresponsive and immobile.

As quietly and furtively as I could, I shuffled along the cold, hard floor, the tiniest of manoeuvres, every breath I took requiring such effort it made me feel sick to my stomach. My muscles were rigid with anticipation, the sound of my clothes dragging against concrete as I moved a sonic boom in my head.

I kept on, pushing myself along, inch by inch, stretching as far as my chain would allow, which wasn't that far at all, and all the while trying to disguise my shallow breathing, trying to be as quiet as I could until I touched something solid. Not quite solid. Heavy, but pliable. Another person? A psychopath or somebody else who was being held prisoner? Somebody just like me? I stopped. I was taking a chance, groping around in the dark, hoping to find a way out of this place. Hoping to escape with my life.

The noise shook me out of my stupor, filling me

with both hope and terror in equal measure. A voice; small and reedy, deadened by fear, but a voice all the same.

'Help. Please help me. I think I'm dying.'

A deep growl, words, low and full of menace, mingled with a roar. Something connecting with the side of my face, the force of it slamming my head into the wall. And then nothing.

21

NEIL

It vibrated through his body, the force of the knock as he tried again, resounding into the night like the blast of a cannon being fired. Neil held his knuckles, rubbing at them with his other hand. He felt sure the people who ran the place lived in a flat above the shop. Hadn't Honnie said that he needed to knock louder if nobody answered straightaway? She had intimated that there would be somebody inside to speak to him. So where were they?

He leaned forward, resting his head against the glass, and stared through the door. Inside, everything was shrouded in darkness, a blanket of grey draped over the shelves, along the floor. He stepped back, looked up at the window above. Honnie had been right. Somebody was home. A dim light shone out through a crack in the curtains. Driven by fear and anger, he knocked again, this time the noise of his knuckles rapping against wood, an inescapable thunderous sound. It reverberated around him, the thud of his fists as he hammered them against the door. Upstairs, the curtains twitched and a face glanced out of the window, pale and ghost-like, and angled downwards, two eyes peering out at him in disdain.

He stopped and waited. Counted the seconds. A light flickered inside the shop. Neil hopped from foot to foot, the cold biting at him. If Fiona was out in these temperatures without a coat, then—

He stopped with that train of thought. He had to focus on finding her. Exhausting himself by worrying about things that may not have happened was futile.

'Yeah?' A young man swung open the door and stood before him, his face wan and pasty, eyes deep set, heavy and tired-looking as if he was fatigued by life. *Me too*, Neil wanted to say. *Me too*.

'I'm sorry to disturb you. I was wondering if you've seen Fiona, my wife. We were here a while back shortly after we moved in and—'

'Not seen 'er. Sorry.'

The door began to close. Desperation coursed through him. 'Are you sure? Honnie said that you might be able to help me find her.'

She hadn't said anything of the sort, he knew that, but here was a youngish-looking lad who could help him comb the island, giving him clues on where to look.

'Can't help yer. As I said, not seen 'er. She's hasn't been in 'ere.'

The slam of the door shook him. He could feel it in his bones, the futility of his requests for help, the insidious creeping fear that was slithering beneath his skin, tightening itself around his vital organs. Neil stood, his breath misting in front of his face, wondering what to do next. Where to go. Who to turn to. He was a stranger to almost everybody on this island. He was alone, nobody around willing to help him.

He broke into a run, clambered back to his car and swung it around, driving at speed in the direction of home. She would be there by now. She would be at home waiting for him. And if she wasn't... well, he wouldn't think about that right now, refused to consider it. He wanted to believe that nothing bad had happened, that all this was a silly mistake. An oversight. She would apologise. He would run her a bath and afterwards they would sit together on the sofa, limbs curled around each other, Fiona tired and wide-eyed, regaling him with tales of how she had got lost, stumbled over, managing to finally get her bearings and make it home. They would drink a glass of wine, eat plates of nibbles, the television on low in the background.

And then reality hit, a punch to his gut. The emptiness of the cottage loomed large in his mind, Fiona's absence knocking all the air out of his lungs. He had to consider the fact that she wouldn't be home when he arrived, breathless and riddled with anxiety. What then? What would he do as he stepped into the darkness of their cottage, the silence of her absence a tangible thing? He ran his fingers through his hair, rubbed at his eyes. He would more than likely run up and down the lane, pulling aside shrubbery, calling out her name, hollering into the night, no longer able to disguise his growing desperation. He would knock on doors in Harbour Lane and ask if anybody had seen her and he would refuse to leave until he got some solid answers. A breath rattled in his chest. Not that he would need to do any door knocking. She would be home when he got there. She would. He just knew it, could feel it in his centre, in the very heart of him. He could sense her presence, see her in his mind's eye as she wandered around the kitchen, rummaging in cupboards wondering what to prepare for their evening meal, perhaps even humming to herself. The radio would be on in the background, the comforting sounds of the soothing voices of the presenters and some light music filling the air, the delicate aroma of her perfume as she drifted around the house closing blinds and curtains lingering in her wake. She would be wondering where he was, checking her watch and pulling the curtains aside to peer outside into the darkness of the night for him. He smiled at the irony and put his foot down, suddenly eager to be home.

Except she wasn't there. He pulled up outside the cottage, his stomach plummeting when he saw that it was shrouded in darkness. No lights on inside. No signs of Fiona. She wasn't home. She was still missing, still out there somewhere on this strange and unfamiliar island with its eccentric residents and their quirky, sometimes violent ways.

Panic suddenly took hold, gripping him. An iron fist of terror crushing his body, stopping him from breathing properly. Had she left him? Had it all suddenly got too much for her and she had upped and left, a spur-of-the-moment thing? He fell out of the car, crashing to the floor, scrambling up to his feet and pelting to the front door, legs liquid with terror. His fingers trembled, the key slipping about in his palm as he pushed it into the lock and turned it.

The door flung open, slamming into the wall with a crash. 'Fiona!' His voice resonated through the hallway, bouncing off the walls and floors, disappearing suddenly, swallowed by the shadows.

Ridiculous, really. He had no idea why he was shouting her name. She wasn't there. He knew it. Deep down he knew that she was gone. On impulse, he ran to their bedroom and flung open the wardrobe door before wildly pulling out drawers to check for missing clothing. A heavy sickness took hold, the ground swaying beneath his feet, walls leaning in drunkenly. They were all still there, her clothes hung up or folded neatly into tidy little piles. She wouldn't leave without taking any of her belongings. He knew that. He knew Fiona. She was always organised. Always prepared. Fastidious in her approach to life.

The suitcases. If they were still there, then she definitely hadn't taken herself off somewhere. His knees cracked as he bent down and leaned into the bottom of the large cupboard at the back of their bedroom. His hand touched upon their luggage set. All still there, even the matching rucksack. Fiona was gone; her clothes and bags were still here.

A tightness crushed his chest. Acid swirled in his stomach, bubbling and burning. What next? What the fuck was he supposed to do next? Ring 999? Was there even a police station on Winters End? He doubted it. He hadn't seen any sort of law enforcement since arriving here. No ambulances, no emergency services. For the first time since moving here, he felt truly alone, paralysed by fear and confusion. Dread seeped into his bones like poison. He couldn't let panic take over. Not yet. There had to be other options open to him, other things to do before he let his emotions rule his head.

Neighbours. He would check with them. Maybe, just maybe, Fiona had come home and had no key so went to them, knocked for help and was currently sitting on their sofa, feet curled up under her backside, cup of coffee in hand while a fire roared in the hearth. Maybe. Or maybe not. Very probably not, but he had to try.

He pulled out his phone and called her again. Still turned off.

Shit!

Bit by bit, everything was slipping away, the odds

of her returning home safely, moving further and further away from him, slipping into near oblivion.

He peered out into the lane. It was blanketed in darkness. With no street lights, he would have to take something to help him see his way to the next house up from theirs. A roughly tarmacked road littered with potholes would be the undoing of him if he stepped out there and fell over with limited visibility.

The heft of the large torch gave him a feeling of invincibility. Fingers curled around the rubber casing, he picked it up off the cabinet in the hallway and headed outside, thoughts that he could use it as a weapon if need be in the forefront of his mind. He shivered, pulled up his collar. It felt colder than it had just a short while back, a wind whipping its way over the clifftop.

Using the torch as a scythe, he fought his way through the shrubbery that flanked their front path, turning left to head up to the next house. The yellow beam from the torch was powerful, but the lack of light pollution was greater, affording him only a marginally better view of the road ahead. He walked with care, the smack of his feet against the road the only sound to be heard. His breath fogged, small grey clouds that ballooned and dissipated rhythmically until he reached a row of overgrown conifers and stopped. Behind them sat a small house shrouded in darkness, the height of the trees obscuring its roofline from view. Words rumbled in his head, strings of syllables running loose as he tried to work out what he would say to these people. He didn't want to appear desperate even though he was. He needed them to take him seriously, to see him as somebody who wasn't unhinged, a potential lunatic. He needed them to be on his side.

The door swung open before he had a chance to knock, a guy he recognised from the pub standing there, watching him.

'I've not seen 'er.'

Neil's eyes widened, his skin rippled with annoyance, words abandoning him. The shadowy figure began his retreat back into the house.

'Please!' It was all he could think to say to stop this man from shutting him out altogether. A reflex to a moment. A knee-jerk reaction to his hopes of getting some help being snuffed out before they had had a chance to properly ignite. 'I just want to talk, to ask you about my wife, find out if you or anybody has seen her. It's just that—'

The slam of the door vibrated around him, another rejection filling him with such a deep sense of gloom, he almost crumpled right there on the spot.

What the fuck was wrong with these people? Where was their decency, their compassion, their humanity? It was clear that word of Fiona's disappearance had spread. So why were they sitting there, inside their warm homes, fingers clutching the curtains as they peered outside, waiting for his arrival so they could take pleasure in turning him away? This was bleak – worse than bleak. It was... he couldn't think of the right words to describe the range of emotions he was feeling. Darkness, dread, terror. They were all there, gurgling up inside him, ready to spill out.

Cold water flooded his veins; his thoughts were disconnected from his body as he trudged farther along the lane, hoping, *praying* that the final house would provide him with some sort of assistance. He wasn't religious, never had been, but desperation had taken over. Maybe it was the passing of time with no word from Fiona or maybe it was the cold receptions his calls for help had been met with. Maybe, he thought, as he slipped through the small, narrow gate that led to the small bungalow at the end of the lane, it was a combination of both. Each frosty response compounded his sense of dread that something terrible had happened to his wife.

Unshakeable images of bodies plunging over clifftops took hold in his mind: her body grey and distended, swollen by the seawater, eyes sealed shut in death. He couldn't think of it, refused to even consider it. It wasn't possible. Fiona would have taken care; she would have rung him if anything untoward had happened.

So why hadn't she? Why was her phone turned off? Where the hell was she?

Grief, terror, frustration all jabbed at him. Helpless. That was how he felt. Helpless and useless. He was doing nothing. He was Fiona's husband, her next of kin, and he couldn't even manage to get neighbours to join in the search for her. What sort of a pathetic man couldn't get anyone to rally round to help find his wife?

This time, he was greeted with a smile and a handshake, the door swinging open after the first knock. Maybe it was a sign. Maybe these people were expecting him. Maybe, just maybe, they had something positive to say, something pleasant and helpful. Something compassionate that would alleviate his near grief.

'Welcome, lad. It's dark out. Get yerself inside 'ere.'

Before he could refuse or protest, stating that he needed to keep looking and just wanted a brief word, he was pulled into the house, warmth wrapping itself around him, embracing him, softening his rigid posture. Making him suddenly weak and pliant. He staggered, the floor see-sawing, tipping him off balance.

'Steady up, fella. Here, sit yerself down.'

Neil felt himself being lowered; his backside perched on the bottom stair of the hallway. He wanted to speak, to ask this wonderfully warm man for help, but nothing would come. He tried opening his mouth, a stream of unintelligible sounds emerging followed by a rasping cry. Not the words he hoped for but an unearthly sound instead. It reverberated in his head, that awful howling noise. He tried to stop it and couldn't. And then the tears came. The tears and the snot, exacerbated by the gentle reassurances of the small man who was leaning down next to him, telling him that everything was going to be all right. It wasn't. He knew that now. He just knew it. He didn't know how – a sixth sense perhaps, some deep-rooted instinct that everything was off balance, out of kilter. But he knew it nonetheless.

A handkerchief was passed down to him, He took it, dabbed at his eyes, wiped his nose, feeling weak and stupid, an insipid creature for allowing the tears to flow. He wasn't one for crying or showing his emotions, never had been, but this had got the better of him, left him feeling wrung out. Hollow.

'Tek yer time, lad. Tek yer time.'

He did just that, sitting loosely, trying to catch his breath, a series of hiccups escaping, his gullet going into spasm as he tried to compose himself.

'Fiona,' he managed to say after a few seconds. 'My wife, Fiona. She's missing. I need help to find her. Please. Please, help me. I don't know what to do.'

22

A cacophony of noises in my head. Static popping and fizzing. And pain. So much pain. Unbearable.

I lifted myself up off the floor, trying to remember the chain of events, trying to recall what had happened. Nausea gripped me, vomit gathering in my abdomen, my gullet going into spasm. I swallowed down the flow of acrid bile that burned at my throat. White noise, loud and discordant, rang in my ears.

Something had definitely taken place, something violent. It flashed before my eyes then: being pushed backwards, hitting the wall, the rear of my head connecting with it at speed. I took a shaky breath and waited, pain shooting up and down my body. I waited until it subsided, until the sickness passed and the fog cleared, thinking back to the few seconds prior to having my head smashed against the wall with such force that I almost passed out. And then it came to me. There was somebody else here with me. Another woman. Distressed, possibly dying. I wasn't alone. She spoke to me. And then out of nowhere, a hand, smacking my face, pushing me backwards. A voice telling me to shut up, to stop talking, that I had better close my stupid mouth if I wanted to remain alive. My head hitting the wall with such ferocity I felt sure my skull would break in half. Then nothing.

I lowered my eyes, rested my chin on my knees. A feeling of helplessness surrounding me. How could I expect to get out of this place when faced with such brutality? Such violence? I was no match for whomever it was had assaulted me. I would try. My God, I would fight them until I dropped with exhaustion but knew that unless something miraculous happened, unless somebody found me and untied me, picking me up and carrying me to a place of safety, then I was done for. Me and this other lady. Both of us doomed.

Oh God, where was she? Had she died? Been killed for daring to speak to me?

I didn't want to think about the possibilities. I didn't want to be alone. I desperately wanted this other woman to be sitting beside me, the two of us together. Allies. Friends. Prisoners.

A grating sound emerged from my throat when I attempted to right myself, to pull myself into an upright position. It was all about knowing, and I didn't know. I had no idea when to speak, when to remain silent. Speaking could rupture our chances of staying alive, of surviving this ordeal. And yet, staying silent meant doing nothing, accepting my fate. I didn't want to die here. I wanted to fight this monster, show them that they had picked on the wrong person. I just didn't know how to do it, how to summon up enough strength to battle an unknown assailant in the darkness, in a strange environment. I was shadow-boxing, fighting off a ghost.

Another sound. A whisper. Then, 'He's gone.'

My heart was a caged bird, wings wildly flapping beneath my ribcage. Despite feeling cold, heat seared over my flesh, creeping up my face. A furnace blazed beneath my skin.

'You're still here? I thought they might have...' The words caught in my throat. I couldn't voice my fear. She was still here. She wasn't dead. I wasn't dead. We were both still trapped here. Together and yet apart. We may as well have been at opposite ends of the country for all the good we could do. We were tied up, slumped on the floor next to each other.

'Where are we?' It was a croak, my voice, raspy with dehydration and fear.

'I don't know. Somewhere where nobody can hear or see us. I've tried screaming. Nobody comes. Nobody hears. It's useless.'

Two voices communicating in the pitch-black. Two despairing souls. I had to know more, to work out where we were. Who put us here. And why.

Slowly but steadily, the pain abated and I was able to think clearly. My flesh felt bruised, sensitive and sore, but I wasn't about to die. Not yet. That thought pushed me into a dark place. I resisted, dragged myself out of it. Nothing final. Not yet. I wasn't ready. I hadn't fought as hard as I could. They hadn't got the better of me. Still some fight left in me.

My eyes were heavy, leaden lids resisting gravity. I rested my head back against the cold brick wall, imagining the smears of blood where I had hit it, where my skull had been slammed against it. This woman – she was the missing lady, the body on the beach. She had to be. I cast my mind back, trying to remember her name; those news articles, the grainy photo of her smiling at the camera, carefree and happy, never thinking that something as grotesque as this would ever happen to her.

Sian. That was it. Her name was Sian Dupre.

'We're going to get out of here,' I said, wondering how we would do it. *If* we could do it. They were just words. Words designed to bolster Sian. To bolster me. I needed to hear them spoken out loud, not have them as fragments of ideas in my head, disconnected and without direction. Maybe if Sian had been here longer than me, she knew about ways in and out of this place. Maybe—

'We get fed and we're allowed to use the toilet three times a day. That's it. Nothing else.'

She began to cry, softly at first but soon turning into a muffled howl. Using my free hand as a lever, I shuffled along the floor to get closer to her. She was nearby, her voice not too far from where I was sitting. A touch, the feeling that somebody else was close by, that was all I could do to help her. It wasn't much but it was something and it was better than nothing. It was better than being alone. Better than sitting slumped and frightened in this horrific place, waiting for death to take us.

I bit at my lip, tasting blood. My teeth were locked into position, my jaw rigid. My ears were attuned to every sound; to the *thud thud* of blood that was pounding at my temples. I counted, trying to control every pocket of air that exited my lungs, trying to keep it low and rhythmic. It was all I could do to stay in control, not let my fear upend me, leaving me weak and wasted. At the mercy of this person who was approaching again, their footsteps growing louder, closer. My innards somersaulted, twisting and squirming within me. A fist grasped at my bowel, steel fingers clasping it tight.

In the corner, a door opened, the squeak of the handle, the click of the lock instantly recognisable. A triangle of light. The sound of something grating along a hard surface. Then the sensation of something touching me. I recoiled, suppressed a shriek, visualised a hand resting against my leg, fingers touching, groping. Then darkness and a slam.

'It's food and a drink.' She was whispering, her voice brisk and full of desperation. 'We need to eat it quickly or it gets taken away.'

'How? I can't see. How are we supposed to eat when it's pitch-black?' It sounded ridiculous, surreal, hearing those words spoken out loud.

A hand grabbed at mine, cold fingers opened my fist, laid something warm and sticky on my palm. Revulsion gripped me. I wanted to vomit, wipe it away, scramble up onto my hands and knees and get out of the room.

'You have to eat it. Or drink something. Here,' she said, touching my leg, fumbling and patting around until she found my other hand, 'take this and drink it. Dehydration is worse than hunger. Trust me, I know.'

I wrapped my fingers around the handle of a tin mug, the thought that it might be poisoned crossing my mind.

'It's water. It's fine. Drink it.'

I listened to her eating, the sounds she made making me gag. I couldn't stomach any food but drank from the mug. The water was cold at least and tasted fresh.

'Who is it?' I said, a dribble of water running down my chin, the cooling effect stark against my hot flesh.

'Who is what?'

'That person, the one who put us here. Who are they?'

'Shh!' The chewing noises stopped, a silence hanging between us.

I sat, waiting, my whole body on edge, every nerve ending screaming at me.

'What?' I hissed into the darkness, my voice low, sibilant.

There was something, a noise deadened by distance, but it was there all the same. Footsteps again. Heavy, cumbersome. The movements of somebody large and graceless moving about.

'Sian, who is it? And what do they want?'

My question was met with a sudden silence. I nudged at her bony leg with mine, our knees banging together, my fingers pressing against her flimsy clothing.

'Who is it, Sian? Who is the person that put us here?'

Any remaining residual heat left my body, leaching out of me in a rush as I listened to her reply, the odour of her rancid breath drifting past me. Even in the darkness, I felt myself leaning, dizziness knocking me sideways onto the floor as she spoke, her voice a rasp in the darkness.

'Who is Sian?'

23

NEIL

He stared at Wilf through blurry eyes, everything dim and distorted. Neave was a small, indistinct figure in the corner of the room, a diminutive woman who rarely spoke. Wilf sat opposite Neil on the sofa, head cocked to one side like he was listening out for a noise from elsewhere.

'Ah wish ah could say that I've seen 'er but we've seen nothing, have we, Neave?'

Neil couldn't bring himself to look at this man, was too afraid to see the expression of hopelessness in his eyes. This house was his last chance, his final point before calling the police.

He looked around the room, for what, he wasn't sure. A sign perhaps, that these people had some element of control, that they could come up with a solution and everything would be magically solved. With their faded velour sofa, grainy photographs dotted around, and a teak coffee table that leaned to one side, a beer mat angled under the leg to keep it stable, he knew that as kind as they were, they wouldn't be able to help him. He was on his own.

'What next, then?' Neil's veneer was slipping, the cracks in his voice now apparent. He coughed, rubbed at his face and tried to straighten his posture. Nobody else was in control on this shitty little island. He had to be. 'Is there a police station on Winters End?' The answer was apparent to him even before Wilf spoke. Of course there wasn't a police station. 'Or an acting police officer?' They didn't have anybody on the island. He wasn't even sure why he asked.

The older man dipped his head, staring at his wife before looking back at Neil. 'We used to 'ave one up until the end of last year. A female officer stationed 'ere on secondment but she left, said it wasn't the job for her after all. Durham Constabulary didn't appoint anybody to fill her role, I'm afraid. They were supposed to but with the pandemic and cutbacks and everything, well, I guess it just weren't their priority.'

'So, what do we do now?' It came out as a squeak, a high-pitched, desperate whine. That's because he was desperate. There was no other way of describing how he felt: the tightness of his chest, the pitching sensation in his stomach, his plummeting sense of hope, they were all indicators that everything was spiralling out of control. His tiny little world spinning off its axis into oblivion. A fat black cloud, its belly engorged with rain, hung over him, heavy and ominous, his internal barometer plunging at an exponential rate.

'I guess we can wait until morning, see if she comes home once it's light, eh? Things always seem brighter once the sun comes up.' Wilf gave him a half-smile, his mouth a thin sympathetic line.

Wait until morning? Neil could hardly breathe. His heart beat solidly, thumping and stampeding beneath his sweater. Perspiration coated his top lip. He was right in what he was thinking. He truly was alone on this, that much was clear. Nobody around to help, no assistance. Just the tender words of a kindly old man and his disabled wife. Nobody had anything to offer him. Nothing concrete that he could use to his advantage to help find Fiona.

'I need to find the number of the Durham Constabulary, the nearest police station on the mainland, or I need to call 999.' He stood up, his legs unsteady. He wasn't sure he could trust them to take him home.

Everything felt skewed, the room spinning, his vision hazy.

'Let's get you a cup of tea, lad. You've gone a funny grey colour.'

All his resistance gone, he slumped back down, the fear of passing out, lying sprawled on this man's carpet, the only thing stopping him from bolting out of the door and into the cold night air. He needed help, there was none to be had. Tea, that was all there was to keep him going. Cups of fucking weak, tepid tea.

Guilt wrapped itself around him like a vice. Guilt, fear, dark thoughts too terrible to consider, they tightened themselves, barbed-wire images cutting into his flesh, working their way under his skin, digging into his bones and settling there. Permanent fixtures reminding him that Fiona was gone. She had been concerned, felt something was awry; he had ignored her, brushed aside her concerns, and now she was missing.

'Ere we are, fella. A biscuit as well. You need the sugar.'

'Aye.' A voice carried across the living room. 'For the shock.' Neave was watching him, her body angled to one side when she attempted to lever herself out of the armchair. Beside her stood a pair of metal crutches propped up against the side of the over-stuffed armchair that had seen better days, its pink patterned fabric reminiscent of a 1970s décor splurge. Grunting, she gave up her attempts to stand and flopped back down, almost disappearing into the folds of cushions that were strategically dotted around her.

He nibbled at the anaemic-looking biscuit, his stomach churning as he swallowed it down, and took a sip of the tea, if only to try to garner some strength. He was going to need it. His instincts told him as much. It was going to be a long night.

'I need to go and make a phone call,' he said finally after taking another sip, his guts still roiling like the crest of a wave. 'I'm also going to go and have another search of the island, maybe take a look at the harbour where the ferry docks, see if I can see anything there.'

'You think she's gone to the mainland then?' Wilf's small eyes narrowed even further, disappearing into the bushy folds of his eyebrows and layers of excess skin.

Neil shrugged. 'It's a possibility.' He stood up, shook his head and sat back down, a deep sigh escaping unchecked. 'Fiona hasn't settled here that well.

She may have gone back to Saltburn on a whim. It's unlikely, but I can't rule it out.'

'Well,' Wilf replied, 'it's just a pity the ferry don't 'ave passenger lists. It's a hop on, hop off jobby, otherwise you coulda checked.'

He knew this, the futility of him going there sitting like tar in his belly. He had to do something. He stood again, this time knowing he would leave. He wouldn't waste time going to the quayside; he would call the police on the mainland, register her as officially missing. And then things would start to happen. Then it would all feel horribly real.

'Thank you for the tea.' His voice carried across the dated living room, ethereal and distant. An echo in his head that didn't sound like him at all, but a frantic man who feared his wife would never come back. A man who feared his wife could be dead.

Wilf's hand on his arm, placed there to help guide him out, felt both alien and heartening. He hardly knew the man; they were, up until a few minutes ago, complete strangers, and yet Wilf had shown him more kindness than anybody else had since arriving here.

'Vince?' Neil said on impulse, spinning around to see the reaction on Wilf's face at the mention of the name. To his credit, his face remained impassive, features unmoving, giving nothing away.

'Yes, ah know Vince, all right. What about 'im?'

A pulse thrummed in Neil's neck, a small hammer banging against his sinews. He clenched his fists, wondering where this would lead. For all he knew, they could be best friends, had grown up together, be related even. He was picking his way through a minefield, unsure of what to say or do next. 'It's just that I called at his house earlier while I was out looking for Fiona. I knocked on his door when I was trying to find Honnie's house.' He stopped, trying to find the right words. Semantics was everything. It made a distinction between being polite or being offensive. Between getting this man on his side or provoking him. Right now, he needed all the friends he could get. Upsetting people unnecessarily wasn't on his agenda. 'And he seemed a bit—'

'Abrupt? Stressed, even?' Wilf gave him a sad smile, his head shaking as he clicked his tongue. 'Aye, well we'd all be a bit curt if we were in 'is position, lad. Got a disabled son, he has. Poor little 'un been stuck in a wheelchair for most of 'is life. And with there being only 'im and the young laddie,' he stopped, as if trying to find the right words, 'well, alls I can say is, he's done a bloody good job so far. Running that pub gets him out of the house, lets 'im see people, otherwise they'd both be stuck in that place getting on each other's wires, if yer know what ah mean.'

Neil sucked in his breath, wishing he could unsay what he had just said. Unthink what he had been thinking.

He began walking away and stopped. 'What happened to his wife, the lad's mother, I mean? Where is she?' Fiona's words filtered into his mind, her worries, all of her fears. The ones he had batted away and thought incredibly stupid and lacking in any substance.

More head shaking from Wilf. A lowering of his voice as one often does when speaking of sombre things. Neil knew then what was coming, was able to feel it somewhere in his abdomen, in the sudden burning of his cold flesh. He knew exactly what was coming next.

'Ah, that was a rotten time for 'im. For both of 'em, truth be told. The young laddie, he didn't really understand what had happened, why she 'ad gone.'

Neil swallowed, rubbed at his face, weariness oozing out of him. He needed to hear this. As much as he didn't want to listen, he knew it was important. He waited. Their eyes locked, a darkness in Wilf's expression, a sadness perhaps that hadn't been there before.

'Why *who* had gone?' Something shifted in the

back of his brain, a dormant thought coming to life and breaking free, something recent. Something Fiona had said to him. It was lodged in the recesses of his mind, concealed in the shadows.

'His wife. The laddie's mother. She went missing a few years back. Rumour 'ad it that it all got to be too much for 'er so she upped and headed back to the mainland.'

Jesus. It was Vin's wife, the missing woman that Fiona had told him about. What was her name? It eluded him, slinking back into the shadows and staying there.

'Aye, it was a right rotten time for 'em both. Thing is, Tim, the young lad, was in the house on 'is own when she disappeared, which was a bit strange. She'd never left him like that before, but I guess folk do odd and unpredictable things when they're under pressure, don't they?'

'I guess they do,' Neil said, his voice steady, belying his true feelings. 'I guess they do.'

'Aye, everyone thinks probably the constant caring for the young 'un got to 'er in the end which is understandable.' Wilf shoved his hands in his pockets and stared off over Neil's shoulder. 'Can't be easy looking after a young lad like that when 'e's in a wheelchair 'an all. I mean,' he lowered his voice to a whisper and glanced behind him, 'Caring for our Neave 'as its ups and downs I can tell yer. We get along well enough most of the time, but it's not all beer an' skittles.'

'Well,' Neil murmured, his mind already elsewhere, 'I reckon you do a wonderful job. Neave seems very happy and settled.' He thought of her crutches, the dated armchair, the grubby-looking carpet, and felt weighed down with a terrible sadness for both of them.

'It's 'er knees and hips, you see. She's on the waiting list for new ones but it seems to be tekkin forever.'

'Here's hoping they get in touch soon then, eh?'

On impulse, Neil reached out and shook Wilf's hand, shocked by the strength of the older man's grip and the sturdiness of his fingers. Here was no feeble individual but somebody who was a damn sight stronger than he appeared to be. Helping another person to get around the house day after day would do that to a man, he guessed, increasing their power and durability, elevating their own personal strength and stamina.

'Aye. And let me know the latest wi' that wife of yours. Winters End does weird things to a person's mind. Yer 'ave to be happy wi' yer own company stuck out 'ere in the middle of nowhere.' He stepped closer and, for one awful moment, Neil thought he was going to reach up and hug him. Instead, he dipped his hand into his pocket and produced a piece of paper. 'Our landline number in case yer need anything. It teks us a while to get to the phone but we're always in.'

'Thank you.' He nodded and took the slip of paper, tucking it into the chest pocket of his jacket. 'You've been really kind and helpful.'

'Anytime, lad,' he said, giving Neil a thin, watery smile. 'Anytime.'

* * *

The cottage was chilly when he arrived back, the darkness compounding his misery, the absence of light and warmth highlighting Fiona's absence and fuelling his anxiety and the torment that plagued him, the lack of knowing where she was almost too much to bear. He knew what he had to do next. It was all he had left, all other avenues closed to him. He'd reached that dead end now, the point he had been dreading.

The plastic casing of the phone was cold in his palm as he punched in the number and held it up to his ear, his breathing erratic and laborious while he waited.

A voice at the other end: a male, brisk, efficient. 'Emergency. Which service?'

Then nothing. A silence while they waited for him to speak.

He let out a trembling breath, sank down to the floor, his legs pushed up against his chest. Tears welled up, threatening to flow. He swallowed, blinked them away, pressed the phone closer to his ear and spoke quietly, almost a whisper. 'It's my wife. She's missing. Please help me. I can't find my wife.'

24

BEFORE

Another day, another dollar. He liked that phrase. He had heard the men on the island say it as they passed each other every morning on the way to work. Most of them were fishermen, going out on their boats at dawn, braving the rough seas to bring back their haul. His dad would have been amongst them if he was alive but he had died a few years ago. Not in the sea but of a heart attack.

'Was probably all them cigarettes he smoked,' his mam had said, her face scrunched up like an old newspaper. One of the other men had told her to shut it and she had told him to piss off. That's how people were round these parts – they told it like it was.

He pulled on his socks and trousers and headed

downstairs for breakfast. Since the cake baking, his mam had been nicer to him. Not nice exactly, but she hadn't been all shouty and slappy, her hands swiping at his arms and legs, her cold, fat fingers clawing at whatever she could catch in order to inflict some sort of pain. He had decided that it was easier to do as he was told; that way he would get fed more often and there'd be no more shouting. No more getting locked in his room. No more talk of that day at the graveyard.

'Where you off to?' It ricocheted around the kitchen, her voice. Like a tennis ball hitting every surface. No escape from it. Bounce, bounce, bounce.

'Out to play.' He grabbed at a piece of toast and pelted outside, giving her no time to protest. No time to say no and drag him back in by his collar, hissing in his face that lads like him didn't deserve to play, that he was bad through and through and that no good would ever come of him.

He knew exactly where he was going. The boys at school had talked about it. He had listened to their conversations, desperate to see the place for himself. It wasn't too far from his house, beyond the old wired-off area. A New Clear bunker. That was what they had said and he hadn't asked what one was for fear of appearing like an idiot. A retard. That was the word they all used when pointing out that somebody was thick.

He didn't want to be one of those thick people so looked up what it was in a book at school and it sounded like an amazing place. He would slither under the wire on his belly and explore the area, find out what was in there. He'd seen it before but never given any real thought to what lay beyond the wire. Besides, it used to have signs there warning people to stay away but now the signs were old and tattered, the letters almost gone, rubbed away by the sea air and strong winds. Nobody had ever bothered to clean them up or paint them. Marcus in his class said the land used to belong to the government but they didn't want it any more and that it was all right for anybody to play there now. So that's what he was going to do. He was going to explore and find out what all the fuss was about. Then he would be able to join in with all the other lads and tell tales of his adventures in the New Clear bunker.

Excitement fizzed in his chest like popping candy, sparks of happiness jumping and dancing around inside of him, throbbing in his veins, making him feel alive and a little bit dizzy.

The sea breeze whipped across his face but, for once, he didn't care. The wind could blow a hoolie and it wouldn't bother him. He had things to do, places to discover. Secrets to unearth. He didn't care that he was doing it alone either. He preferred it that way. This would be his adventure. He could do whatever he wanted. The possibilities were endless. His own playground full of dark secrets and hidey-holes.

He closed the back gate behind him with an almost silent click and headed over to the barren field behind his house, imagining himself to be a spy. Like a character out of James Bond on a special mission. A secret top mission that only he and his superiors knew about. His mam would have a fit if she knew where he was headed. It was close to the cliff path. Too close. But that didn't bother him. Spies didn't need to worry about things like that because they had superpowers; they could escape from all kinds of dangerous situations unscathed. He sped up, almost running. He was invincible. Once he snuck under that wire, he would suddenly become unstoppable. He didn't know how he knew that; it was just a feeling he had. A strong feeling that he couldn't shake. He was big and powerful, as strong as the old oak tree up on the far side of the island. No wind could ever fell it. He was like that. Nobody could ever put him off his stride.

Shrubbery lined the perimeter of the area, concealing it, giving it the look of a scrub of barren land. But it wasn't that at all. It had secrets. Secrets and mysteries that tore at his sense of curiosity, firing up his imagination. He needed to get inside, see what it was like. He pushed the length of bushes and undergrowth aside, noticing that the wire was all but gone, parts of it perished, other parts torn and straggly, ruined by years of neglect and the elements that battered it on a daily basis. More candy-popping explosions in his stomach as he dropped to the ground and snaked his way in like a commando about to attack an unsuspecting enemy. Another thought that made his insides fizz and explode. He preferred that feeling. Unlike the ants in his brain, it made him feel good. Happy and excited. The ants bit at him, forcing him to do things he knew he shouldn't do. Bad things that, once done, could not be undone.

The low trailing pieces of wire snagged at his clothes when he slid under. He untangled himself, not caring that his sweater had bits of cotton sticking up after being caught. Things like that didn't matter when you were a top agent carrying out a secret mission on government land. Nobody knew he was here. It was his special plan. His own special undertaking. Something he had to do all on his own. That meant a lot to him, to not be directed by anybody else, to have some ownership over his days and how he spent them. No teachers telling him what to do. No mam yelling at him and spanking him. No boys in the schoolyard screaming his name, shouting that he was a useless nobody. A pathetic loner.

Wind screeched across the area, pushing at his back, invisible fingers urging him on, guiding him. Telling him to keep going. He imagined somebody standing behind him, shoving him forwards. An unseen guide. His ally.

It only took a couple of minutes to spot it. That was, he decided, his special skill – having the ability to seek out hidden areas that others couldn't find. It was the raised mound of grass that gave it away. He followed it around to the other side, the wind cooling his face. His hands and throat burned with anticipation. He dropped to his knees to see a small opening that reached his shoulders. Like a hobbit hole. He shivered and bent down, peering at it through narrowed eyes. A tangle of knotted weeds obscured the door, years of growth blocking the entrance to his very own den. His special secret space. Nobody had been here for years and years. Everybody knew it was here but nobody except him had been brave enough to dare to venture this far. He was the only one with enough courage to do it. The popping candy in his belly exploded into a plethora of fireworks, a glorious display of patterns and bright colours that burst inside him, firing off in all directions.

His hands shook as he leaned forwards and grabbed a handful of foliage, pulling and tugging, dragging it away from the metal door beneath. Sharp thorns and small barbs tore at his fingers. It didn't stop him though. He carried on tearing and grabbing, yelping as the small points and spikes stabbed at his skin, until he could see a handle, a small metal circular thing, like a miniature steering wheel. Even before he touched it or attempted to move it, he knew it would be locked. Places like this didn't reveal themselves so easily. He might have only been in junior school but he knew a problem when he saw one. It didn't matter. He was in no rush, nothing pressing. He had days, weeks, months, years even, to work out how to get inside. Nobody knew he was there. He was concealed by the shrubbery and undergrowth, the doorway to this special secret place covered by a huge tangle of weeds that were woven around the perimeter of the entire area. Nobody cared about this place. Nobody except him. He was its new owner. Its precious keeper.

The protector of the New Clear bunker, the place that nobody else dared visit.

25

'I don't know what you mean?' My voice was lost in the thud of approaching footsteps, the scraping sound of somebody opening a door and pushing it ajar.

A triangular spread of light appeared in the doorway, flooding a small area with a bright ochre hue. A figure silhouetted, their body shape a lumpen mass, too hazy and unclear to make out properly, appeared. It stood, the silhouetted form, dark and ominous-looking, in full cinematic glory, framed against a backdrop of blazing light. It lumbered towards me, the dark shape, and bent down, grabbing at my plate and cup. I leaned forward and held on to the mug of water, the fingers of my free hand clasped around it tightly. I was ready to do battle, to hang on to the filthy tin mug and to fight my corner. A rage burned inside of me. I may have been chained up like an animal, my feet bound, but my spirit wasn't broken. Not yet. I still had some fight left in me. Enough to stand my ground. Enough to insist I had access to clean fresh water. At some point I may come undone and capitulate to this person's demands, but we hadn't reached that point just yet. If this monster had wanted me dead, they would have done it by now. They hadn't. I was still here, still breathing. Still plotting and planning. For now.

'Suit yerself.' A slight tussle before they let go of the mug and backed away, but not before I managed to get a look at their face.

Much like their body, their features were bland and unremarkable, with pasty skin and dead-looking eyes. Instantly forgettable and yet, at the same time, utterly terrifying. *They* were now recognizable as a *he*, that much I could tell. No longer an amorphous lump, I was able to see that my attacker was a large, lumbering monster of a man. Too big to fight off. For now. The dead look in his eyes told me that he wasn't the brightest of people. Perhaps I could outwit him, talk him round. Or maybe not. It's not easy reasoning with a sick-minded person.

The crack of light disappeared, the door pulled to with a dull thud and we were left alone once more, a thundering silence ringing in my ears. Beside me, I could hear breathing, could sense the other woman watching me.

Her voice was husky. 'Why did you call me Sian earlier?'

Exhaustion rattled at my chest. My head thumped, an ache setting in behind my eyes. 'Because that's who you are, isn't it?'

I thought of Sian Dupre, her face, wishing I'd turned when the door was open, taken a long hard look at this person sitting beside me.

'No.' Her voice was clear, verging on angry. 'I'm not called Sian.'

My head swam. I was unsure how to articulate what I was about to say without appearing unhinged. The banging of my heart in my chest made me nauseous. I needed to speak slowly, clearly. Get the story right. But one thing first. Before all that.

'So who are you?'

I knew what her answer was going to be before she replied. It was the only thing left that made any sense. Not that it did make sense. The whole debacle was wrong and horribly cruel. I mouthed the words before she was able to even say them, the name rolling off my tongue with practised ease.

Myra. The lady next to me was Myra Simons. Missing for so long, everyone thinking she had become depressed and taken her own life when in reality it had been taken from her and she had been held here against her will. Kept captive by somebody in this damp, dank place.

I wanted to weep, thinking of how long she had been here, all these years, all the things that had been taken from her. Her life put on hold by a maniac.

I wanted to hear her story, to find out whether it was similar to mine, that she had been attacked, struck from behind and brought here in an unconscious state. She tried to speak but was too weak. I moved closer and reached across, horrified to feel bone through her clothes. She was emaciated, her skin pale and shrivelled. Beside her was a slip of paper. I snatched it up with my free hand and shoved it beneath my legs before reaching back and stuffing it into my pocket.

The door swung open, slamming into the wall with such force, my whole body juddered. I shrank away from him, my body curling up into a ball. It was instinctive, a way of protecting myself from his loose fists and violent temper.

'Stop talking!' he roared into the room, the sound and strength of his voice stilling my blood, turning my insides to water. 'I don't want to hear your voice again, d'you hear me?'

I didn't reply, was too terrified say anything. And yet, a part of me refused to back down. In spite of his size, his obvious strength and deranged ways, I wouldn't let him see how frightened I was. Disgust rippled through me as I saw him standing there, his face lined with fury. I unfurled myself and sat upright, doing my utmost to show him I wasn't scared of him even though my nerve endings were alight, my brain screaming at me to look away, not rile him any further. Sometimes it's easier to ignore those thoughts, to override our initial reactions and do what we think is right, not what our senses think is safe and acceptable. We have to push those boundaries, be brave and search for answers. So I sat there, back straight, muscles flexed and ready – ready for what, I didn't quite know – and stared at him, at his pale, flabby face, his dark eyes and rounded posture, at his huge hands and blackened nails. At his seething anger and lumbering, unwieldy body. He was a shocking sight, like a creature from a movie of old with a face carved out of clay, his complexion pale and craggy, his narrowed eyes full of hatred.

He took a step towards me and I could see then in greater detail his decayed face, his pockmarked, flabby skin. He had the look of somebody who had aged badly, lacked self-care and daylight. Is this what he did? Lived his life in a darkened room, hiding away from the rest of the people on the island? I didn't recognise him, hadn't seen him before now, but then, I hadn't met everybody on Winters End.

There was so much I wanted to say, to ask. So many words stored up inside my head. I knew then to stay quiet, to pick my moments carefully. He was clearly a very powerful man. I wasn't weak. I wasn't feeble or stupid for getting trapped by him. He was a monster, a huge wall of a man. I stood no chance.

'Toilet,' he said, his finger pointing at nobody in particular.

I didn't say or do anything, not even daring to breathe. I was slumped here in the semi-darkness, my surroundings unknown. Chained up in a dark room somewhere, held captive by this monster of a man with a face like melted putty and hands as large as shovels.

'Don't move.' He was standing over me, his finger pointing in my face. Flecks of spittle coated his mouth, his rubbery lips quivering as he spoke. 'Just wait.'

I didn't respond and kept my gaze lowered, refusing to let him see my fear. Or my anger. I would show him nothing, this beast of a man. For once, being deceitful and lying with impunity would pave the way to better things. Or at least I hoped so.

In the corner of the room was a broken wooden chair and next to it was an old metal filing cabinet, its drawers open, the contents strewn around, pieces of yellowed paper and Manila folders littering the floor. A bare bulb hung overhead, accentuating the starkness of the white walls. Aside from the toilet in the corner, there was little else around. Apart, that is, from the metal chains hanging from walls that were keeping me prisoner in this place, like cattle.

I wanted to speak, every sinew straining, a series of questions burning at my brain. I asked them over and over in my head. *Who are you? Where am I? Why are you doing this?* I wasn't gagged but the walls were solid. Very little chance of anybody hearing me should I decide to scream for my life, to holler and yell until my throat was hoarse. I tried to visualise this place, to recall some of the deserted buildings I had passed on my travels across Winters End. A basement, perhaps? A derelict farmhouse or an old barn? I thought of the run-down place I had passed on my walk and knew we couldn't be there. The windows had been broken, the brickwork crumbling. This room was somewhere remote, its walls thick and intact.

'Right,' he said, leaning down towards me. A large forefinger was pointed in my face, crescents of dirt lodged under the nail. 'Toilet. And no messin' about.'

I wanted to scream and lash out and gnash my teeth at this monstrosity of a man. To tell him to fuck off and leave me alone. The reek from his armpit when he leaned across to unlock the chain on my wrist was unbearable. His breath was even worse, a rancid, stale stink that hung around my face.

'Get up. Now.' The stench of his fetid breath continued to linger, his eyes scanning my face, my breasts, my legs.

Please God, no. Anything but that.

His big hands pulled me up off the floor and led me to the cubicle. I glanced down at the figure of a rake-thin Myra, at her shrivelled features and lank hair, her emaciated body and ragged clothes, and suppressed a sob. This was wrong. Everything was wrong. It wasn't happening. It couldn't be. I thought of Neil, of our little cottage. Our new life on this isolated island, and wanted to scream at this monster, tell him that he had no fucking right to be doing this to me. To us. How dare he rip apart my world like this? A world I had carefully constructed to keep my sanity intact. A thousand thoughts crossed my mind as he wrestled with me, forcing me upright: how deranged this whole thing was, how much I missed Neil and needed him, how I wished I had appreciated the small things, things I may never ever see again. Blue skies, distant birdsong, the feel of the wind in my hair, the soft breeze as it caressed my face. I yearned for them all.

Rope cut into my ankles as I slipped and hobbled my way into the cubicle. The door was slammed shut behind me, his grunts filtering through the thin laminated surface of the flimsy door. I looked up and saw nothing but the same concrete ceiling. No escape hatches. No loose boards. Of course not. I took a deep breath and undid my trousers and pants, lowering myself onto the squalid cracked toilet seat, shame burning at me. What if I stayed in the cubicle, waited for him to break down the door then threw myself at him, knocking him over? I could do that. I was injured, my head still sore, but I was strong enough to put up a fight if I caught him unawares. My feet were tied up but my hands were free. Surely, I could do something? I thought of his size, the sheer bulk of his body. His height and the unmistakable brutality of the man, but decided to do something regardless. I leaned down, my fingers frantically working at the rope. Air swelled in my throat. I swallowed it down, trying to remain silent, my gasps and grunts contained within me while I picked at the strands of thick rope with my nails.

'Hurry up. Got a knife out 'ere so don't try any funny stuff. I ain't in the mood for it, you hear me?'

Was that possible, that he did actually have a knife on him? I hadn't seen one. It was an idle threat; I was sure of it. A stupid, childish way of keeping me in line. A stupid, unsophisticated way of—

'Now! Open the door or I'll batter it down.'

'I need more time.' My voice wobbled. I took a few deep breaths, rubbed at my face. 'I'm on my period. I need a sanitary towel.'

A grunt. Footsteps faded away, returning within seconds. I waited, bracing myself, trying to gather what little strength I had.

'Not got anything like that in this place. Here, use this.'

A toilet roll was thrown over the top of the cubicle. I pulled up my trousers, closed my eyes and leaned back against the cold porcelain of the toilet, wondering what to do when I unlocked the door, whether

I should take my chances and risk his wrath or be the submissive woman he expected me to be. The sound of my feet squeaking against the concrete floor thrummed in my ears. I bent over and picked up the loose piece of rope, shoving it deep into my pocket. It had been a crudely tied knot. No need for anything too elaborate or too tight. I was chained to a wall. That was his thinking. That is, if there was any thinking behind this macabre set-up. I didn't want to give this monster any credibility for his actions. Maybe he was just too ham-fisted to tie a tighter knot, his brain too addled to carry out any intricate methods of imprisonment. He had solid concrete walls. What else did he need?

'I won't be a minute,' I said weakly, hoping the thought of me bleeding would sour any ideas he had of creeping up on me while I was chained up, doing unthinkable things to me that would leave an indelible stain on my memory. On my bruised and battered body.

I knew what I had to do next. It crackled in my head, the idea that I could do it. And the repercussions that would take place if it all went wrong. The dreadful punishments this man could mete out to me. Visions of him lying on top of me, his hands tearing at my clothes, filled my head, his large hands roaming over my flesh. His fists being driven into my body. I shuddered and shut out those thoughts. No matter. I had to do something. I refused to give in to this creature, to abide by his hideous, warped rules. The time was right. Time to do something before I became starved, dehydrated, and stripped of all strength. Before I became Myra, trapped in this filthy place for years on end. That thought made my head spin, forcing me to take action. I had to get out.

I flexed my fingers, my feet, and my arms, loosening them. Readying myself for my next move. I had to do this. As frightening and risky as it was, I couldn't let him keep me here. Neil was out there, waiting for me. Wondering where I was. Perhaps even thinking that I was dead, had fallen over the edge of the cliff or, worse still, had stood there willingly, my mood so low that I had taken the dreadful decision to leave him forever, everything too bleak for me to continue.

I slid the bolt across before tentatively pushing at the door, wondering how close he was. Wondering if he would grab me as soon as it was opened. There was no point in waiting. I had to do this. I promised myself I would put up a fight and that was what I would do. I took a breath, braced myself, my body bent low, my arms tensed and ready, my hands curled into fists, shoulders tight, and with an almighty roar that pro-pelled me into action and caught him unawares, I threw myself out, Neil's face, his sweet, sweet face blooming in my mind, telling me I could do this. Telling me to live, that I had to get out of there and back home where he was waiting for me.

26

NEIL

Forty-eight hours? Forty-eight fucking hours before they would do anything to try and find her? It had to be some kind of sick joke, surely?

He'd given in too easily, that was the problem, had acquiesced and put down the phone before he'd had a chance to think of what needed to be said to catapult them into action. The body on the beach. That would have worked, surely? Or that other missing woman, the ornithologist. Maybe Fiona was right and they were one and the same. Seems that she had been right about a lot of things lately. All those things, if he had said them, would have helped build a bigger picture, given the police more reasons to suspect that something was terribly wrong on the island. But he hadn't.

He let himself be manipulated by the smooth-talking person on the other end of the line who knew exactly what to say while he stuttered and stammered, his mind a whirling vortex of fear and confusion, perspiration coating his top lip, gathering in tiny iridescent pearls around his hairline. By the time he had finished speaking to them, he was a sweating wreck, fear and confusion turning him into a gibbering mess of a man.

He needed to call them back, ask for an officer – no, a whole team, actually – to be sent over to Winters End. He would demand they comb the island from end to end. His shoulders slumped, his body buckling as he sat down on the floor, fingers splayed over his face, tears leaking through. He hadn't done enough. Once again, he had let down the one person he cared deeply about and was failing to fight his wife's corner when she needed him the most. And now, rather than getting out there and tearing around the island leaving nowhere unsearched, he was sitting here, weeping into his hands, his body wracked with sobs like a big fucking baby.

The creaking of the floor, the rustle of his clothing, they all thundered in his ears as he stood up, his large fingers sweeping downwards over his sweater, his trousers, rearranging himself, straightening the crumpled fabric. A firm, austere plan, that was what he needed, a way of locating Fiona, making sure she came back home safely. It's what Fiona would do. For all of her worries and anxieties, she always made sure she got the job done, saw things through to the very end. He would do the same. He would find her, no matter how long it took, how arduous a task it proved to be. He was her husband, she was his wife. He loved her.

But he needed to do one thing first. A painful task that would make his toes curl with shame. It would also cause endless worry and he didn't want that but couldn't think what else to do.

His hand trembled as he punched in the number, even more so than his call to the emergency services. This was a personal call, so much emotion behind it.

Chrissie picked up after two rings. He winced, had hoped that it was going to be Kate who answered. Wished it had been her. He remembered with a certain amount of horrible clarity the strained relationship Chrissie and Fiona had. His sister's partner was a tough one to deal with, her coarse edges difficult to smooth. The money debacle had simply finalised any chances they had of her ever softening towards them. He had considered calling Fiona's parents but didn't want to worry them unnecessarily. All he wanted to know was whether Fiona had contacted any of them, whether she had made the decision to head back home to the mainland and was currently safe with Dot and Ralph, his parents-in-law, the two people who stuck by them without complaint.

His chest hummed and vibrated. It was difficult to find the right words, words that wouldn't cause worry, wouldn't elicit the wrong response from this woman. Words that wouldn't cause another argument. He just wanted to find his wife.

'Chrissie? Is Kate there?'

A short silence, the sound of low breathing followed by the clatter of the phone being placed on a hard surface. Thrown probably. With force.

'Hello?'

Hearing his sister's voice almost brought him to his knees. Lovely Kate. Ugly visions of her being dominated by her headstrong partner took form in his mind. He hoped that wasn't the case. She deserved kindness and happiness and so much more.

'Kate? It's me.' His voice was thick with emotion, a tightness pulling at the back of his throat.

'Neil? Are you okay? You sound, I dunno, a bit different. What's up?'

Something had to be up. They both knew it. Contact had been sporadic, almost non-existent since they had paid back the money. He had wanted to get in touch, to say hello and let her know that things were still okay between them and felt sure that Kate had wanted to as well, but everything was too raw, the atmosphere too strained to take the step and call one another. And now here he was, clutching at straws, unsure how to ask his sister for help, unsure how to tell her how desperate and worried he was. Unsure how to tell her that Fiona was missing and that he was frightened she had fled back to Saltburn, never to return. She had been the one who had initially wanted to move to Winters End but only because of his stupidity and the mess he had created. She had craved solitude and obscurity, somewhere where nobody knew of her crime. And now she was gone.

'Neil? Look, I know things haven't been easy for any of us but I'm really glad you've called.' She lowered her voice to not quite a whisper but a soft, gentle utterance. He guessed she was trying to evade being heard by Chrissie. 'I've been meaning to ring you but things here have been – tricky.' She continued, jumping in before he could interject with any comments about her partner. 'I mean, not awful or anything, just – well, you know how it is. But it is getting better, I promise. I don't want to lose touch with you or Fiona. I've missed you.'

A lump rose in his throat. Lovely, forgiving Kate. Always thoughtful. Always tender, ready to lend a helping hand.

He bit at his lip, willing his brain to work as it should, for the sentences to come spilling out of him. He could do this. He just needed to calm down, start thinking rationally, to stop acting like a child. Fiona would have spoken by now, found the guts to say what needed to be said. She would—

'Neil, what's the matter? You're starting to scare me. Can you please say something? What's going on?'

And so he said it, the words pouring out of him, hot and unsteady, his syllables clipped and disjointed. He asked if she had heard from Fiona, told her of his fears that she had fled home to her parents' house, her mind fractured by their recent past.

'Neil, no—'

'So, I think that maybe if I can find out whether Dot and Ralph have—'

'Neil!'

He stopped speaking, his ears buzzing, his head aching from the sheer effort of unloading his anxieties on to Kate.

'Fiona isn't with Dot and Ralph.'

'How do you know?' Something grew in his chest, something that was stopping him from breathing. A ferocious, rapidly expanding fear unfurling itself like a sleeping monster that was awakening and coming to life, claws sharpened, teeth bared.

'Because I've just seen them. I've just got back from town and they were there, parked up next to my car. We chatted for a couple of minutes. They asked if I had heard from you or Fiona, said a telephone call was long overdue.'

The air was heavy with his fear, the sour stench of terror rising out of his pores.

'So, if she's not with her parents and she's not with you, then where the fuck is she, Neil? Where has Fiona gone?'

A twisting, tumbling sensation took hold in his stomach, his head full of serrated edges as he slumped to the floor. For the second time that day, he felt himself sinking into the darkest of places, a tight corner full of shadows and sneering, unforgiving faces. Nobody around to help him, nowhere to go that he knew or recognised. It was as if everything he had always taken for granted and accepted as real and per-ceptible was being pulled away from him, leaving him cold and vulnerable, exposed to the elements, roughed up by the howling wind and pelting rain un-til, eventually, there would be nothing left of him, just a pile of dry, crumbling bones.

'I don't know,' was all he was able to say. 'I honestly don't know.'

The wooden floor felt cold and hard beneath him as he continued to sit there, the phone clutched between his freezing fingers.

'Neil, what's going on? Are you there?'

Kate's voice was a distant clanging, a tinny echo. A jumble of words with no meaning.

He sat up, desperation doing its damnedest to pull him back down.

'Neil! What the fuck is happening? Speak to me.'

'I don't know,' was all he could manage to utter, his mouth lacking in moisture, his tongue suddenly horribly dry and too big for his mouth. 'I honestly and truly don't know.'

27

BEFORE

It took a few attempts and several visits where he brought some of his dad's old tools, digging and wrenching at the door with screwdrivers, before he was able to get inside. But in the end, he did it. And it was worth the effort. The New Clear bunker had been everything he dreamed of and more. The popping candy had exploded in his belly when he first saw it, a thousand fireworks going off, firing in all directions, warming up and softening his pulpy flesh, burning their way through his veins, making him feel important and vital. Nobody else had ever managed to get in. He was the first. He was the special one. The clever one. It was his and his alone. His secret place. Somewhere he could go when things got difficult. An escape room. That's what it was: his very own escape room. Two escape rooms, actually. He headed through the first small area to another bigger room, more excitement bubbling up in his belly when he spotted it.

He had wandered around, torch in hand, slack-jawed as he took it all in. The walls were white and featureless like a prison cell but that didn't bother him. He had spent the next half hour pretending to be a prisoner, working out what crime he had committed. Breaking and entering. He liked the sound of that one. He had broken into the New Clear bunker so was obviously good at it. A professional, even. Or he could be a weapons expert, storing them in here, selling knives and guns to other criminals. The possibilities were endless.

It occurred to him that he needed to keep the place hidden. Nobody else would be allowed to see it. He would conceal the entrance with branches and shrubbery, hide it away from the rest of the people on the island. They didn't need to know that he had opened it up and he definitely didn't want the other boys at school discovering his new special place.

Time ticked away as he explored the small area, the thought of leaving, going back home, looming large in his mind. But he would come back. Every day if need be.

Which was exactly what he did. He needed nobody else. Just him, his imagination, and his bunker.

* * *

It was a cold day in March, decades later, the weather
bitingly cold, the sea dark and frantic, when he pur-
sued his first one. It had been a slow build-up of resentment and loathing when he finally decided that
the time was right. He didn't take her back there, to
his secret place, simply knocked her to the ground instead and drank in her discomfort and pain, feeding
on it like a predator. It was a practice run for the future. He had it in him – the anger, the frustration. The
hatred. He knew it then, that it was a lead-up to something bigger. Something better, more ferocious. Something final. It excited him, that thought, that he had
the strength, the ability, the power to do those things.
It made him stand up just that little bit taller, gave
him the confidence to face the world and its tormen-
tors. The confidence to face his mam and her daily
taunts and sick little rituals.

He had stood over his victim after pushing her
down, watching her, even giving her a little kick
whenever she moved or squirmed. Or just whenever
he felt like it, whenever he felt the urge to do it. Anger

travelling down his body, through his muscles to the end of his large steel-toe-capped boots. She wasn't dead. It wouldn't have mattered if she was. She was a nobody to him. An irritant. The type of female who looked down on him, sneering whenever she passed by, her lip curled at him in contempt. That's how they were round these parts – superior, aloof, indifferent. Bitches, each and every one of them.

He had grown tired of watching her and left, and when she had eventually come round she had gone into the local pub, shouting the odds about him, telling everyone what a fucking maniac he was, how he should be locked away from the rest of the is-landers. How he should never have been born. That one had stung. He had heard that particular trope be-fore from his mam. She used to say it often: that he should have been the one who died. He should have been the one who was crushed by a gravestone, his skull smashed into a hundred tiny pieces, his ribs pushed deep into his lungs beneath the weight of the ancient granite slab.

As cutting as those comments were about him being depraved and a psychopath and how he should be shut away from his family and friends, they didn't stop him. Nothing would have stopped him. He knew that. It was just how he was: a personality flaw carved deep into his soul. Part of his genetic make-up. Maybe his mam had always known it and that was why she hated him.

The next time he got the longing, it had been for real, a taster of what it felt like to do it properly, to finish somebody for good. It was something to whet his appetite, get his juices flowing. And it was easy too. They all made it so easy for him. Stupid and pathetic, that's what they were. If they didn't have the bravery or nous to fight back, then as far as he could see, they didn't deserve to breathe the same air as him. They thought they were superior to him. They were wrong. He was the bright one, the strong one. The one who made a difference to the island, ridding it of its pests and vermin, cleaning up the place, making sure only the worthy walked the land.

It didn't take too long and the best thing was nobody suspected a thing. He was cleverer than they realised, cleverer than even he realised. He had seen her from his boat, swimming gracefully, long-limbed and competent. She had stopped, waved at him and mouthed something that he couldn't make out. It had been a disparaging remark, he felt sure of it. They always were. Any words thrown his way were always loaded with malice and distrust and loathing. He had moved closer to her and leaned down, his hand cupped around his ear. She had tried to speak again but he hadn't been interested in any of her words, only in what came next.

Her demise was swift. For somebody so fit and agile, and purportedly capable in the water, her struggles were brief, his palm pressing down on the top of her head until she stopped thrashing about and lay there, her hair fanned out around her in the icy water.

Rumours abounded that she been caught in a riptide, that even the most experienced of swimmers could run into trouble in the unpredictable and fast-changing currents of the North Sea. Nobody suspected him. That thrilled him, kept the excitement coursing through him. But those feelings didn't last. For a long time after killing her, his everyday routine had felt low and empty, his life flatlining. Nothing could match those feelings of excitement, the stirrings of joy that had tingled in his veins when he realised she was dead. He needed to do it again, to reach those dizzy euphoric heights that only that sort of finality could bring.

He hadn't planned on it happening that day. It just did. He was supposed to stay hidden after another altercation with his mam, but the warmth of the day was too difficult to resist, the outside air a delicious soft taste on his tongue, the salt of the sea coating his mouth, lodging in his gums and sticking to his teeth. It felt good to be free, to feel the breeze on his face, to have the heat of the late sun kiss his flesh with the gentlest of touches. No work that day. Nobody at home telling him what to do, how stupid he was. How useless and unwanted he was.

It was an unchallenging task getting around the island, making sure nobody saw him. He waited until the light began to fade. So few people around, so many overgrown footpaths and dimly lit lanes. It was so easy. A piece of piss.

The front door was unlocked making it oh-so simple for him. It was her own fault. She was asking for it, leaving herself wide open like that. Anybody could have wandered in, done something terrible to her. And he did. That always made him smile, that sentence, the way he was able to justify his actions.

Nobody saw him creep inside the house. She was alone. He knew that. Her husband was away working in Newcastle. He was free to do as he pleased. No male protector around to stop him. He may have spent his days holed away from everybody, stuck in his poky little room on his own, but he still knew what was going on around him. He had ears, a brain, was able to work out what was going on in other people's lives.

The light in the living room was dim but he could see that she wasn't in there. Neither was she in the kitchen. Or the dining room. Then came the telltale creak from upstairs.

Electricity surged through him at the thought of going up there. Maybe she was in the bath, or getting undressed in the bedroom. A tingle took hold in his groin, a twinge of excitement as he pictured her sprawled out on the bed, underwear strewn over the floor. Waiting for him. Murmuring his name over and over.

Slowly, he made his way up, his footsteps muffled against the thick pile of the carpet. Darts of desire speared his abdomen, burning his flesh. He stopped at the top, listening for something. Anything. He needed a clue, a sense of direction. Something to guide him, something to tell him where she was.

The bathroom was empty, the door ajar. Which left one of the bedrooms. Giddy with desire, he tip-toed to what he guessed must be the main bedroom. She would be in there, waiting for him. Calling his name, licking her lips. Spreading her legs.

'Who is it?' The sound of her voice cooled his ardour, like an iceberg smashing into him, knocking him sideways. Tipping him into the freezing ocean. He hated her. He hated her voice, he hated her house.

He hated the way she had already spoiled everything before it had even had a chance to begin.

'If you've come for the milk money, I've left it under the plant pot next to the front window.'

A creak, a movement. She was coming closer, heading out onto the landing. He stopped, rooted to the spot. All of a sudden, it was real. It was happening. Freezing water lapped around him, stopping him from thinking clearly, numbing his brain, his movements.

More creaking, floorboards shifting and groaning. A pain took hold in his belly. This wasn't how he thought it would be. It was different from the other time. Trickier. Scarier. Something swirled and churned inside him, his bowels bloated with fear. She could shut herself away in the bedroom if she saw him, pick up her phone. Make life difficult for him. Last time was unbelievably easy. One push and she was sucked under the sea, dark water swallowing her slim body, turning her skin blue. That had excited him, made him want to scream with joy, to open up his lungs and holler that he was here and he had a right to live as others did. He had been alone the other time, nobody around, just the two of them and the deep, cold sea. But this. This one was different. It felt as if he was trapped, confined in a small space. His escape routes limited.

A darkness spread across the banister as she appeared, her shadow trailing down the stairs, zigzagging down the wall. She opened her mouth to say something. He had to silence her, to stop the scream from getting out. He stepped forwards, hands outstretched, their bodies colliding.

In the end it proved to be easy, the fluidity and seamlessness of it restoring his equilibrium. One swift push, that was all it took. One surge of strength and she was gone, her body toppling downwards, the sound of her bones as they hit each step making his soul soar and his senses sing like a bird that has taken to the skies after being freed from captivity. That was how he felt. Every killing allowed a little more daylight back into his life. Another step closer to the warmth of the sunshine.

The tingling in his groin returned as he stared down at her unmoving body, her open eyes and lifeless form, the way her legs were splayed, the fact that her blouse had shifted, a soft, shiny breast slightly visible beneath the white fabric.

A gasp emerged from his throat. He moved his fingers, trailing them over the front of his trousers, undoing the zip, slipping them inside his underwear, rubbing at the flaccid lump of flesh there, willing it to life. A rage overcame him. He wanted to roar and beat his fists against the nearest wall. It was always the same. It was useless. He was useless.

As quietly and nimbly as a feral cat, he raced downstairs and out of the front door, wiping the handle as he left. That much he knew – to not leave any evidence behind, anything that could incriminate him. Not that it would matter. He was a nobody around these parts: an invisible man, a ghost. Everybody knew this couldn't have been his fault, not least because as far as anybody knew, he was already dead.

28

I hit a wall. That was how it felt, my arched body slamming into a mountain of a man. A hot wave of pain flared up and down my arm where I barged at him, the crunch of the bones in my shoulder causing me to gasp. He was silent at first, as if my actions took a few seconds to register in his brain. Then he moved, his sudden roar, the heat of his breath like an erupting volcano, white-hot anger spilling and spreading around the room, bubbling and dispersing around me. Fear rooted me to the spot, stopping me from moving. I felt paralysed, time slowing down, dulling my thinking. I knew that I had to do something. My life depended on it. He couldn't win. I wouldn't let him. I forced myself out of my terror-induced stupor, throwing off the shackles of fear, breaking free and springing into action. This was my only chance. I knew that. I couldn't give in, not when I had created an opportunity and made the first move to try and escape. I had to give it my best shot. Be my best self. My strongest self. For me, for Neil, and for Myra. Quiet, emaciated Myra who was slumped on the floor, silent and unmoving. The thought of spending another day in this place filled me with such horror I could hardly breathe. She had been here for years. I wouldn't let that happen. I needed my freedom, my life back to how it was. I needed Neil.

'No running! You need to stop it. Sit down, stupid bitch. Sit the fuck down!'

His words sailed over my head. They held no meaning for me and posed no threat. I wouldn't do as he asked. I wouldn't give him the pleasure of seeing me capitulate to his demands. I was going to be sturdier than that. I was going to put up the biggest fight of my life which would hopefully take him by surprise, catching him completely off guard, giving me a distinct advantage.

A loud buzzing filled my head, insects swarming around my brain. He made a move towards me, his bulky frame towering over me, arms curled in front of him as if he planned on scooping me up and crushing me. He was large but I was smaller and more agile, nimbler than he could ever hope to be.

I needed a weapon, something sharp, and if there was anything close by I had to get to it before he did. I didn't believe he had a knife. He would have been holding it by now, brandishing it as a way of scaring me, keeping me in line. All he had was his hands and his superior strength.

We began our macabre dance, my feet shuffling, my body darting about trying to avoid his grasp. If he lunged at me, I would be trapped beneath his bulk, my body crushed by his inescapable weight and solidity.

While he let out a loud bark of disapproval, I pushed past him, slipping beneath his outstretched arm and out of his reach. It wouldn't last long, my advantage, I knew that. I had to find something to use against him. Something heavy and sharp. Flames burned at my head, behind my eyes, marring my vision. My blood bubbled and boiled. I needed to stop, to think clearly, not get bogged down by my own growing terror. The terror that was very real. If I didn't succeed, then I would die. He would pick me up as if I was made of air and he would crush me between his large, crooked fingers, blood and bone slithering out onto the concrete floor.

I was driven on by my reflexes, no time for meticulous planning or forethought. Putting my whole weight behind the metal filing cabinet, I ran at it and pushed, a scream rushing up my throat and out of my mouth. It gave me strength, that scream, and I watched as the cabinet toppled, the drawers falling forwards, the metallic crashing sound it made as it hit the ground, bouncing around the room, rattling in my ears.

Luck played its part. It certainly wasn't intentional but for once the gods were smiling down on me as the corner of the heavy cabinet caught his ankle, a shard of twisted metal digging into his lower leg. His howl was animalistic; the cry of a wild creature caught in a snare.

It wouldn't be enough to stop him but it was enough to give me some extra time to work out what to do next. The key for the chain that was shackling Myra was in his pocket. I stood no chance of retrieving it so I could free her. She was too weak to move anyway. I had to do this thing on my own. Whatever *this thing* was. I had no idea what my next move would be. Not a clue. While he struggled with his injury, grasping at his leg and trying to stop the flow of blood, I took a chance and ran for the door. I didn't recall him locking it but couldn't be certain. It opened, not exactly with ease, but with a heavy groan. I put every-thing I had behind it, every bit of strength and energy within me, leaning and pushing, shocked at the weight and sturdiness of it. What did I expect? An easy escape route accompanied by signposts? There was a reason Myra had been here for so long. This place was a fortress, hidden somewhere on Winters End. Nobody knew about it. If I didn't get out this time, then I felt sure I would never see daylight ever again.

Myra was ominously silent, any noise she may have been making drowned out by his shouts and roars, and his growling protestations. I wanted to stop, to look down at her, at her bony body and grey face, but didn't have time. It was now or never. So I left them both behind, ignoring his shrieks and cries for me to sit the fuck back down, to stop or he would kill me, and squeezed through the crack in the door, step-ping out into the unknown. I had no idea what I was going to be greeted with, no time to think about it or prepare. All I knew was I had to get out of there, had to keep on going. No looking back. No hesitating. Just freedom.

My chest was fit to burst, my heart banging furi-ously against my ribcage when I stumbled into the next room and saw a door that looked suspiciously like the kind of metal structure that would have a huge locking mechanism. Behind me, I could hear him stumbling about, his huge, ungainly frame banging into walls as he attempted to scramble up and right himself. I didn't have time to stand around thinking about exits and locks and bolts. I had to get out.

The handle was cold and heavy as I turned it and prayed. It moved. Trying to contain my cry of desperation that was gilded with hope was impossible. Even heavier than the other door, it still moved a fraction; its weight, although still providing some resistance, didn't stop it completely. I grasped it with both hands and pulled, my fingers slipping against the smooth metallic surface of the circular handle.

'No!'

He threw himself at me, his massive, towering body slamming into me with force. I felt my chin hit the edge of the door, my teeth biting down on my tongue as my jaws clamped together. A swill of blood filled my mouth, travelling down my throat, making me choke and gag. Tears misted my vision, my face burned hot. I could feel his large, sweaty hands pressed around my lower body, his fingers pushing into my waist.

I don't know how we did it, but we ended up on

the floor, our bodies locked together. Still, my hand remained curled around the edge of the door. If he decided to slam it shut, I would lose my fingers. I needed to do something else, something forceful to stop him. I began to twist and turn, attempting to loosen his grip on my torso. It was vice-like, the hold he had on me, his large, fat fingers pressing against my hip bones and into my flesh. He was strong but he wasn't dexterous. I imagined him pressing so hard that he ruptured my vital organs, lacerating my liver and puncturing my spleen. As quickly and nimbly as I could, I began to twist my body, bending and turning, my legs kicking out at him. Once again, I got lucky and felt my foot hit against something soft. I quickly glanced behind me and saw my heel catch the side of his face. Blood was seeping out, thin ruby rivulets springing out of the long gash just below his eye. It was fractional, the slackening of his fingers, but I took advantage of it and jumped up, dancing away from his lumbering frame. I did the thing that I knew would render him useless and brought my foot back, slamming it between his legs with a burst of energy and hatred that I didn't know I possessed. He let out a high-pitched scream and began rocking about on the floor, curled up into a foetal position, hands clasped at his groin. Soon his pain would dissipate and he would be up on his feet, grabbing at me, pinning me down. The shock and agony of my kick wouldn't last for long, certainly not long enough for me to escape. He would scramble to his feet and follow me and when he caught me, he would almost certainly kill me, his huge fingers clasped around my windpipe, stopping me from breathing until I turned blue and collapsed to the floor, my limbs floppy and inert like a rag doll. I wasn't about to let that happen so brought my foot back and kicked him again as hard as I could, the sensation of my toes meeting with the soft skin of his scrotum filling me with a sense of elation and relief. His head jerked back, his mouth opening as a scream filled the room. I could see the back of his throat, his rotten teeth, the pink hue of his tongue and the globules of saliva that spilled from his lips. Then I turned and once more curled my fingertips around the edge of the steel door and pulled.

29

NEIL

'There's no way for you to get here.' Neil's voice was croaky, his hopes diminishing. 'The last ferry is in an hour.'

'Neil, I can get to the quayside in less than twenty minutes. Don't try to talk me out of it. I'm on my way.' Kate's voice was like being immersed in a warm bath.

'But what about Chrissie? Things are already tricky between you. You can't—'

'You're my brother. You need my help. That's all there is to it. Stay where you are. I'm on my way.'

'Hang on!' He was gasping, finding it hard to get enough air into his lungs. 'I'm going back out to look for her. I'll leave the door unlocked. Nobody is going to break in. If you get here and I'm not at the cottage, call me on my mobile.' He didn't give Kate any time to reply or to protest, cutting in before she could say anything in return. She had their address, would be able to find them without any problem on Winters End, the tiny, sinister place they now called home. The tiny, menacing island that was slowly turning their lives into a living nightmare. He wasn't entirely certain about his assurances that nobody would enter their unlocked cottage after tonight. He wasn't certain about anything any more. Not here on Winters End, where all the usual rules and protocols didn't apply. 'And I'll contact the police again while I'm out.' He ended the call before Kate could reply. Before she could try to persuade him to change his mind and stay put until she arrived. There was no way he was going to sit and do nothing for the next hour. Time was precious. The day was ebbing away, almost gone completely. Every minute counted.

Once again, he rang Fiona, his hand trembling as he held his mobile to his ear, unsurprised but also bitterly disappointed to discover her phone was still turned off. His head swam. She wasn't on the mainland. She was still here somewhere on the island. Thoughts of the sea sprang into his mind. The sea and the cliff path. Everything always came back to the sea and that stupid fucking cliff path.

Fucking hell!

He headed back out to his car, torch in hand, and all but threw himself into the seat, his weepiness now replaced by a growing anger at how almost everyone around him had turned their backs, refusing to help him. What was wrong with these people? With this island? How had he not seen it before now? Was he so wrapped up in his own life that, unlike Fiona, he had been blind to how selfish and strange these people were? She had known it from the very beginning and he hadn't been able to see it. If he was being truthful, it was because he hadn't wanted to see it. There were signs there but he had ignored them. Blocked them out. He had been lazy and selfish.

His foot pressed down hard on the accelerator, the engine revving wildly while he thought about what to do next. Driving around in the dark would solve nothing. He needed a plan, somewhere to go. Something more concrete than simply scanning nearby bushes and thickets in the hope of finding her. He thought about what the police would do and decided to retrace Fiona's route to the last place he knew for sure she had visited. Once more he would go and see Honnie. He would comb the entire area, searching every hedgerow, every piece of woodland. He would call out Fiona's name, and while he was doing that, he would ring the police again, insist they send somebody out to the island tonight. Not in forty-eight hours. Not tomorrow, but tonight. And only after he had done all of that would he allow himself to think about the unthinkable. Only after he had exhausted every other avenue would he turn to look at the sea, the one place that meant his hopes of her survival in that icy cold ferocious place were almost non-existent. If somebody had taken her, if she had fallen and was lying somewhere waiting for help, then there was a chance of getting her back home. A fall into the sea was final, the thought of Fiona thrashing about before sinking beneath the cold, dark waves making him weak with despair and chilling his blood. He dismissed that image, those macabre thoughts, and concentrated on what he was going to do next, the thought of Kate arriving within the next hour or so fortifying him, giving him enough impetus and energy to keep going. Two heads had to be better than one. Kate didn't know Winters End but then neither did he. Not really. Her fresh eyes, however, might just see things he had missed.

Pushing his foot to the floor, not caring that the heavy growl of the engine would alarm neighbours in the lane, he set off, aware that he was wasting time, his mind raking over unimportant stuff, things that could wait.

The journey to Honnie's house took just a couple of minutes, his breakneck speed halving the time it would usually have taken. He stepped out of his vehicle. First, he would speak again to this woman, then when he was sure she didn't have anything else to tell him, he would search the whole area. It's what the police would do. They would re-enact Fiona's last known movements and her visit to Honnie was exactly that.

* * *

'Told you earlier. She left 'ere. Not seen 'er since.' The old woman's face was scrunched up, deep lines and grooves stretched across her skin, resembling an old, faded newspaper, discarded and damaged by the elements and the passing of time, thought Neil as he watched her from the darkness of the doorstep.

'Did she say where she was going? Any clues at all as to what she was going to do next?' There was a pleading quality to his tone, a desperation that this old lady was impervious to, her hardened countenance showing no signs of cracking or softening. Could she not see how upset and desperate he was? How much he needed her help? What was wrong with everyone on Winters End? Why were they all so fucking reluctant to get involved?

Honnie shook her head and attempted to shut the door. Neil moved forward, placing his palm on the door frame, pushing his foot over the threshold.

'Where is she then, Honora?' He hoped the use of her full name would shock her into action, make her realise how serious this was, that he wasn't about to take no for an answer. 'If she left your house hours ago, why hasn't she arrived back home?'

'She's your wife, in't she? You should know the answer to that question, not me.' A shrug of her shoulders accompanied by a move back into the shadows of her hallway.

Neil felt a rage rising within him, travelling up his abdomen, combusting into a white-hot furnace that burned at his innards, flickering flames licking at his stomach and throat with such intensity that he had to stop himself from lunging at Honnie and placing his fingers around her windpipe until she begged for him to stop.

Shame bloomed in his chest. He took a shaky breath, turned his head to the breeze to allow the air to cool his red-hot face. She was an old lady living here alone and none of this was her fault. This was insane. The whole scenario was insane, nothing making any sense.

'Honnie, please! Please help me?' He was begging and it wasn't pleasant, sitting uncomfortably with him, but it was better than the hatred and desperation he had felt just a few seconds ago. Those emotions were useless, sapping his energy, hindering his search for Fiona.

'Look, get yerself 'ome. There's nowt I can do. Your wife going missing hasn't got anythin' to do wi' me or mine.'

'What about the others?' The words spilled out of him. He hadn't meant to ask but the words had been said now and he couldn't unsay them.

Her eyes narrowed, a suspicious glint in them. 'What others? What you on about? I'm busy, stuff to be getting' on with so if yer don't mind...'

It was out of character, what he did next, so far removed from his usual behaviour that he felt sure he had been possessed, his movements directed by somebody other than him. 'The other women on the island who got injured or died or just went missing. What about them? What happened to them?' He pushed Honnie against the wall as he rushed forward and stepped into the hallway, slamming the door behind him and turning the key, slipping it into his pocket in case she got any ideas about trying to escape. He wanted answers. He wanted some assistance, a way out of this godawful mess. She wasn't hurt. In fact, she looked like the type of woman who could hold her own, not some feeble, incapacitated old lady who was unable to look after herself. A small amount of guilt nudged its way into his brain but he ignored it. This was something he needed to do. It was about time he started being more forceful. His wife was missing, possibly even dead, and as far as he knew, this old woman was the last person to see her. It was her duty as a citizen of this island to start answering some questions, to come to his aid. What sort of person would turf another out on to the street when such a terrible thing was taking place? She was purportedly Fiona's friend but was acting like a complete stranger.

He placed his hand on her shoulder, ignoring her initial resistance, and pushed her along, guiding her into the tiny living room before sitting opposite her and staring deep into her eyes.

'What do you think has happened to Fiona, Honnie? Where the fuck is my wife?'

30

BEFORE

She knew after the first one, firing questions at him all evening. Where had he been when it happened? Had he seen anything untoward while he was out? He couldn't hide anything from her. She just knew. He tried to lie, to tell her he'd been too far out at sea to notice anything taking place and even though he prided himself on being able to keep secrets, he couldn't hide it from her because no matter how adept he was at being deceitful, she was better. They had both spent a lifetime living dishonestly, showing one face to the outside world and wearing another behind closed doors. They were more alike than either of them cared to admit. And so he had told her, staring down at his hands as he recalled the incident, how the swimmer had got tangled up in his nets and how he had tried to free her. He couldn't tell her the real story, how the thrill of it had aroused him, made him want more, but it didn't matter because she didn't believe him anyway. She knew him better than he knew himself, shouting at him that he was a liar and how he should have died at birth and was never wanted anyway. It didn't bother him that much. He'd heard it all before. Water off a duck's back was what it was. She was probably right. He wasn't like other people, his brain wired up differently from everybody else, but so what? Everyone got their kicks in different ways. Some people on the island killed themselves off slowly with the drink, living a boring existence, spending every day in the pub until their liver became so diseased, they could hardly get out of bed. The only difference between him and them was that he killed other people, not himself.

She had shut him in the cellar, the one that had been locked up since his dad's death all those years ago. He should have fought back, told her no, that he was bigger and stronger than she was, but there was something about her, the way she wielded power over him. It made him capitulate, weepy with resentment and worry. He needed her. He'd never be able to live anywhere else although there was that one special place that he still visited when things became too much for him, that wonderful secret place he called his own. Forgotten and neglected by everyone else, it was the epicentre of his world.

She told him the following morning what she had done, how she had taken his boat out and rammed it into the rocks. Even the most experienced of fishermen struggle in those waters, she had said, everyone knew it. She had had to do it, she had told him, to stop any blame from coming to her door. She was a proud woman and had a reputation to maintain. She wasn't about to let him ruin what she had worked hard to construct.

He did it even more after that, not only to satisfy his urges, to inject some sparkle into his life, but also to get back at her, to make her realise she couldn't control everything about him. They didn't speak about it. Ever. It was as if none of it had ever happened. He stayed hidden away but knew the island like the back of his hand, was adept at getting about and remaining concealed and unseen. Except for that one time. The one time when he was spotted by an unsuspecting passer-by. Their eyes had met and that was when he knew that it didn't matter anyway, being seen like that, because his mam wouldn't have been able to take his boat out on her own and wreck it – she had needed somebody to help her, somebody who would keep her secret and take it with him to his grave. They had both turned their backs that day, scuttling away like nothing had happened. Like they hadn't just seen one another, their gazes locking even though he was supposed to be dead.

Days he waited for the gossip about his appearance to begin. Those days turned into weeks, the weeks turning into months. No whispers. Nothing was said. Everything remained as it was. If Davey Fairhurst had told anybody, then they too had kept it secret. The best-kept secret on Winters End. He knew then that his guesses about Davey helping his mam were true. Nobody would ever get to know about his secret life, his hidden existence. He was a dead man walking. A ghost in their midst. Free to do whatever he pleased, whenever he wanted to do it. And nobody could do anything about it because how do you blame somebody and make them stop when they're already dead?

31

The door was heavy but not impossible to shift. It gave way with a screeching groan and I wondered how nobody had heard or seen anything untoward going on in this place until I peered out and surveyed the nearby area. Much like our new back garden, it was set in a patch of wasteland surrounded by waist-high weeds and yards and yards of gnarled hedgerows. Nothing around, nobody nearby to see us. Nobody close by to hear me scream. I couldn't believe that on such a small island, this place actually existed. It was dark, but even amidst the gloom I could see that there were no houses around, no flickering lights or people milling about their living rooms, half-hidden by closed blinds or curtains. I had no idea where we were but knew that, much like the cliff path, it was a deserted, lonely area, nobody nearby to help me. Whatever I managed to do in the next few desperate moments, I would have to do it unaided. My thoughts flew back to Myra; how I had left her alone, escaping on my own. I couldn't help it. Time had been against me, adrenaline flowing, marring my thinking. I was fuelled by fear, acting on impulse, no time to plan things logically and with no emergency services on the island, I wasn't sure what would now happen, how I would get any help. Whether I would get far enough to reach somebody. I hoped he was still lying on the floor, writhing in agony. I hoped I had kicked him hard enough to make sure he couldn't get back up for as long as it would take me to reach the nearest house and scream for somebody to do something. But I couldn't be sure. It would probably take more than a couple of kicks to his testicles to fell a man of his stature.

I scrambled out, falling onto my hands and knees when I attempted to fight my way through the tangle of bushes and shrubbery that was growing around the perimeter of the doorway, and quickly righted myself. I wanted to glance back, to see if he was there, but there wasn't any time to hang around. For all the power I put into that kick, and it was powerful, I knew that he would soon be up on his feet, fury driving him on, travelling from his head to his fists at lightning speed. I may have temporarily injured him but he wouldn't stay on the ground for long. He was an immense, ungainly creature, a mountain of a man with hands the size of large rocks. The thought of him pinning me to the floor, raining blows down on me with his fists, made me weak with terror and dread. I had to get up, to keep moving, not stop until I was absolutely certain that I was safe.

My feet were leaden as I broke into a sprint, gravity suddenly intensifying, the force of it pulling me downwards. My breathing was erratic, my chest tight when I tried to speed up my movements. It felt nightmarish, like trying to wade through treacle. He would be after me soon. Any second now, I would hear him, the heavy, unmistakable clump of his footsteps causing the ground to shift, his thunderous movements spelling out my demise if I didn't get to a place of safety. I got lucky last time. I was certain it wouldn't happen again. I now needed energy and a certain amount of skill to get home in one piece and would have to dig deep into my reserves to find it.

Rabbit holes littered the landscape as I ran, my ankles twisting and weakening every time I stumbled across one and fell, the sheer depth of them making me gasp. Flames bit at my calves, shooting pains stabbing at my ankles, but still I gained traction, managing to dodge the next few holes, jumping and weaving through the darkness. And then I heard it. I heard him, his voice hollering behind me, getting closer as I headed deeper into the loneliness and opacity of the night. His shouts and screams weren't anything that I could decode or decipher, just a torrent of furious sounds, animalistic and voluble, echoing into the still night air. I had really angered him, ratcheted up his temper and propensity for more violence. I had no choice. I had to get out of there, minimise the chances of being beaten or raped, even. The thought of it made me sick to my stomach, bile rising and burning at my gullet as I picked up speed to try to make my escape.

The roar of my own breathing filled my ears, the pounding of my heart battered at my neck and chest, but still, even above the sound of that cacophony of clashing noises in my head, I could hear him behind me, the sound of his voice growing closer, the gap between us narrowing, his height and the length of his strides giving him a distinct advantage over me. I had my agility, my slim frame allowing me to dodge and weave his grasp should he get close enough to try to grab at me, but he had the sturdiness and mass of a hundred men, there was no denying that fact.

'Fucking bitch! You're all fucking bitches!'

The deep roaring of his voice was enough to catapult me into action, my body pushing forward against the prevailing wind and the rain which had started to pour down, soaking my clothes and blurring my vision. In no time at all, the ground would turn to mulch, impeding my progress, so I ran as fast as I could before it became too muddy. I ran into the night with no idea of where I was headed, my screams for help ripping through the air, obliterating his insults and obscenities, my high-pitched shrieks far harder to ignore than his low rumbling and hollering. They sliced through everything, my cries for help. I made sure of it. After being ignored for so long, sneered at, insulted and told it was all in my head, I was determined this time to be heard.

Huge droplets of rain fell in my mouth and on my head, soaking my hair and separating it into thick clumps that hung in my eyes like chunks of wet rope. It picked up speed, the downpour, water running down my neck, saturating every part of me. I was freezing, my hands and feet so very, very cold. Still I ran, on and on, trying to escape his roars and to put some distance between us, to get away from the sound of the heavy footfall behind me. Trying to escape his grasping hands and destructive, damaged mind. I would not let him catch me. I would live through this, get back to my tiny little cottage, to my husband and my life. A vast, monstrous being wouldn't be enough to stop me. I'd survived a recent trauma and come out of the other end bruised and dented, but not completely broken. I wouldn't let him be the one to break me. He was a monster, a psychopath. A nobody.

Those thoughts put more fuel into my tank, driving me onwards. Forcing me towards Neil and Prosperity Cottage, the only home I now had.

32

NEIL

Her eyes were glazed over, a bluish, jelly-like film coating her pupils and irises. Neil sat, thinking how distant and cold she seemed, how trying to meet her gaze was like staring into the face of a dead fish. He couldn't quite comprehend how Fiona had become friends with this woman. It wasn't the age difference; that didn't matter. It was something else. Something less measurable than the passing of years. It was a feeling he had that something wasn't quite right with the woman, her cool demeanour a façade for something more sinister. Frightening even. He wasn't given to feeling scared or fragile but her manner unnerved him, had him shifting in his seat despite trying to act brave and confident in the hope she would crack and tell him what he needed to know.

'Already told yer. I don't know anything about yer wife.'

He couldn't swear to it but thought he saw a smile, the corners of her mouth twitching in mild amusement. A spark ignited inside his chest. He stood up and walked around the place, scanning for clues, his eyes searching every corner of her dated living room, seeing if Fiona had left any trace of herself behind. Disappointment undulated through him, rippling over his skin when he realised there was nothing of Fiona here. No forgotten bag or purse or comb. No mislaid bank cards or wallets. Not a damn thing. It was as if she had never been here at all.

'But she was in your house with you earlier, wasn't she, here in this room?' He kept his voice low, non-threatening. He needed Honnie on his side. She was the last person to see Fiona. Upsetting her would narrow his chances of ever finding his wife. If his voice came across as accusatory, then she would remain quiet, telling him nothing at all.

'Told yer that as well. She was 'ere, then she left. Not sure what else you want me ter say.'

'The truth?' He waited for her reply or absence of one that could indicate that she knew something about what was going on here. Because there was something going on. Everything was skewed, the people on the island clamming up when he approached them, slamming doors closed in his face. Pretending they were busy. Honnie knew. She may not have known Fiona's exact whereabouts but there was something she was hiding. Some awful, dark piece of information that could unlock this whole mystery.

'I know nowt.' She cocked her head to one side and stared at him with those cold fish eyes.

He held his silence, determined to wait it out. Seconds ticked by. He had asked enough questions. It was now time for Honnie to start speaking. He hoped the protracted stillness would unnerve her, even though it was clear that she was a tough one and wouldn't break easily. He hoped his subdued, quiet manner would push her into revealing things she wouldn't ordinarily say.

A knock at the door broke the awkward hush in the room, the thumping sound echoing through the house. Neil's blood sizzled, the hairs on the back of his neck stood on end.

'Aren't you going to get that?' He stared at her, remembering the key in his pocket. 'Or shall I go and answer it?'

The edges of her mouth dropped, a look of derision on her face. Another brief silence followed by the faintest of noises, a distant crowing of sounds coming from outside. Then more knocking, louder this time, more insistent. Demanding.

'I think somebody really, really wants to talk to you, Honnie.' He nodded towards the hallway then glanced back at the elderly lady who was staring at him, her head lowered, hands curled at her sides. He could see the ridge of her knuckles as they pushed at her grey, waxy skin, her irritation now visible.

Neil watched her stand, noticed her cumbersome movements, how she rocked from side to side when she left the room. He listened out for her searching about, possibly for another key, but heard only the slamming of cupboard doors and drawers being pulled open and shut again. He waited, his breathing low and controlled, then stiffened as she entered the room holding something.

'Say nothing or it gets plunged deep into your chest.' Honnie's voice was a whisper. She approached Neil, a finger placed over her mouth to indicate that he needed to shut up, a large knife clutched tightly in her other hand.

Neil eyed her up and down, carefully weighing up his options. She was elderly, not exactly frail or frag-ile-looking, but he guessed that she was in her late seventies or early eighties. Surely, he had the agility and enough strength to overpower her? Then he took another look at the knife. It was at least ten inches long and appeared to be some sort of hunting blade, not your average bread knife. It had a jagged edge and a thick leather handle. Large and, he guessed by looking at it, sharp enough to slice him wide open if it made contact with his skin. Would she be strong enough to cause him untold and lasting damage? Strong enough to kill him?

Another knock at the door and the sound of footsteps fading, then growing closer, stopping by the front window. A shadow outlined in the fabric of the curtains. 'Honnie! You in there? You need ta come outside. Summat's going on out 'ere. Summat weird.'

Neil continued to watch her, never taking his eyes away from that blade. She shook her head and glanced at the window, making a shushing sound and keeping her finger placed at her pursed lips, her jelly-like eyes boring into him.

All he needed to do was create a distraction by tapping at the window or shouting. In the time it would take for her to come running at him, he could dodge and dart about, knock her to the floor and remove the knife from her grasp. She would break a bone with the fall, become weakened and immobile.

There was so much he could do, so many ways he could get the person outside to help him. And yet he remained rooted to the spot. It was like being frozen in time. He had to snap out of it, break out of his self-induced torpor and do something – anything. Outside, the rain began to beat against the window, pounding at it like bullets hitting the glass.

'Here! I'm in here!' His voice ricocheted around the room, the depth and volume of it a surprise even to him. 'And she's got a knife!'

A movement outside. Nothing from Honnie – not a single sound, no steps towards him. Just an eerie stillness and a scornful stare. Time slowed down, his limbs and mind disconnected from each other. The key. He had the key. She was blocking the doorway. He looked at the window – old, small and single-glazed. In one swift movement he brought his arm back and elbowed the glass, shattering it into fragments that landed at his feet. Wind drove the rain in, the curtains billowed, becoming saturated in seconds, turning a dark crimson colour and dripping onto the floor in ragged splodges.

'That'll do yer no good. Him outside knows what's what. He knows all right.' Honnie nodded towards the glassless wooden frame and squinted at the dark figure that was waiting outside.

An arm reached through the broken shards, large fingers pulling away the remaining pieces of glass from the splintered surround.

'In 'ere, Davey,' Honnie said with a growl. 'He's in 'ere. Get yerself inside. I've got somebody here who seems intent on causing us a load of bother. We need to do something and I can't do it on me own. I need a hand.'

Neil swallowed and rubbed at his brow with the back of his hand. Two of them against one. And Davey was a biggish guy. With him and the knife that was currently clutched in Honnie's hand, Neil knew that he stood no chance. He glanced down at the shards of glass, thinking he could use one of them as a weapon to defend himself. They were all too small. Not nearly large enough to deter Honnie or Davey. He could only hope that Kate would call the police, have them out searching for Fiona. Because if she didn't and she arrived here trying to find him first, well then, they were both as good as dead.

33

I ran and I ran from him, my legs shaky and unsteady, my chest burning. Our cries and screams merged into a cacophonous noise that was deadened by the roar of the wind and the crashing of the savage sea below us. He was gaining ground. I had to leave him behind, to close that gap between us, but I was so tired, flames dancing and flickering beneath my breastbone, streaks of pain snaking up my calves. I could hear him when I slowed down to catch my breath, his shouts like that of an animal in its death throes. He didn't sound human. More like some sort of chimera. A freak of nature. A monster.

My feet slipped and slid in the wet soil as I set off

again, the ground now spongy and slippery beneath my feet. It was quickly becoming a quagmire. I needed to be careful but at the same time I couldn't let the wet conditions slow me down. It would be the undoing of me, to come this far and lose because of a bit of bad weather. I refused to die at his hands, not in that terrible dank place, nor out here. I would make it back to the cottage. I would get back home somehow, I would lock all the windows and doors, I would ring Neil and tell him to call the police, and then I would be safe. And then the police would catch him and he would spend the rest of his life where he belonged – behind bars.

But all of that was still ahead of me. I was jumping the gun and had yet to get away from him and leave him far behind and that was proving difficult as the rain grew heavier and the terrain more treacherous. Everything felt heavy, my wet clothes weighing me down, sticking to my skin and hindering my progress. Wisps of damp hair continually marred my vision, clinging to my forehead and my eyelashes. I swept them back and stared ahead, realising with a jolt that I was close to somewhere with houses. Suddenly feverish with excitement, I let out another scream for help, my pitch and tone enough to shatter glass, and felt the adrenaline coursing through me, my legs in-jected with a sudden surge of power and energy. I ig-nored the pain and the pounding in my head where he had hit me and focused only on reaching those dwellings, thinking of the people inside, how they would open their doors and help me. I kept on, the burn in my calves telling me I was picking up speed, the tightness in my chest so painful I was sure my lungs would burst, but still I did it, running and run-ning because my life depended on it.

They were close now, those few houses, but I could tell by the howling behind me, the commands for me to stop, that he was closer. I had to open up the gap, make sure he couldn't catch me. I tried to move faster but the mud slowed me down, my feet sticking to its viscid surface, the rabbit holes now turning into large, sloppy craters. My only hope was that his less-than-dexterous frame would fall harder than I ever could and that he would remain there on the ground, his large body rocking about in pain, too injured and too cumbersome to get back up again, his limbs slip-ping about in the loam while I continued on, widening the distance between us.

'Fucking slut!' It was a roar, every syllable enunci-ated with such venom and hatred that it almost stopped me in my tracks. Almost, but not quite. His anger was palpable. I didn't want to get caught by a man who could crush me without blinking. I didn't want to get caught by a man who had undressed me with his eyes, his gaze travelling over my breasts and hips. There was so much spite and malevolence in his tone. So much animosity and anger. I was a nobody to him. A warm body he could use however he pleased.

Those thoughts put steel in my blood, giving me enough strength to keep going. I headed towards the tiny row of lights, my eyes fixed on the distant rooflines. Brambles and nettles tore and stung at my limbs, the pain soon dissipating, adrenaline masking it as I ploughed on, fire combusting in my chest and burning its way through my veins. I thought back to how romantic and enticing it had all looked as we sailed in on the ferry all those weeks ago and how quickly everything had soured, how I should have taken notice of my initial rumblings of fear and discontent and turned around and headed back to the mainland. Too late now. Everything was too damn late. This could be where it all ended. Or not. I wasn't about to give in without a fight. Those houses were my salvation. My lifeline.

Behind me, the hollering and insults and stream

of invectives grew louder, more threatening. I tried to drown them out with my shrieks and cries for help and just when I thought I would collapse from exhaustion, I saw something. A figure ahead of me, standing motionless before moving away from me and towards the direction of the lights. Moving away. They turned and began to walk in the opposite direction. I wanted to drop to my knees and weep, to shout to the heavens above that I would die if somebody didn't come to my aid. What was wrong with the people of this island? I was in distress. I was injured and in dire need of help. What sort of sick individual would turn their back on somebody who was clearly distressed? Somebody who was being chased and hunted down like a wild animal. What the fuck was wrong with the people of Winters End?

My life began to flash before me – both good and bad. My achievements and sins, all of them there in glorious cinematic technicolour for me to see. Maybe this was it. Maybe for all my bravado and desperate attempts to escape, convincing myself I could actually do it, perhaps this really was the end. Perhaps my demise would happen out here in the mud under a veil of heavy rain. Positive thoughts don't always transfer themselves into actual realities. Thinking something doesn't necessarily make it so.

I began to weaken then, stumbling about in the sodden terrain. Until something happened. The figure in the distance appeared once more, turning to face me before moving in my direction. I had no idea if it was friend or foe, whether they meant me harm or would help me, but was prepared to take my chances and opened my mouth to scream for help, my voice travelling across the darkness of the night. I prayed to every god I could think of that the figure was Neil but knew that the chances of it being my husband were slim. Still I prayed, hoping against hope.

The thought of collapsing into his arms gave me the impetus to keep going, to battle against the howling wind and the driving rain, to reach this person and beg them to help keep me safe. My feet slipped and twisted beneath me. I lunged to the ground time and time again as the storm grew in strength, the downpour a fierce beast, wild and unforgiving, and each time, clambered back up again. Mud clung to my skin, my clothes; it stuck to my hair, was streaked over my face, the earthy pungent smell of it smeared inside my nostrils and my mouth. I retched, spat out stringy lengths of brown saliva, my throat rough as sandpaper, and carried on running, each breath a ragged heave that came from so deep inside my chest, I felt my lungs would explode with the effort of it, and all the while behind me, his voice was carried by the prevailing wind, his threats to kill me, to tear me from limb to limb and rip my beating heart from my body with his bare hands, continued. All I could focus on was that figure in the distance, reaching them and hoping that whomever it was that was walking my way had enough compassion and common sense to do something, to stop this monster from harming me.

I wiped at my eyes with the back of my hand, slipping time and time again in the thick mud, my legs like rubber as they scissored beneath me, but I didn't stop. I wouldn't. Not until I reached safety. The person in the distance began to run towards me, their arms pumping furiously at their sides, legs moving manically, machine-like in their strength and rhythm. I stopped, tears and snot streaming, relief washing over me, expanding in my chest before I began moving again, fear and a sense of liberation forcing me on. He was behind me. I couldn't forget that. The monster was gaining ground, getting closer and closer. No time to stand still, to think that I was finally free because I wasn't. Not yet.

The blurred, shadowy outline of the running person slowly took form as we stumbled towards one another, their features gradually coming into focus. I screwed up my eyes, my breathing a deep, desperate roar when I was finally able to see who it was. I stopped, suddenly weak, unable to take another gasp, and brought my hand up to my mouth to suppress the howl of relief that forced its way out when I realised who it actually was.

34

NEIL

'It's over, Honnie. Put the knife down, yer daft old woman. It's all over. Enough is enough.' Davey stood in the living room, his hair slick with rain. It ran down his face, hanging in small drops from the tip of his nose and landing on the threadbare rug. 'Been goin' on for too long, this 'as. Time to put an end to it all.'

Neil stared at him before flicking his gaze over to Honnie. She was shaking her head, her eyes dark, narrow slits. 'He might be a bit deranged, all soft in the head like, but he's still my lad. I'll not 'ave anybody trying to tek 'im away from me.' She nodded at Davey and jutted out her bottom lip. 'And you should know what I'm talking about. You should be stickin' up for 'im as well.'

'Oh, for Christ's sake, Honnie, put that fuckin' knife down, will yer? It's over!' He began to walk towards her, hand outstretched, palm turned upwards. Neil wanted to pull him back, to tell him to leave her be, that she was angry and unpredictable. Somebody who had been pushed into a corner and was lashing out. She may have been an elderly lady but she had the stance and build of somebody who could handle herself, not a frail-looking thing who would crumple and break if confronted. Her gait was lopsided and her vision wasn't great but she was sturdily built and gutsy, not fearful of this situation and definitely not frightened of either man.

'Tek it off me at your peril, Davey. You're as much to blame for all of this as I am. You know what's been goin' on and you've done nowt to stop it. You've done nowt to stop 'im.'

Davey shook his head and glanced at Neil then turned back to Honnie, his hand outstretched, his tone firm. Authoritative. 'Gimme the knife, Honnie. I'm fed up to the back teeth of this carry-on and the destruction he's caused. We all are.'

'Never. I'm not one for givin' up, Davey Fairhurst. I'll never back down to anyone. Ever.' She swung around and fixed her gaze on him. 'Where's your allegiance for the lad, eh Davey? Where's your allegiance and loyalty for him?'

'He's not a lad any longer, Honnie. He's a grown man an' it's about time he started accepting consequences for 'is behaviour, not treated like some naughty schoolboy who's stolen apples from a bloody tree. This has to stop, Honnie. It all has to stop.' He glanced at Neil, then back at Honnie, at the knife clutched tightly in her palm, her thick white fingers curled around it. 'We've all 'ad enough. All of us.'

'You did this to 'im, Davey Fairhurst. You turned 'im into what he is today.'

Neil waited, hoping she would lose focus, the conversation knocking her off course and lessening her grip on that knife. Weakening her resistance.

'Me?' Davey's voice rose an octave, became louder, aggressive. 'How the fuck is any o' this my fault?' He took a step towards her. Neil braced himself, readying himself for what came next, flexing his fingers and curling them into fists. He had to keep an eye on that blade, see where it went next. Stop it from being pushed deep into Davey's chest. Stop it from being pushed deep into his own chest. 'You're the one who locked 'im away in that cellar down there, blamed 'im for the death of your girl. If anyone's at fault for the way he is, it's you, his own bloody mother.'

'Aye, and if he goes down for this, we go down with 'im. Bet you hadn't thought of that, had yer?'

'I'm willin' to do whatever it takes to get this thing over with.'

Honnie fell silent, Neil watching her as she mulled over Davey's words, his own mind trying to keep pace with the conversation, to pull all the threads together and come up with a coherent, plausible theory.

'Willin' to go to prison?'

Davey nodded, kept his spine rigid, his eyes firmly fixed on Honnie's. 'Aye, if that's what it takes. I'll do me time, pay for me sins. What about you, Honnie Armstrong? Will you own up to what you've done, to the part you played in all of this, or will you continue to lie like yer have for as long as I can remember?'

Her laugh filled the room, ringing around them, forcing Neil to momentarily shut his eyes and take a breath to attempt to still his thrashing heart. It was manic, her guffawing. The laugh of somebody who had reached the point of no return. She would do whatever needed to be done to save her boy. To save herself.

'Continue to lie? Continue to lie?' Her last sentence was a roar. Crests of foamy saliva gathered around her mouth.

Neil considered running at her, wrestling the knife

out of her hand while her attention was elsewhere.

'You wanna talk about lies, Davey Fairhurst? How about finally owning up about yer son? About the fact that my boy is your boy as well? How about tellin' the rest of the island that yer took pity on a lonely older woman whose husband was a useless specimen who smoked an' drank more than he earned and how that pity went too far one night and resulted in my lad bein' born?'

Everything began to mesh together in Neil's head. The gossiping, the whispers in the pub. There were still holes in this story that he needed to work out but parts of it were finally slotting into place.

Neil flicked his eyes over to Davey who looked as if all life had ebbed out of him. His face was the colour of ash, his stance suddenly floppy as if he was unable to stay upright, the weight of the world balanced precariously on his shoulders.

'And now your son has my wife.' Neil's voice was uncharacteristically low and menacing. A throaty hiss. 'Where is he? Where has he taken her, Honnie? Davey, do you know? You have to tell me if you do because we all know he might just kill her and if he does, you two will be held responsible. So tell me, what the fuck has your psychopathic son done with my wife?'

35

'He's back there and getting closer! We need to keep going, to get away as fast as we can or he'll kill us both!'

Kate stared at me, rain dripping off her eyelashes, running down her face, her coat. She was slick with water, hardly recognisable amidst the raging storm and torrential downpour.

'Who's behind you? Fiona, what the hell is going on?' She was shouting, her voice still difficult to hear above the noise of the rain as it poured around us.

'Don't waste time talking. Please, just run!' I grabbed at Kate's hand and dragged her along with me, relief and terror merging in a hot rush in my veins.

'Over there! Back the way you came. We need to get over there.' I pointed to the lights ahead, too tired to say anything else. Explanations could come later. If there was going to be a later. He was still gaining ground, determined to catch up with me. For such a clumsy, unwieldy man, he was deeply tenacious, but then so was I. My will to live was strong. Stronger than his determined efforts to kill me.

We held one another, Kate and I, as we pounded through the mud, making our way over the uneven ground that was full of holes and small hillocks, our hands slippery with water, our fingers interlocked so tightly my hand began to go numb. On a few occasions I skidded, my legs like elastic, my vision impaired by the inclement weather, but she was there for me, pulling me along, keeping me upright. What I wanted to do at that point was stop and hold her close, to thank her for coming all this way for me, for braving the choppy waters and ferry ride over to Winters End, but we didn't have time. That would come later when we were home. It kept me going – the thought of Kate and Neil and our little cottage. Prosperity Cottage. It filled me with hope and a sense of optimism that soon this would all be over, that my captor would be arrested and shipped off to the mainland where he would spend the rest of his life behind bars for his heinous crimes. But we weren't at that point just yet. We were close, but not completely safe.

'Look!' She pointed ahead, her long, slender finger wobbling with what I presumed to be relief combined with terror at finding herself in this unspeakable predicament. She had come here for me with no idea of what she was letting herself in for. And she had stayed and was currently helping me to safety. Our rift didn't run that deep. There was hope for me yet. For us. All of us. 'I can see somebody over there by the light.'

She was right. A figure was visible, the dark frame silhouetted through the haze of the driving rain, their stance crooked, angled to one side as if whomever it was was unable to hold themselves up properly. We watched them as they took a step, then another. A stagger forwards then a sudden drop to the ground. My hand flew to my mouth as the figure fell. Tears sprang to my eyes, burning at my lids. Even the freezing rain couldn't cool the furnace that raged in my head, searing over my cold, wet flesh and travelling down my spine, small bolts of electricity jarring me, stabbing at me again and again and again. It was Neil. He was the figure in the distance. I could see through the murk, was able to recognise his willowy frame, his thin, muscular legs. My Neil. My husband.

Laid on the ground. Injured. In pain. Possibly even dying.

'I heard something earlier, before I headed over to you.' Kate turned to me, her eyes wide with realisation. 'I heard shouting coming from one of the houses. I'd been to your cottage and Neil wasn't there. I tried ringing him but he didn't answer so I just drove around looking for you both. I didn't expect to see anything and when I heard that shouting, I got frightened and...' I shook my head and pulled her closer to me but she pushed me away. 'If I'd tried to find out what that noise was, maybe I could have helped Neil. We'd both be here now with you. He might be badly injured, Fiona. Oh God, I don't think I could bear it if I could have done something and didn't.'

'We don't know what's happened, Kate.' I grabbed her arm and pulled her along. 'Come on, we have to get over there. He might be okay. He might just have—'

The roar from behind made me dizzy with shock and a realisation that the monster behind us was gaining ground, was even closer than I realised. We had stopped, lost our momentum. Lost track of time. And now he was almost upon us.

'Run, Kate. Now!'

Her body was like lead when I tugged at her hand.

She capitulated, loosening her stance after a few seconds and running alongside me.

'He's coming,' I panted. 'And if he catches us, he'll kill us.'

There wasn't enough time to explain any further. Not that I had an answer to any of this. I had no idea who he was or what he wanted with me. Why he hated me. Except it wasn't just me. He hated women. All the women of Winters End. He hated them all. The other deaths – he was behind them, I just knew it, and if we didn't escape, my name would be alongside those others, my grave next to theirs up in the churchyard of St Augustine's.

For such a tiny island, the distance to those lights felt like a hundred miles away, the time to reach them stretching out ahead of us with no end in sight. But then I heard him. I heard Neil, recognised his voice. His groan. That awful, guttural groan as he lay on the ground, his hand clutched to his midriff. Kate reached him before I did, my legs weakened by the run. Even in the dim light, I could see the blood.

Oh God, so much blood!

'Police,' he said, his head turned to us, his voice gravelly. 'Call them now. She's got a knife.'

I looked up into the face of Honnie. She had made her way over and was staring down at us, the blade of the knife smeared with a dark substance. I swallowed down bile, a thousand thoughts whirring through my brain. I had no idea what to do next, how to react and stood motionless but it didn't matter because Kate took over, running at Honnie, her body bent forwards, arms folded at her chest, the force of the collision knocking the knife out of Honnie's hand. It spun in the air as if it had a life of its own and landed at my feet. I bent down and picked it up, clutching it tightly. Determined to hold on to it. This was our lifeline, our only form of defence. Honnie turned and came at me, as powerful as the storm that raged around us, but I was nimble. Exhausted but agile all the same. I darted to one side, slaloming out of her way. At the edge of my vision, I could see Kate on her phone, speaking to someone.

Please let it be the police. Please, please let it be the police!

'Come on now, lass. Don't be daft. Hand it over.' Honnie was standing in front of me, her body suddenly seeming to take up so much more space than I remembered. I could see the expression on her face, the look in her eyes that told me she had done this to Neil. She had stabbed my husband. The only person in the world I loved more than life itself and he was lying on the floor, bleeding out. I had thought she was my friend. I had thought wrong.

I shook my head, droplets of rain circling around me in a swift, rhythmic spray. 'No. What have you done, Honnie? What the hell have you done to my husband?'

She stood there, saying nothing, her body braced for a struggle. And then, as if out of nowhere, came the approaching shadow and the unearthly hollering. I took a long, shaky breath and turned to see Davey running at us. I clung on to the knife, my fingers curled around it, my palm pressed hard against the wet leather handle, fear pulsing through me. One elderly lady I could manage; a grown man full of fury might prove to be too much for my slightly built body. A sharp, bloodied blade was the only thing standing between us. That and my fear.

I felt my blood begin to bubble, terror heating up my flesh. I watched Davey, I watched Honnie. I feared for Neil and prayed that Kate had managed to get through to somebody who could help us. If she hadn't, then we would surely be dead in the next few minutes, our bodies laid out next to Neil. All of us spread out on the wet loam, life ebbing away from us as the rain continued to fall and the wind traversed over our bodies as if we didn't even exist.

Oh God, Neil, please don't die!

Tears pricked at my eyes; a hard, rock-like lump became wedged in my throat. Davey was just feet away. Behind me, I could hear the cries of the monster who had imprisoned me, the man whose name I didn't even know. I felt faint and queasy. This was the part where it all came to an end, the odds stacked against me, Neil and Kate. We were injured and disadvantaged, our chances of escaping this unscathed minimal to zero.

'Give me the knife.' Davey's voice carried over the noise of the pounding rain.

I shook my head, clasped it tighter, my hand trembling violently, my legs liquid with dread.

'For fuck's sake! I'm on your bloody side, woman. Now gimme that knife or we're all dead.'

Another sound cut through the thick pounding of the downpour and the howling wind: an overhead rumbling, accompanied by a distant blue light that was moving closer. I dared to glance away for just a second and saw it coming closer, descending and landing close by. My lifesavers. Our lifesavers. Maybe we would survive this. Just maybe Neil would be saved.

I gasped, cried, turned to look at Kate who was

slowly making her way over to where I was standing. It was over. It was all over.

The blow caught me by surprise, stars bursting behind my eyes, pain pinballing through my skull. A blue light overhead, people screaming. Then nothing.

36

NEIL

He tried to control his breathing, to keep it regular and low. No gasping. He had to conserve what little energy he had left. She took them both by surprise, lunging herself at Davey when he tried to take the knife from her. Davey managed to throw her off but wasn't fast enough to stop her from turning her attentions to Neil. He took the brunt of her anger, the knife catching him in his side then slicing across his arm when he backed away from her. It hurt like hell. A deep, throbbing pain that ran through his middle, setting his flesh alight; flames licking around his ribs and his stomach, his internal organs a furnace of agony. He managed to stagger to the door and unlock it while Davey continued to wrestle with her. Davey wasn't a particularly big guy and years of drinking had ravaged his body, sapping his strength and leaving him weakened against her. Also, Honnie had a knife, always a distinct advantage, but somehow Davey managed to remain unscathed, just a few scratches on his hands from the struggle.

It was as Neil was stumbling from the room, his mind focused on his wound, his hands clutched to his side to try to stem the bleeding, that she caught him again, the knife slicing through his abdomen. He ran from the house while he could before the deep gash took its toll and he passed out. He made his escape, leaving Honnie and Davey inside, Davey scolding the old woman, trying to reason with her. If Neil could just reach his phone and call the emergency services, then maybe he would live through this. Maybe. The signal on the island was sketchy at best. Perhaps they would take him seriously this time now that everything had sunk to its lowest point. Fuck their forty-eight-hour wait. This was a bloodbath.

He could hear them shouting as he staggered out into the darkness of the evening, their clipped, raised voices taking on an ethereal quality as everything grew dim and dulled around him. He was bleeding badly, his hands clutched to his midriff. He needed help or he was going to die.

Everything hurt. Every single part of him. He stared ahead, eyes narrowed against the driving rain that battered his face and his body. Even the elements were working against him. A searing pain tore through his flesh, his ribs feeling like they were breaking in two when he attempted to reach into his pocket for his phone, his innards exploding beneath his skin. He needed to keep calm, to get to that mobile and scream down the handset that they had got it wrong and that his missing wife was here and probably injured, possibly dead, and that he was going to die too if they didn't get somebody out here to help him, but it was so damn hard, exhaustion washing over him, leaving him stripped of all strength and completely helpless. His couldn't get his hands to work properly, his fingers lacking their usual co-ordination and dexterity, everything decelerating around him. Life in slow motion, his body gradually shutting down, his thoughts blurred and sluggish. He was so tired, so very, very tired. At least his agony was easing, a numbness setting in where only a few moments ago there was deep, gut-wrenching pain. He didn't feel himself drop to his knees but realised when he looked down that he was closer to the ground, mud slopping around him, making it difficult for him to stay upright. And he was cold. Really cold, his body like ice.

He just needed to lie down for a few seconds, to focus on his breathing, rest himself. Just a few seconds, that was all he needed. A few moments to gather his thoughts.

He closed his eyes. It was pointless trying to fight off the fatigue. Above him, he could hear a whirring sound. He thought of aircrafts and spaceships, his mind drifting away to a world of fantasy where nothing and nobody mattered. He just wanted to nap, to close his eyes and sleep for a hundred years, to escape to a place where he would be safe and warm, where Fiona would be waiting for him, smiling and unharmed.

The noise thumped in his head, pounding through his bones. The ground bounced beneath him. There was something bright overhead, something hovering. That was the last thing he remembered before everything fell silent – the swirl of a blue light. That and the screams and shouts circling him, amplified in his brain. Echoes of voices that prickled his flesh and penetrated his consciousness, and then his vision attenuating, shadows and shapes flickering at the edge of his line of sight until eventually there was nothing but darkness.

37

I required thirty-two stitches to the back of my head. I was lucky to not suffer from a fractured skull, although my injuries were still considered to be extremely serious. That's what the doctors and nurses told me when I awoke and turned to see a drip attached to the cannula in the back of my wrist, the overhead strip lights blinding me. He had used a rock to attack me. Not his huge fists after all. Even a man of that size needed more than just his own strength to knock out his victims. Everything had almost been at an end, the police helicopter landing close by, but even at that point, he still refused to give in, bringing that jagged lump of stone down on my head with such force I was knocked unconscious and airlifted to hospital for emergency treatment for a bleed on my brain. I don't consider myself lucky, far from it, but I am glad to be alive. Had it not been for Davey risking his life and dragging him off me, I wouldn't be here now, living to tell the tale.

Duncan. That's his name. The unremarkable name of the man who almost killed me, smashing my skull to smithereens, or at least trying to. The name of the man who killed those poor women, although that has yet to be proven in a court of law. The same man who attacked and murdered Sian Dupre. Her body was found in Honnie's cellar, the place where Duncan had been living since his own mother faked his death to shift the blame from him and keep any trouble away from her door. She knew what he had done, what he was capable of. What he had yet to do. She has denied it. Of course she has. But she knew. Why else did she pretend her only son was dead, locking him away from the rest of the people of the island? Duncan Armstrong and Honnie Armstrong, the people who almost took my life and the life of my husband. Almost, but not quite. Neil spent nearly two weeks in the ICU after suffering massive blood loss, having his liver lacerated and his lung punctured. But like me, he's alive. We're both here – damaged but not dead. Bruised and battered but not beaten.

We don't know yet how many were involved in the cover-up. So far, only Honnie and Davey have been arrested and been held for questioning but I get the feeling more will follow. Poor Ewan is having to deal with the aftermath, administering prayers and delivering sermons to a half-empty church, everyone either feeling shamefaced and requiring heavy-duty penance or too embarrassed to attend.

'I'm so very sorry you had to go through this, Fiona,' Ewan said, his voice brimming with sorrow as he sat at my bedside two days ago. 'I've prayed for you and Neil every day since this happened.'

I smiled and didn't try to pull away when he grasped my hand. It felt reassuring, the solidity of his touch, the closeness of his spiritual presence. Maybe I would start attending church at some point, if only to see Ewan's lovely smiling face and to listen to his sermons. Not everyone who attends believes, do they? People have their own reasons for going to church. Ewan and his comforting, benign companionship would be mine. None of what happened was his fault. He, like me, was relatively new to Winters End. How could he have known? There wasn't a damn thing he could have done to put a stop to my attack.

'I spoke to Neil and he mentioned about—'

There was a sudden silence. He didn't have to say

anything else. We both knew what he was referring to. I closed my eyes briefly and sighed, giving myself a couple of seconds to think about what I was going to say next, to work it through without sounding unbalanced. He was talking about my reports of Myra and how she had spoken to me. How she had helped me get through my ordeal just by being there. And yet she wasn't. There, that is. She was beside me physically but Myra had long since departed this world. I have been over it again and again in my head, what took place in that bunker, how I was sure I heard her voice, how I was certain she had passed me a message that I tucked away in my pocket. The message that she had written to her family soon after she had been captured, knowing she wouldn't make it out of there alive. A message telling them who was behind her disappearance and telling them how much she loved them both. The medics who cut off my clothes retrieved it. I cried once I was able, for both Myra and her family. I cried about the fact that nobody on the island claimed to know about the bunker and its existence. Had they known and searched it, Myra may have been found alive, and I might never have been subjected to such a vicious assault by an unhinged man who should have been sectioned many years ago. But it's too late for all that now, for all those what ifs and if onlys. I don't be-

lieve in ghosts or the afterlife and I have no explanation for what happened in that room, except that
Myra's presence beside me gave me enough impetus
to escape, making me feel less isolated, more able to
take on Duncan's gargantuan frame and leave that
hideous place behind me. The coroner's report said
that Myra had probably died just a few days after cap-
ture, the wounds he inflicted on her too traumatic for
her to have survived without medical attention. They
found her skeleton next to where I was chained up,
her corpse still dressed in the clothes she was captured in. My guess is that before he chained her up,
Myra was able to reach the bits of paper scattered
around the room and write the note just before she
died. How I found it is still something I cannot explain. Perhaps it was laid on the floor next to where I
was slumped. I don't have an explanation for it except
that I was frightened and dazed and my mind played
tricks on me, put events in my head that didn't really
happen. I don't suppose I will ever really know and I
shouldn't spend time raking over it. It happened and I
survived. I'm doing my best to put it all behind me
and focus on the future.

Somebody on Winters End definitely tried to warn
us about Duncan with the mysterious notes but we've
yet to find out who. I doubt it was Ewan. Maybe we'll

never discover who it was or maybe, with the passing of years, the truth will out. It usually does.

A remembrance service was held for Myra. It was beautiful and emotive and at the same time despairing and deeply sad. Many of the islanders were there, Honnie and Davey's absence duly noted. Wilf arrived with Neave in a wheelchair, both wearing their Sunday best. My heart swelled with a deep fondness for them, for the efforts they had made to get there. I spoke to Wilf, determined to thank them for how welcome they had made me and Neil feel after our arrival on the island.

'I'm so happy to see you and your wife here, Wilf.'

He narrowed his eyes and laughed, shaking his head and placing his hand on mine, tapping at my fingers before removing it and smiling. 'Ah, you must be referring to Neave. Easy mistake to make, lovey. Neave isn't my wife.' He looked over at where she was sitting, embroiled in a conversation with Ewan. 'Neave is my sister.'

We chatted for a short while before going our separate ways, each of us mingling and talking to other locals. His sister. It struck me then how I was possibly the only wife on the island. The last one to survive. I didn't know that for sure but it was something that lingered in my mind. I hoped that with Duncan's absence, things would start to change around the place, that the population would grow and blossom, more people coming here to live. More women wandering about the place.

As for me and Neil? We're getting better. Slowly but surely. Our bodies are gradually returning to normal, our relationship stronger than it's ever been. We have common bonds that will bind us together for the rest of our lives.

38

PRESENT DAY

The water is choppy, the fog finally lifting. A distant swirl of grey is all that remains of the mist that has enveloped Winters End for the past two days. A ray of dappled sunlight sits at our feet, small spots of ochre that dance about with the moving clouds and gentle breeze.

'There it is.' Neil points to the small object out at sea.

'Come on,' I reply. 'Let's sit and wait over there.'

We perch on a large nearby rock, Neil's walking stick resting against its craggy surface.

'I'm nervous,' I say, my throat hoarse and gravelly.

His touch is reassuring, the weight of his hand on mine, the way he squeezes my fingers with his, a reminder that I'm never alone. We've come a long way, Neil and I, and still have far to travel. Or at least I hope we do. I suffer from bouts of sporadic dizziness and Neil is learning to walk unaided but we're heading in the right direction, our bodies and minds angled towards a common goal – happiness. A pain- and worry-free future. I feel we've earned it. Life will still throw hurdles our way because that's what life does. It happens to the best of us, and we'll do our utmost to overcome them with as much grace and dignity as we can muster, but I hope that the worst is behind us. Lying in a hospital bed gave me lots of time to think. Despite my recent visits to church where I regularly absorb Ewan's supportive and wise words, I'm still not a religious person. I do, however, believe in some sort of karma. Perhaps what we endured was punishment for my crime. If so, then we deserve to now live our lives without having to continually apologise. Our parents came to visit while we were in hospital and I hope that was their way of telling us that the past is firmly behind us and that we can all move forward together.

'There,' I say, tipping my head to one side and pointing out to sea. 'They're nearly here. I hope the crossing wasn't too rough for them.' The weather in the North Sea has for the past week or so been erratic and unpredictable, fog enveloping us, accompanied by strong winds and heavy rain. It doesn't bother me so much any more, the bleakness of it. We're accustomed to Winters End's strange ways and windswept landscape. Anything else would perturb me, make me think something was awry.

'At least it's not a long journey,' Neil says, removing his hand from mine and standing up. I watch him, the instinctive gut reaction to help him so strong it almost hurts. I suppress it, knowing how important being independent is to him. I'm growing used to his lopsided gait as much as my own occasional wobble when a bout of dizziness takes hold.

The ferry docks up and we wait as cars drive off and passengers disembark, small groups of tourists clutching their binoculars and cameras, hoping while they are here to catch sight of the rare birds that nest here, building their homes high up in the crevices and overhanging rocks of the cliffs.

'There they are.' I take a deep breath and grab at Neil's free hand, our fingers interlocked in an act of love and solidarity.

My breathing is laboured, my chest tight with anxiety when I spot them. My mum gives me a wave, as does Neil's mum. Chrissie smiles and raises her hand and that's when I know everything is going to be just

fine. Chrissie, the person I felt sure would never forgive us, is here with Kate. Relief flowers in my gut,
small tendrils of hope unfurling and spreading. It's
going to be okay. After all my worries and sleepless
nights every time I thought about this visit, everything
is going to be okay.

Finding a holiday home for them to stay in was a
stroke of luck. Vince told us about a lodge on the west
of the island and gave us the number of the owners.
We've been seeing a lot of him and his boy lately, our
lives intersecting. Turns out we have more in
common than we ever thought, Neil and I calling
around his house a couple of times a week to see if
they need any help to keep their garden in shape.
We're not exactly fit or agile, our injuries slowing us
down, but we enjoy gardening and it's good for us
both physically and mentally to keep moving. We
don't let the adverse and often brutal weather conditions slow us down. We've also made a lot of friends
since the incident, venturing out to The Bucket of
Blood for lunch every Sunday afternoon. The local
pub now feels like a warm, welcoming place. Not
quite our second home but definitely an improvement on how it used to be. Vince has been persuaded
to let some of the islanders give it a makeover, bright-
ening up the bar with some pastel-coloured paint and

new flooring. We'll take our guests while they're here, show them that Winters End is a changed place, people relaxed and happy. Everyone friendly and welcoming.

My parents are staying in our spare room. While recuperating, I pottered around the cottage, cleaning it at a leisurely pace, doing the odd painting and touch-up job. It's amazing what new curtains and fresh flowers can do for a room. I'm hoping they will like it. It's got a lovely view of the garden, something else we've managed to spruce up. Wilf and Neave brought over some cuttings after we arrived home from the hospital and Wilf even planted them in the garden for us. Everyone has been terribly kind. Many thought we would leave, go back to Saltburn, too terrified to continue living here, but we didn't. We've stayed, weathered the worst of storms, far worse than anything the North Sea can throw at us. Freezing fog, howling gales and torrential rain are nothing compared to what Neil and I have been through. As far as we are concerned, things can only improve. None of us can predict the future and we certainly can't control it, but we have the power to limit our exposure to any damage or upset we may encounter.

'Come on,' Neil says softly, his voice full of his usual warmth and happiness, 'let's go and say hello. I think some smiles and hugs are long overdue, don't you?'

We walk forward together towards our family members. That's how we live our lives on Winters End now, with composure and dignity, and always moving forwards, never looking back.

ACKNOWLEDGMENTS

So many people to thank and then the terror of missing anybody out but I'm going give it my best shot, so here goes. First and foremost, I'd like to give my thanks to Boldwood Books for giving me free rein with my ideas and letting me loose with them without any interference along the way! I'm delighted and honoured to be a part of your team. Huge thanks go to my editor, Emily Ruston, for her careful guidance and making sure my flowery prose doesn't over-blossom and take over the entire story. Emily, you are amazing and my stories would be nothing without your edits and educated supervision. This book would be a very different story without you! I look forward to working with you in the future. I would also like to extend a big thank you to Ross Dickinson for his superb proof-reading skills. Ross, you are a star.

Bloggers and readers are the lifeblood of authors. We rely on you to read our books and spread the word and you all do it so brilliantly so thank you for taking time out of your busy day to get my books noticed and read by others, and thank you for your positive reviews. Every single one counts!

Writing can be a lonely profession and chatting to other authors helps keep me sane so a huge thank you to Anita Waller and Valerie Keogh. Our chats are my lifeline to the outside world when my writing starts to absorb my life. Thank you also for listening to my frequent queries and moans when things don't go the way I want them to.

I would like to thank the members of my wonderful ARC group for your continued support and timely reviews. You guys are fabulous and I'm continually in awe of how you manage to read my books and get brilliantly written reviews out on time, so thank you again for that.

I'm fortunate to have so many supportive friends and family members. I daren't name them all for fear of forgetting somebody but you all know who you are and I love that you're there for me. If I've missed anybody out, I apologise but know that it's a genuine oversight and I'm still immensely grateful to you!

MORE FROM J. A. BAKER

We hope you enjoyed reading *The Last Wife*. If you did, please leave a review.

If you'd like to gift a copy, this book is also available as an ebook, hardback, large print, digital audio download and audiobook CD.

Sign up to J. A. Baker's mailing list for news, competitions and updates on future books.

https://bit.ly/JABakerNews

Local Girl Missing, another twisty psychological thriller from J. A. Baker, is available now...

ABOUT THE AUTHOR

J. A. Baker is a successful psychological thriller writer of numerous books, previously published by Bloodhound. Born and brought up in Middlesbrough, she still lives in the North East, which inspires the settings for her books. *Local Girl Missing* was her first title for Boldwood.

Follow J. A. Baker on social media:

facebook.com/thewriterjude

twitter.com/thewriterjude

instagram.com/jabakerauthor

THE *Murder* LIST

THE MURDER LIST IS A NEWSLETTER DEDICATED TO ALL THINGS CRIME AND THRILLER FICTION!

SIGN UP TO MAKE SURE YOU'RE ON OUR HIT LIST FOR GRIPPING PAGE-TURNERS AND HEARTSTOPPING READS.

SIGN UP TO OUR NEWSLETTER

BIT.LY/THEMURDERLISTNEWS

Boldwood

Boldwood Books is an award-winning fiction publishing company seeking out the best stories from around the world.

Find out more at www.boldwoodbooks.com

Join our reader community for brilliant books, competitions and offers!

Follow us
@BoldwoodBooks
@BookandTonic

Sign up to our weekly deals newsletter

https://bit.ly/BoldwoodBNewsletter